SCARLET SANDS

Udayan Mukherjee was born in Calcutta. He had a two-decade long career as an award-winning financial journalist, serving as lead anchor and Managing Editor of CNBC. He is the author of *Dark Circles*, *Essential Items: And Other Tales from a Land in Lockdown*, *A Death in the Himalayas: A Neville Wadia Mystery* and *No Way In,* which received the 2023 Valley of Words Award for Fiction. *Scarlet Sands* is the second instalment in the Neville Wadia Mystery series.

Praise for Udayan Mukherjee

'Udayan is a truly gifted writer' – Vivek Shanbhag, author of *Ghachar Ghochar*

'A powerful writer whose prose tugs at your heart strings' – Karan Thapar, *Hindustan Times*

'A skilful narrator of our troubled times' – Benyamin, author of *Goat Days (Aadujeevitham)*

'Mukherjee's prose is beautiful' – *Wire*

'If you have been desperate for an Indian mystery novel that is written very well, just dive into *A Death in the Himalayas* ... of a higher quality and more honest than many so-called literary novels' – Manu Joseph

'Udayan Mukherjee ably juggles local and racial politics in *A Death in the Himalayas* ... light, breezy and intriguing reading' – *Firstpost*

'[*A Death in the Himalayas*] may be a page-turner, but certain pages make you linger' – *Hindu*

'[*No Way In*] is a pacy, immersive read ... goes where news stories seldom tread – *Hindu*

'*Essential Items* is as a beautifully crafted set of observations on the state of the nation during the difficult months of the lockdown in India' – *Mint Lounge*

'[*Dark Circles* is] a fictional piece that deftly explores human relationships and their complexities ...' – *Hindustan Times*

'*Dark Circles* has one of the most realistic depictions of depression in recent fiction' – *Hindu*

'*Dark Circles* is a sensitive study of the anguish of its main characters' – *Indian Express*

SCARLET SANDS

UDAYAN MUKHERJEE

PICADOR INDIA

First published in 2024 by Picador India
an imprint of Pan Macmillan Publishing India Private Limited
707 Kailash Building
26 K. G. Marg, New Delhi 110001
www.panmacmillan.co.in

Pan Macmillan, The Smithson, 6 Briset Street, Farringdon, London EC1M 5NR
Associated companies throughout the world
www.panmacmillan.com

ISBN 978-93-6113-138-7

1 3 5 7 9 8 6 4 2

Typeset in Dante MT Std by R. Ajith Kumar, New Delhi
Printed and bound in India by Thomson Press India Ltd.

FSC www.fsc.org
MIX
Paper | Supporting responsible forestry
FSC® C010615

For Tinnie

Prologue

DAWN WAS BREAKING OVER A DESOLATE VAGATOR beach, the darkest hour almost reluctantly giving way to a faint lightening of the horizon, its sheen reflected on gently lapping waves. There wasn't much of a moon, and all that was on offer was silhouettes – rocky outcrops, coconut palms and a few shanties. A damp wind wafted about, as if clearing the decks for the day to take over. It was perfectly still, except for the distant sound of a pickup truck driving away, odd for this ungodly hour, odder still in Goa.

There wasn't a soul in sight, but a closer look at the barren stretch of sand revealed the outline of a human form. A white man in the vest and Bermudas lay resting on his stomach, face turned to the side, legs splayed, arms by his body. It could have been a tourist who had too much to drink the night before and passed out on the sand. But there was something wrong about the positioning of the limbs – they weren't quite those of a sleeping man. Till one reached the head, that is. The dark brown hair was all matted and glued to the skull, with a resin more potent than ordinary sea water. The skull itself had caved in, revealing a concavity so grotesque that there could be only one conclusion: this man would not see the day that was about to unfold. He lay dead, his head shattered from some brutal impact. It seemed so incongruous – here the sun was preparing to light up the world with its wondrous radiance, while there in the sand lay a man whose life had been cruelly extinguished. How could one ever reconcile these beginnings and endings, the delights and horrors that stalked our everyday lives?

The waves began to tentatively creep up on the corpse, one step forward and two steps back, as if they had an inkling of the dreadful sight they were about to encounter. They continued to edge closer, until finally one powerful surge pushed them over the lifeless body. Others followed, and there was something calming about this almost cleansing ritual, the waves washing the body of its pitiful fate. The sea, as old as time, was no stranger to death, yet it seemed to mourn a life that had been taken away far too soon. Unfairly, too, from the look of it.

1

'COME ON, THEN. YOU HAVE BEEN AT IT FOR A WHILE. Say something,' urged the young man by the window, the sunlight streaming in catching a hint of mischief in his eyes.

The girl opposite him smiled. She had an open face, but tinged with melancholy, as if grief had already touched her young years.

'I didn't realize we were in it.'

'Ah, Julie,' he teased gently. 'Since we sat down, all you've done is steal glances in that direction. I may as well not be here. That's alright, as long as we can make a game of it.'

She reached out and stroked his hand. Mark was right.

It was four o'clock on a Sunday afternoon at the Boston Tea Party Club in Cheltenham – a name that sounded grand for what was really like any other roadside cafe, just nicely done up inside. A line of blue leather-upholstered sofas were backed up against wood-panelled walls, all around the room. The bright blue combined well with the warmth of the wood to produce a stylish effect. Distressed wood tables added a mildly bohemian charm, making it seem less stuffy.

The Sunday lunch crowd had already left, and the place was empty, except for the young couple in one corner and an ageing woman who sat alone on the other side.

Mark and Julie had this thing going between them. Sometimes, in a public place like a park or a cafe, they would pick a solitary person and try to guess the story of their life – where they hailed from, their line of work, what they could be thinking, what their day had been like, and so on. Julie, training to be a psychotherapist, was generally fond of people-watching. Mark played along. Sometimes it could be fun.

'Alright, Mark,' Julie said, playfully. 'Let's hear what you make of her.'

Mark glanced over at the woman by the stained-glass partition. She appeared to be in her late fifties, or maybe sixty. The heavily lined face made her look older than she probably was. She sat with an untouched glass of lemonade, eyes constantly darting out of the window that looked onto the street. Her right hand rose every other minute to stroke a jade earring. Once, she looked furtively at the two of them, but never again.

'So, Sherlock?' prodded Julie, in a teasing voice.

'Mm, she is obviously waiting for someone. Maybe a

lover? Seems tense. Probably not local, considering how long she studied that menu before ordering her drink. Your turn.'

'Not local, indeed. But I doubt it's a clandestine tryst. Feels more like a meeting with someone she has a strained relationship with – perhaps a sibling, daughter, or even an estranged friend. She seems a bit on edge, a touch anxious. But there's something else, Mark. I sense sorrow in her eyes. Some recent tragedy, perhaps. Don't you see?'

Mark was about to challenge this deduction as highly speculative but his reply was interrupted by the jangle of a bell as the cafe door opened to let in two middle-aged women. Their subject rose from her sofa and greeted them, 'Hello there, I am Grace. You must be Dorothy and …'

'Rachel,' one of them completed.

The women hugged each other. For strangers, as they evidently were, the embraces were warm. As if they knew each other, just hadn't met before.

'There goes my story,' Mark muttered. Julie put a finger to her lips. It wasn't a very large room, so it was easy to pick up the conversation unless one deliberately kept it down.

'I am so glad you could make it. It's quite a journey, especially for you Dorothy, all the way from America.'

'Some things are just too important, Grace, wouldn't you say? I ran into Rachel at the station. Obviously,

I didn't know her but somehow, I had this sense she was one of us. So, I asked if she was headed to the Boston Tea Party. And so she was.'

Rachel smiled. She looked like someone who lived alone in a cottage filled with cats – it was easy to imagine her reclining with a book on a sofa with one of them on her lap, another curled up by her feet. Her voice was gentle, like a kind nurse's. 'It's so good of you to go through all this trouble, Grace. Getting in touch with everyone, organizing this. How many of us, finally, by the way?'

'Well, three others, who should be here any minute. It's only the six of us but I thought it would be enough to start a conversation, at least. I have mails from at least twenty others who said they couldn't make the journey but are here with us in spirit.'

'Twenty, you say? Even that would have been too few, right? I mean there are two hundred and forty-five of us, that's what I read. Two forty-five in the last twelve years. What's that, an average of twenty murders every year? So, yes, bloody hell, we need to start that conversation, as you say,' said Dorothy, in her pronounced American accent, and not quite in Rachel's gentle tone.

Mark clutched Julie's hand, silently mouthing the word 'murders' with a stunned expression. She nodded, patting his hand to keep him from blurting out something. She wasn't any less startled – the meeting had just taken an unexpected turn.

Grace was peering out the window and turned to the others, saying, 'I think the others have arrived. I can see them on the footpath, waiting for someone to cross the street.'

The door opened again and in walked the remainder of the party – three women who couldn't have looked more different from one another, one notably younger than the other two. Greetings were exchanged, more hugs followed. Once they had taken their seats on the blue sofas and chairs, occupying one corner of the cafe, Grace continued, 'I think it may be best if I introduced all of you briefly, though you may know a bit about each other already. I am Grace Wright, as you all know. Hannah Wright's mother. This is Dorothy Parker from Philadelphia, mother of Nicole Parker. Rachel Kelly, Rebecca's mom. Ludmila Lebedev from Moscow, Damir's mother. Mia Davies, sister of Joshua Davies, and Ella Jarvinen from Finland, whose son Leo's death and botched-up investigation gives us fresh cause to knock on the doors of every concerned authority again. In the hope that others won't lose their loved ones as we have.' An obviously rehearsed opening spiel, somewhat trite, yet one which made Julie's throat tighten as she listened on, trying her best to look away from the assembled group.

Ella spoke up next, haltingly. It was apparent that she was wrestling with her emotions and also with her limited command over English. 'Thank you, Grace. The way you fought for the last decade to get justice for your daughter gives me so much courage. It's been incredibly hard to carry on, and sometimes I just feel like giving up. But then I read last month that Hannah's killer was finally arrested and convicted in India. It gives me hope that justice might come for Leo, too.' She paused and lowered her head.

Ludmila, who sat next to Ella, wrapped her ample arm around the woman's frail shoulders.

'Where do things stand with the case now, Ella?' Dorothy inquired.

'There's been some progress. First, they said it was an accidental death. But after I insisted on a second autopsy, it proved that the skull injuries were caused by blows using a heavy object. There is a possibility the case might be reassigned to the Central Bureau of Investigation there. I'm waiting to hear from them.'

The youngest in the group gasped, placing a hand over her mouth. 'Oh my god! This is exactly what happened to Joshua last year. When they found his body on Anjuna beach, the police insisted that the head wounds were from him hitting his head on rocks near the sea, before he got washed away. After they handed his body over to mum, we got a second autopsy done here in the UK. Mum sent the new results back to the Goa police, but they refused to reopen the case, despite her repeated requests. It was only after we heard about the conviction in Hannah's case that mum wrote to Grace and she suggested we try again.'

Ella shrugged. 'That's what they do, Mia. They always call it accidental, till you can apply some diplomatic pressure on them.'

Grace, who had been listening with the resigned look of one who had been through all this before, spoke up. 'Don't give up, is all I can say. My girl was raped and murdered, and they tried to pass it off as a drug overdose. For ten years, I had to fight them till they acknowledged it as a violent crime. I suppose that's why we are here today, right? My Hannah won't come back but we must try and put an end to this. Enough is enough. And Mia, you must use the autopsy report to push the doors open. Something may happen this time.'

'You mentioned something about writing to the Indian PM, Grace?' Ludmila asked.

'Yes, indeed. We need intervention from the top. You see, over the years, on my trips to the courts in Goa, I met a few sympathetic journalists. One of them suggested I write to the PM's office and send a copy of the letter to the media. That would create a stir. But now, I think we should send a joint letter, signed by all of us and as many families of victims we can round up. There are sixty in Britain alone. Our plea should be simple: transfer all pending investigations to a commission appointed by the Supreme Court of India.'

'I also think we should push our Home Ministries to issue travel advisories warning tourists about Goa. That may prevent future episodes,' suggested Rachel.

A waiter hovered nearby, waiting for the opportunity to take their orders. Sensing a pause, he finally spoke up.

The women looked blankly at each other's faces, as if refreshment was the last thing on their minds. Finally, Dorothy took charge, and asking each one of them, placed orders of Lapsang Souchong, Moroccan mint tea, sparkling elderflower, hot chocolate and a salted caramel milkshake.

Once the waiter had left, Mia turned to Grace. 'Mum has told me a lot about you, but I wanted to ask – did you have to travel to Goa often over the years? I mean, for follow-ups with the police and courts?'

'Don't ask. I have practically bankrupted myself in the process, not to speak of the frustration of returning empty-handed every time. Thankfully, the media there took my side, else they would have buried the file long ago.' Grace said this and looked up at Mia, as if a sudden thought had struck her.

'Why? Are you planning to go?'

'I have to. You know that mum went last year but she can't handle it anymore. Plus, I think there is someone there who might help.'

The beverages arrived, and the women gathered around, making plans. Their voices rose in outrage, dipped in despair. If one of them sounded downbeat, the others were quick to offer words of solace. How frail they seemed, how damaged; yet how undeniably strong.

Julie realized they would all take back much more from the meeting than a renewed resolve to pursue action. There was a potent solidarity among these women that transcended their shared grief.

A call came in from Stockholm and Grace put it on speaker phone for everyone to hear – another bereaved mother. But the line was bad, and the call was abruptly disconnected.

At that moment, Julie stood up, motioning to Mark, and they quickly departed from their corner. As they made their way out, they heard Grace asking Mia when she intended to leave for Goa.

'Next week actually. I should have done it long ago,' Mia's steely voice echoed as the door closed behind them.

2

NEVILLE STOOD ON THE BALCONY OF THEIR BUNGALOW in Assagaon, preparing a drink for his wife. Oddly, she had taken to cashew feni, some new brand called Cazulo. Nice bottle, he had to concede, though the smell still made his stomach turn. Shehnaz swore it was unlike any she had tasted before. It would have to be, as Neville remembered distinctly how much she once detested the spirit, revered as it was in this land. For good measure, he added a dash of bitters, an orange peel and topped it off with ice and soda, hoping that would suppress the pong. For himself, he poured a measure of Hapusa gin, another not-inexpensive local hit which claimed to use Himalayan juniper berries. Every week, a new gin seemed to hit the shelves in Goan supermarkets. RIP Blue Riband, not a day too soon either, thought Neville. They raised their glasses. 'To rain.'

It was seven in the evening on a rained-out August day in Goa. The past week had been relentless. They loved it but could imagine the plight of people who had to travel to work every day braving this weather. Everything around them seemed lush and verdant. The trees looked happy to have been born in Goa. The only worry was snakes, which Shehnaz was mortified by. This was the season.

Neville walked into the house and turned the lights on. The sight of the rooms through the glass doors gave Shehnaz's heart a lift. It had been nearly three months since they had moved in and every day, on their return from walks, they would look at each other and smile, thinking the same thing. They had lucked out.

What added to their relief, in no small measure, was the tumultuous period that preceded their move. Neville and Shehnaz had decided to sell their cottage in Birtola in the lap of a quaint Himalayan village; a place they had intended to grow old in. But it was not to be. There had been a gruesome murder and the circumstances that followed made it difficult for them to stay on. The victim had been their neighbour Clare Watson and the future of the estate where they had their dwelling was shrouded in uncertainty following the outcome of the case. At any rate, a miasma of the events would have lingered over the place, spoiling the perfection of the setting. After packing up from Birtola, they spent some time in Shehnaz's flat in Colaba, only to realize that they had lost their taste for city life. They now preferred a quieter place with the option of visiting the city occasionally, not the other way around. The balance had shifted. Neville and Shehnaz could never have expected to grow weary of Mumbai, their beloved city where they were both born – Neville in Kalbadevi and Shehnaz in Colaba. For sixty years, Mumbai had been their universe, where Neville rose to acquire a near celebrity status in his career with the Bombay police while Shehnaz enjoyed a long and successful stint as the editor of the city's biggest newspaper. In the eyes of the Mumbai chatterati, they were a power couple.

But the years wore Neville down. Finally, it was the grisly murder of a teenaged girl at the hands of a feared underworld don that led to his unravelling. He took a long sabbatical from the force before returning for another stint, but things were never quite the same. Till, around his sixtieth birthday, they took the plunge and decided to shift to the mountains of Kumaon. Unfortunately, their idyll was short-lived, forcing them to seek another nest.

Goa had been the obvious choice. Growing up in Bombay, it had always been the go-to place for quick getaways. The state had reasonably good infrastructure and was just a short flight away from Mumbai, where Neville and Shehnaz still held apartments. The climate, barring certain months, was a challenge, but one couldn't have it all. Besides, which place was blessed with good weather, all year round?

After the Birtola murder, they were both clear that they would rent for a while before deciding to put down roots in any place. This business of buying and selling houses was not one to be indulged in more frequently than was absolutely necessary.

Originally, they aimed to rent one of the charming old Goan bungalows around the villages of Moira or Aldona, away from the din and bustle of touristy North Goa. However, their broker suggested a drive through Assagaon instead.

'For people like you, Assagaon will be better, sir. Aldona may be cheaper, but you won't be able to step out of your home and stroll across to some posh restaurant there. Or a trendy boutique, for that matter. And those places, they get too quiet after sunset. Here, you have both scenery and action,' had been his exact words.

Shehnaz had been inclined to dismiss this advice, but Neville said a drive through couldn't harm them. They had been stunned at the transformation of Assagaon. What used to be a quiet, lush village with gentle hillocks and dense groves, now bristled with cafes, shops, galleries, bars and large incongruous dwellings. The neighbourhood remained leafy but had turned trendy and chic, just as the broker promised. Apparently, it had become the most sought-after place to reside in, with the property prices the broker mentioned making them jump in their seats. Why, it would put some Mumbai localities in the shade.

Before Neville could tell their broker that it was way too expensive, he surprised them by announcing that one could still find some old bungalows on lease. It turned out that many of them had ownership issues. The titles were not owned by any one person and there were usually many claimants, legitimate or not, making it impossible to do a clean sale. The next best option was to rent these houses out to city folk and split the rent between members of the family. The property didn't change hands yet generated a neat pile of cash each month. Some of the owners had been far-sighted enough to plough back part of the rental proceeds towards interior restoration, to suit the tastes of their demanding lessees. The better the condition, the higher the rent, after all. It was to such a bungalow that Neville and Shehnaz were led, at the end of their Assagaon excursion. The broker had it all mapped out. The moment the car stopped outside the house, Shehnaz let out a shriek of delight. The broker had smiled smugly,

'What did I tell you, madam?'

There was no date plaque at the entrance, but Neville reckoned it couldn't have been built later than mid to late nineteenth century. There was a name plaque though bearing the name *Sossegado*, the Portuguese word for *susegad* – a term they associated with the relaxed and contented attitude that characterized life in Goa. A rusted iron gate led to a green courtyard, overgrown with bushes and shrubs, flanked by two towering trees – one jackfruit, the other mango. There was some land at the back too, where there had been an attempt to clean up, though it could hardly be called a garden. In it, Shehnaz could already see herself toiling away in the humid afternoons.

In the centre, stood the bungalow itself. It featured a balcony with an ornately carved railing, glass-panelled doors opening into a spacious living area and a front study. The back portion of the house had three large bedrooms with ensuite bathrooms and a delightful kitchen. Two of the bathrooms even had proper bathtubs. The ceilings were high with wooden rafters running along the slanted roof, tiled from outside. The wood-framed windows were huge, each almost six feet tall, with oyster shells fitted inside. The old mosaic tiling on the floor was still intact, only scuffed or chipped in some places. The outside walls of the house were a dazzling shade of green while the walls inside were ochre yellow, with the exception of the study which was turquoise. These colours, which may have looked bizarre in any other city, seemed to fit in perfectly here.

'How Mediterranean!' Shehnaz exclaimed.

'Old Portuguese villas, madam; where will you find them today?' the broker remarked, proprietorially.

Neville corrected him. 'Not really. The Portuguese had little to do with most of these houses. They were designed and built by Goans like you. You can say they were inspired by European architecture, but these are Goan bungalows, really.'

Seeing the broker's face fall, Shehnaz rushed to his rescue. 'Why not take credit for a lovely house?' she offered, and the broker grinned back.

The bungalow was available for lease and the rent, though stiff, would easily be covered by the monthly proceeds from Neville's apartment in Kalbadevi. Neville and Shehnaz conferred and made an offer which was accepted. They had the house on lease for two years – enough time for them to figure out if Goa was where they wanted to be and which part of it would be ideal.

'Let's treat it like a long holiday while we make up our minds. Do the tourist number full on, what say?' beamed Shehnaz.

Neville smiled indulgently, knowing how quickly his wife would tire of the city set they saw milling around the restaurants every week. It was only a matter of time before she would be tugging at his sleeve to hop across to Aldona and check it out. But Neville wondered how long it would be before that too became another Assagaon. The march never stopped.

Anyway, here they were, a few months into their new life, savouring the delightful monsoon and the many charms of Assagaon. In fact, that very afternoon, they had lunched at a popular local eatery and were still reeling from the effects of it.

'We shouldn't be doing this too often, you know, Neville. Gosh, I must have put on five kilos since we shifted here.'

'Nonsense. You are just recovering from the forced deprivation of Birtola,' Neville teased.

Shehnaz laughed. It was so true. In that mountain village, you felt jubilant if you got your hands on a sprig of basil. Heaven knows how they managed two years, given their fondness for good food. As habitual city dwellers, the lack of high-quality provisions and produce had been an everyday challenge in the hills.

As a concession to the lunch, Neville hadn't laid out the roasted cashews, their staple snack with an evening drink. But then, Martin arrived bearing a plate.

Martin, their housekeeper, had come with the bungalow. He, along with his wife Agnes, took care of their every need and fed them till they were about to drop. Martin was a funny man. At their first meeting, he had said, pointing to the house, 'This is the bride, sir. And I am the dowry. I come with her.'

'Ah. But dowries are gifts, right? So, no salary, I am guessing?' Neville had teased. Martin's comeback had been instant.

'Then I am the bride, sir and she is the dowry,' this time, pointing at Agnes. Shehnaz had known instantly they would get along.

'What's this, Martin?' Shehnaz inquired, now eyeing the plate.

'Agnes sent some Goan sausages chopped up with onion, madam.'

'Oh dear. We are stuffed from lunch.'

Neville thought he caught a whiff of feni from where Martin stood, just hoping it wasn't from the Cazulo bottle. Martin didn't try to hide that he enjoyed his drink but was supposed to imbibe only after duty hours. Neville didn't bother bringing it up. Martin left the plate on the table and slinked off.

Shehnaz had smelt the feni too. 'It's alright, Neville. What else does one do here on a wet evening like this?'

'Right. Which reminds me, we have been invited to a party on Saturday.'

'Again? Where now?'

'At Ravi and Ramola's. Ravi called to say there would be a person of my interest at the party.'

Shehnaz cocked an eyebrow. Neville put up both his palms to indicate he hadn't the faintest who it may be. Ravi and Ramola Tekchandani lived down the lane in a ridiculous looking house called *Alicante* which was part Roman, part Greater Kailash in design and large enough to host a small regiment. Shehnaz had bumped into Ramola at one of the Assagaon boutiques and since then they had dined twice at Alicante and once at theirs. Their company wasn't particularly interesting, but it gave them an opportunity to meet the swish set of Assagaon and get a sense of neighbourhood life, essential for their private evening amusement.

Shehnaz reached out and picked up a piece of sausage, shooting Neville a guilty glance. The stuff was irresistible. A clearing of the throat. Martin had returned.

'Dinner, sir? Agnes sent me to ask.'

Neville patted his stomach. 'Nothing too heavy for me, Martin. Shehnaz?'

'What did you get today from the market?'

'Red spinach, madam. And we have kingfish slices, fresh.'

'Well, you have a meal then. Sauté the spinach like you guys do and shallow fry a few pieces of fish. Just don't dunk it in the recheado masala, OK?'

'Martin, seems like a lot of tourists for this time of the year, no?' Neville remarked.

'Not unusual, sir, around the Independence Day weekend. In fact, over the last few years, this has almost become a mini peak season. The rains are pleasant, the weather cool and there are some office and school holidays in the city. Hotels are mostly full around this time.'

'But seems like these are Indian tourists, not many foreigners. What happened to the Russians on bikes?' Shehnaz asked.

'Madam, they have left.'

'Left? But they even had road signs in Russian; don't you remember, Neville?'

'Yeah, but all that was a while back, dear. When this place used to be a green hill. I think the last time we came to Goa was about seven–eight years ago, right? A lot has changed.'

Martin spoke up. 'Yes sir. There was some trouble with the Russians – drugs and all. The government cracked down on those gangs. Since then, the Russian tourist influx has reduced a lot. But it's not as if foreigners don't come, mostly in winter.'

'Right, I remember the crime scene being quite bad out here back then. Still the same?'

'Bad things happen, sir. But Goa gets worse publicity than other places. Perhaps that's why the tourist seasons haven't been as good in recent years.'

Neville's phone rang. Martin took that as a cue to return to the kitchen, or to the glass that waited.

'Hello?'

'Yes, it is.'

'Peter? This is a surprise. How are you?'

A brief conversation followed. Shehnaz listened in with a look of utter surprise on her face. Peter Watson – it had to be him – had been their neighbour in Birtola. His wife, Clare, had been found murdered in a forest, not far from the mountain cottage Neville and Shehnaz had settled in. Clare had been a friend, and despite every intention of not getting involved, Neville had not only got dragged in but managed to solve the case over the course of two nerve-wracking weeks in that pristine setting. After that episode, Peter had shifted back to London, where he was presumably calling from. They had not been in touch since that episode in October last year.

Neville put the phone down on the table and gaped at Shehnaz in mild bewilderment. 'Peter Watson, would you believe it? Apparently, his second cousin, a boy named Joshua Davies, was found dead on Anjuna beach in May last year. The police claimed it was accidental, but subsequent autopsies have proved that he was bludgeoned to death. I vaguely remember reading about it. It became quite a high profile case, unless I am confusing it with another.'

'How strange for Peter to lose two relatives this way, in this country. Anyway, why was he calling you?'

'Ah yes, apparently the victim's sister Mia, quite close to Peter, is coming down to Goa to look into her brother's death.'

'Look into? Is she a cop? Lawyer?'

'Neither. A currency trader. I guess she will push to have the case reopened and the perpetrator brought to justice. Peter says he advised her against it, but she's determined to go ahead. In fact, she's on her way to India as we speak.'

'And Peter wants you to help her, is that it?'

'Yes, he has an impression that I am well-connected with the police administration and can open doors for her. At the very least, look out for her while she's here.'

Shehnaz sighed. Neville shot her a nervous glance before saying, 'I still can't help but have a soft spot for Peter, after all that he's been through, you know.'

'Next thing you know ...'

'Shehnaz, the poor girl lost her brother in such a terrible way. She's coming to a country for the first time, knows no one here. How could I refuse?' Neville pleaded.

She didn't respond. It had started to rain again, a steady drizzle swirling around as the wind picked up. No deluge, but in the orange light of the sodium streetlamps, it looked like a great whirlwind. A gust blew onto the veranda, almost knocking over the glasses. They picked them up and went inside, where Agnes was laying out dinner.

Neville asked, 'Agnes, did you guys hear about a man named Joshua Davies who was—'

He didn't have to finish.

'Of course, sir. The Anjuna beach murder. It was in the papers every day at the time. The boy's mother had also come down to talk to the police. Such a sad story.'

'I see. So, it was reported as a murder?'

Agnes looked baffled. 'What else, sir? His head was bashed in. But obviously the police were reluctant to pursue it.'

'Why obviously?'

She seemed hesitant. 'Sir, this is all hearsay, but everyone thought there was Angelo Lobo's hand behind it. You know, the minister.'

Agnes scurried away before Neville could ask any further questions.

They finished their meal in silence. Shehnaz appeared distracted.

They lay in bed, reading quietly, when Shehnaz put her hand out and clasped Neville's. 'When does the girl land?'

'Mia? Friday afternoon. Why?'

'We should arrange for her to be picked up and brought here. I'll get Agnes to prepare a bedroom. She can stay with us over the weekend and then move to wherever she is planning to go. I think that will be better.'

'Are you sure?'

'Of course.'

As Neville switched off the light, he whispered, 'Goodnight darling. And thank you.'

'Night, you silly man.'

A wave of relief washed over Neville as he lay staring at the dark outline of wooden beams across the sloping ceiling. When he hung up the phone, he had feared Shehnaz would put her foot down more vehemently this time, quelling even the smallest possibility of any entanglement in another homicide. Her foremost concern was Neville's peace of mind, having witnessed how close to the brink of a complete breakdown his job had driven him in the days before he walked away. He was the first to admit that those fears were not unfounded, yet there was a kernel of something, perhaps his innate sense of humanity, that made it nearly impossible for him to turn away those in desperate need. It was a lesson from his father, one that sustained him through the dark years grappling with evil. Refusing to help was simply not an option. Neville knew that despite everything, Shehnaz was cut from the same cloth. When it came to the crunch, she would fling herself, along with him, into the path of danger to help people.

Yet, along with that ripple of relief, and affection for his wife, Neville felt the stirrings of anxiety. He may have solved the Birtola case but was he really in a position to assist Peter's cousin effectively? More importantly, was it even safe for her to come to these shores poking her stick in what could be a den of snakes? Memories surfaced, as they often did; an image of Mariam Sheikh floating up in his head. He had promised to protect the girl from her mobster father, only to see her brutally murdered shortly after testifying. It was a failure, a betrayal that haunted him still. In his bid to help Peter's cousin, was he exposing another young girl to grievous harm? Neville tossed fitfully, as this unsettling thought took hold of him.

3

DSP MICHAEL ALVARES SAT IN THE BACK SEAT OF HIS JEEP, parked a short distance from the Anjuna police station. He had a folded copy of the morning newspaper on his lap. Seated next to him was police Inspector Mahesh Rane, the head of the Anjuna station. Alvares tapped on the paper, and asked, 'Have you seen this, Rane?'

'Yes, sir.'

'This shit has reached the Prime Minister's Office. I told you the moment they nabbed the guy in the Hannah Wright case, didn't I? That gave them the oxygen they needed. Now all these old cases will be pried open, one by one. Mark my words.'

Rane looked pensive. 'But sir, our worry is the Anjuna case, right? The Finland one is the headache of the Canacona station, isn't it?'

'Use your damn head, Rane. What did the second autopsy reveal? I've already received a call from Kamble at the Foreigners Branch, CID. It's only a matter of time before it lands on our doorstep as well. If the boy's family was anywhere as dogged as that Finnish bitch, the case would already be with the CBI.'

'Sir, in that one, the investigating officer has been suspended.'

Alvares nodded, grimly. That very prospect had been vexing him since morning. If the case went to the CBI, the two of them were screwed.

'Should we reach out to …'

'No, Rane. Let's wait and see which way the wind blows. And keep your trap shut. As far as we are concerned, this is still a closed case. There's no fresh evidence, except for that bloody autopsy report. More than a year has passed. We need to keep our cool. Understood?'

Rane slid out of the jeep, saluted and walked towards the station. Alvares lit a cigarette absentmindedly, then another and sat around for a while, observing a young white couple leaning against their motorcycle sipping coconut water through straws. They looked dishevelled, grimy, as if they hadn't bathed in weeks. His phone rang.

'Good morning, sir.'

'Yes, I did. Nothing to worry about yet, I think. I'm keeping a close eye on it, sir.'

Being a cop in Goa was no longer fun. Alvares missed the good old days.

4

MIA'S FLIGHT TOUCHED DOWN AT DABOLIM AIRPORT AT two in the afternoon. Earlier that day, she had arrived in Mumbai from London, before catching a connecting flight to Goa. She was tired but felt fully alert as she stepped out of the airport. Martin was waiting with a placard bearing her name.

'Welcome to Goa, madam. I have come from Mr Wadia's residence.'

'Thank you very much for coming. Shall we walk to the car park?'

'No, madam, please wait here. I will fetch the car.'

Martin walked away. Mia stood amidst a bunch of boisterous young men clad in neon coloured beach shirts, bermudas and straw hats; the kind of regulation jollity one expected at most seaside destinations. One of them passed around cans of beer. Mia wondered if it was legal to drink in public places in India. She stepped aside and noticed giant street hoardings advertising casinos, hotels and even gambling yachts. It seemed like a big thing in Goa.

Martin returned in a compact sedan and insisted on lifting her suitcase into the trunk. Mia took the front seat next to the driver's, which Martin wasn't expecting.

They set off.

'First time in Goa, madam?'

'Yes, it is. Has there been a lot of rain, of late?' Mia inquired, breathing in the moist air.

'Oh yes. This is the season for rain. But nothing to worry about, especially with Martin at the wheel.'

The wet tarmac reflected the overcast sky. Soon, they turned onto a narrow, winding road flanked by dense vegetation. It was like driving through a tropical forest, till the road opened up to reveal still waters – Mia couldn't tell if it was a river or the sea. There were hardly any waves. Small hillocks rose from the water in the distance and the soil was red. The sides of these hills had been gouged out and they looked like gaping wounds. It made Mia shudder. She turned towards Martin.

'So, how long have you been working with Neville?' she asked.

'Only three months, madam. My wife and I are caretakers of the villa Mr Wadia has rented. People keep changing but we remain with the house.'

'Sir and madam are both very nice. Very proper,' Martin added.

Mia smiled. An odd word for a caretaker to use for his employers, though Peter had had very good things to say about them, too. As they drove on, she admired the verdant surroundings, imagining how she may have enjoyed being here were it not for the grim history that connected her to the place and the job she had come to finish, come what may.

Mia hadn't been sure how her request for leave would be received by her boss at the investment bank she worked for. She was prepared to put in her papers, if it came to that, but Clive had been remarkably supportive. He had sanctioned a three-month leave with the possibility of extension. Her job would be waiting there when she returned. Mia was grateful; such concessions were not easy to come by in the industry she worked in.

Hotels in Goa that charged by the night were turning out to be too expensive for such a long stay, so she had booked herself a small furnished apartment in Anjuna for a month. However, the first message she received upon switching her phone on after landing in Bombay was from Neville, informing her that a car would be waiting at the Goa airport to take her to his place. Assagaon was quite a drive away – they crossed a bridge over the Sal River and another over the Mandovi, from which she could glimpse yachts parked in the water. The larger ones resembled the floating casinos she had seen on billboards.

'Do a lot of tourists come here for the casinos?' Mia asked Martin.

He made a face. 'Yes, madam. Goa has become a drinking and gambling joint. Not that anyone in the tourism trade is complaining. If people don't come, there is no money to go around. So, whatever brings them in.'

After another twenty minutes, Martin said they were nearly there as they drove into a genteel neighbourhood. The car stopped in front of a large cottage surrounded by moss-covered walls and overgrown vegetation. Martin got out, retrieved the suitcase, and opened the gate for her. Mia entered to see a tall, handsome man striding towards her, with wiry grey hair closely cropped, fair skin browned by the sun, and a prominent nose. Mia guessed he was in his sixties.

'Hello, Mia. I am Neville.'

'Hi Neville. It's very nice to meet you. Peter sends his best.'

On the balcony, a petite woman stood with her arms open wide. 'Welcome to Goa, Mia. And to our humble abode. I am Shehnaz.'

Mia liked her immediately. Shehnaz had a way of making you feel welcome without much effort. She was slight – bordering on frail – with a pixie cut, dressed stylishly in a sleeveless black tunic and lavender culottes. Rubies in her ears glinted in the sunlight.

'Hello Shehnaz. I am so sorry to impose upon you this way. But when Peter suggested it, I couldn't refuse, considering how big a help it would be to have someone I know here.'

'Come on, Mia. It's the least we can do. There is no reason to feel awkward in the least. Come, let me show you to your room.'

On entering the house, Mia gave out a low gasp. 'Oh, my word! What an utterly delightful house.'

She looked up at the ceilings, down at the mosaic and all the antique furniture draped in the beautiful upholstery Shehnaz had procured. 'I feel like I am in some Spanish heritage villa. It is remarkable what you've done here, Shehnaz.'

'Well, it isn't exactly ours; we have it only for two years. Then, we will see.'

They walked into Mia's bedroom. The moss green paisley bedcover Shehnaz had arranged that morning looked perfect against the yellow walls. Through the open window, they could see leaves glistening in the rain and two blood-red hibiscus flowers leaning onto the grille.

'Your room, for as long as you want it, Mia. And whenever after that. I mean it. It's just the two of us in this house.'

Mia reached out and touched Shehnaz's arm. 'I don't know how to thank you. This is so ... so settling for me, I cannot tell you.'

Shehnaz smiled. There was no need to. She knew. 'There is hot water. I imagine you will want a shower?

We'll be outside, on the veranda. Please join us for tea when you are ready.'

Shehnaz walked out, closing the door gently behind her.

Neville was waiting. He poured out a cup for her from the teapot.

'She seems very nice. Makes me feel even smaller for having reacted so churlishly the other day.'

'Don't say that, darling. I understand where that comes from. But I tell myself, maybe the universe is always conspiring to put people in our path who need help.'

'You mean *your* path, surely?'

'Are they any different, dear?'

'Touché.'

In a few moments, Mia joined them. Shehnaz offered her tea and mince cutlets made by Agnes. Mia, having had only half a foul sandwich on the flight, wolfed down two of them. It was only then that she reclined on the chair, resting her tired back. Her eyes closed from the comfort of her surroundings. She appeared to be fading, but when she spoke, it was to say:

'I know I have only just arrived, but would it be too much to ask if Martin could drive me to Anjuna beach for a few minutes? I want to stand there for a moment. I'm sorry if this is inconvenient.'

The request was unexpected, but Shehnaz realized why she had made it.

'Why Martin? Finish your tea and we will drive you. It will take less than fifteen minutes,' Neville said. 'We have light until at least half past six.'

Mia drained her cup and stood up. Neville fetched the keys from Martin, and they got into the car. Once they were seated, Shehnaz said, 'You know, Mia, this car has been all over – from the northern Himalayas to the Konkan beach via Bombay. Neville treats it with care worthy of an ageing parent.'

'All Parsis do, dear.'

The sky had cleared slightly, but it was still humid. Ordinarily, he wouldn't, but thinking of their newly arrived guest from cooler climes, Neville turned on the air conditioning. He asked gingerly, 'You wish to go to Anjuna proper or ...'

'Oh yes, let me tell you.' Mia looked at her phone. 'It's Ozran beach actually, also called Little Vagator? Right next to the popular Anjuna beach, apparently.'

'I know the place.'

They reached the beach in just over ten minutes. As soon as Mia stepped out of the car, a flock of vendors swooped in bearing all kinds of hats, ornaments and trinkets.

'Madam, take this hat. Very strong sun, soon your skin will be black.'

'Very lucky bracelet, madam. You find top class boyfriend.'

The women giggled at their own pitches. Shehnaz

shooed them away good-naturedly and said to Mia, 'Earlier I would get irritated, but they have to make a living as well, right? Once, I even bought a sarong from them for Agnes. Come, we need to take the stairs down to the beach. This way.'

They walked down the stone steps towards the sea. It was overcast and the palm trees swayed gently in the breeze. The beach wasn't terribly crowded but a few tourists waded in the water. A red flag fluttered, warning swimmers not to go too far. This was the season for accidents. The first thing which struck Mia was how rocky the beach was. Large mounds of grey, hard rock lay strewn across the sand, some even jutting out of the water. In parts, they looked like the ruins of an old fort. A few metres in, there was almost a small island of rock. Mia took off her slippers.

'Shehnaz, can I leave them here? I will just dip my toes and be back.'

With that, she strode in purposefully. Shehnaz was about to stop her, but Neville shook his head. He could guess what was going through Mia's head.

Mia waded in with swift, strong strides. By the time she reached the rock, the water was nearly at her waist. She climbed over and stood there, staring out at the sea, her back to them. Shehnaz felt a tug in her chest, seeing the girl standing there all alone at the very spot where her brother may have washed up.

Soon after, they heard a loud whistle and saw a coast

guard waving frantically at Mia, asking her to return to the shore. Mia stepped back into the water and waded back. Shehnaz had bought a beach towel from one of the vendors and handed it to her. The sky had darkened again, and it looked like it would start pouring, but Mia remained rooted to the spot, staring fixedly at the same rock, as if under a spell. As they watched, a hand went up to her mouth with a slight tremor. Shehnaz was quick to spot it, and she moved to put an arm around Mia's shoulders but before she could get there, Mia turned and buried her face into her neck. Her body convulsed with sobs. Shehnaz clasped the girl to her tiny frame, murmuring something into her ear. In a few moments, the shaking stopped, and Mia stepped back, her face drenched with tears, looking thoroughly embarrassed.

'I am so sorry. I don't know what came over me but …'

'Shush. It's alright, Mia. I cannot even begin to imagine what you must feel standing on this beach.'

Neville wanted to say something but couldn't bring himself to. Any promise he made would be comforting but empty. So how could he? He didn't know the first thing about what had happened to Joshua Davies in the summer of the year gone by. Looking up at the sky, he said, 'Come, we should head back. It may rain.'

They walked silently back to the car. Curiously, the vendors who watched them from a distance stayed away this time. Perhaps they had seen something.

The rain came down hard as soon as they stepped through the gates of the house, making them scamper the last few yards to the veranda. Martin had set out glasses and an ice bucket on the table. The liquor Neville kept locked away, knowing better than to put temptation in the path of a fond drinker.

'I think we should advance our tipple hour a bit today. What do you say, Shehnaz?'

'I second it whole heartedly. I could do with a drink, and I'm sure Mia wouldn't mind one either.'

Mia smiled, with effort.

'What will it be, Mia? I think we have everything in the bar. There should be some wine too, if you prefer.'

'Oh no, not at all. I'm fine with whatever you're having. Really.'

'I will have whisky, Shehnaz will have feni – a local spirit distilled from cashew nuts – and there's gin or vodka if you want. And beer in the fridge.'

Mia gave it some thought before saying, 'Would I come across as a brat if I said I'd like to try a sip of the feni from Shehnaz's glass, and if I don't take to it, opt for gin and tonic instead?'

'No, you would come across as wise, showing the first signs of shedding your formality,' said Shehnaz with a smile.

All this talk of drinking had lightened their mood a bit. Neville hoped that the drink would help lift some of the heaviness that had settled on them during the drive back from the beach. He poured. Mia took a sip from Shehnaz's glass and shuddered. 'I'm sorry, but this is too strong a taste for me. Can I settle for the gin, please?'

Neville laughed. 'Of course. And if it's any comfort, I hate that stuff myself. But to each their own. Here you go.'

They clinked glasses.

'To healing,' Shehnaz said, and the moment felt solemn. In wafted Martin, ready to dispel the gloom.

'Madam, I got prawns and chonak today. And Agnes has made sorpotel.'

Shehnaz clapped her hands. 'You eat everything, Mia? Any allergies?'

'Shucks, I forgot completely!' Mia jumped up from her chair and excusing herself, rushed into the house. She returned in a minute, holding a bottle of single malt in her hand. Extending it to Shehnaz, she said, 'A small gift. I didn't know what to get, but Peter said both of you are fond of whisky. I should have got you something for the house, but ...'

'Thank you very much, Mia. You needn't have, but it is much appreciated. And yes, we remember sharing malts with Peter up in Birtola. Till ...'

'Shehnaz was asking about any food allergies,' Neville butted in, before the mood turned sullen again.

'Oh, no, none at all. I eat everything and in large quantities, too, though you wouldn't guess looking at me.'

That was true. Mia had a schoolgirl's slimness, though Shehnaz guessed she was pushing thirty. She decided to ask, 'How many years apart were you and Joshua?'

'Two. I am twenty-nine and Josh … well, he would have been twenty-seven. He died two days before his twenty-sixth. I even mailed him a card – he loved handwritten cards – but I guess it never reached him.'

Since returning from the beach, Neville had been contemplating the right time for him to ask Mia about the circumstances leading to her brother's death. He wasn't sure if it was too soon but felt that there would never be a good time to ask those questions. He needed to know if he was going to be of any help.

'Mia, I know you have just arrived and must be tired, but whenever you feel ready, I would like you to tell me more. About yourself, Joshua, how he came to be in Goa, where the investigation has led to so far.'

Mia sat up. Her demeanour had changed. 'Yes, I was thinking of that, too. It may take all evening though.'

Shehnaz raised a hand. 'Just give me a moment. Let me settle the kitchen so we aren't interrupted. Dinner at half past eight, nine?'

Mia nodded, and Shehnaz disappeared inside. Mia swiped her phone and held it out to Neville. A picture of a young man – fair, slightly built, like his sister; clean-shaven, dark brown hair combed back, intelligent eyes. No other immediate resemblance to Mia except for the snub nose. In the picture, he stood on a bridge. It looked familiar.

'Is this Paris?'

'Yes.'

Shehnaz had returned and stood over Neville's shoulder, peering into the phone. Mia took a sip from her glass and began. 'Josh and I were born in Cornwall. My grandfather and Peter's grandmother were siblings. My father was an only child and worked at Barclays all his life. We went to school in Cornwall before moving to London for college. After dad passed away suddenly from cancer a few years ago, Mum came to stay with me in London for a while. Now she is back in Cornwall, but she isn't the same; Josh's death broke her.'

Neville handed the phone back to Mia. She glanced at it and turned it back towards them – a picture of Mia and Josh, as college students, posing with their mother. Mia had her mother's face.

'So, after college I went into finance. You could say Peter had some influence in that. We weren't that close during our Cornwall days, but in London, we met quite often. I spent many weekends at Peter and Clare's, and they showed me around. They lived in an amazing house in Camden. Peter is very successful, as you know. Guess I was impressed with all that. Josh, on the other hand, had no interest in a career in management or finance. He studied economics at University College but was always fascinated by the world of corruption and white-collar crime.'

Neville and Shehnaz exchanged a furtive look.

'I know it is an odd thing, but he would spend hours asking Peter about the great financial crisis of 2008. You know, the Lehman brothers, Bear Sterns and all those names. My father had been deeply affected by it, and Josh would have seen it all up close at home. More than me, as I had already come away to London by that time. It may have been born then, this interest.'

'What did he do after he graduated?' Neville asked.

'He became a journalist. A financial journalist, at first.'

'Quite your opposite then. You the banker, your brother out to expose their wily ways,' quipped Shehnaz.

'You could say that. But soon, his interest began to wander outside the narrow world of finance. I think he realized that his real passion was for unearthing stuff that was illegal, exploitative. He quit his pink paper job and started working on documentaries and writing long-format investigative pieces on a variety of subjects. Freelance.'

'Money wasn't a consideration then?' Neville asked.

'No. You see, we always had money in the family. My grandfather was a very wealthy man, coming from a lineage of Welsh landowners with assets that accumulated over the years. My father was an only son, so it all came down to the two of us. We have well-endowed trusts in our names and frankly there is no need to work for a living. I do what I do, but it freed up Josh to pursue what he really wanted.'

Mia was a captivating narrator. Neville liked the way she was filling in the blanks without much prodding, and an image was beginning to form in his head.

'Three years ago, Josh joined this outfit called the Bureau of Investigative Reportage. The BIR specializes in publishing explosive exposés on pretty much every subject. Their reporters spend months chasing a story, which they then offer to reputed international publications. They don't pay much but command immense respect in the world of journalism.'

'I think I have heard of them. Didn't they break the story about the Swiss bank accounts of several prominent billionaires?' Neville asked.

'Exactly. So, Josh's investigations ranged from child abuse in European churches to banking scams to trafficking in North Africa. He never told me what he was working on, only sent me postcards from whichever country he was digging in. And he didn't carry a BIR card.'

'An incognito investigative reporter, would that describe him accurately?' Shehnaz inquired.

'Yes, but at greater risk. Not that it seems to matter that much anymore, but accredited international journalists still carry some immunity with them, more than a nosy tourist at any rate.'

'And you think Joshua was in Goa on such an assignment?' Neville asked it in a matter-of-fact way though he knew how much hinged on the answer.

'Yes. He had to be. He had never been to India before, and I can't think of any other reason why he would suddenly come and park himself here for months. He was on a story. Here's the card he sent me.'

Mia dug into her clutch and produced a postcard. A picture of the sun setting on the sea, from what looked like Morjim beach to Neville. Just one line scrawled in biro: *Mine eyes dazzle. But there's trouble in paradise, sis. Hugs, Josh.* Dated 11 March.

'That makes it clearer, doesn't it?' Shehnaz remarked. 'Were his messages always so cryptic?'

'Yeah, Josh was like that. Deliberately mysterious. Fat lot of good it did him,' Mia's voice was thick with resentment.

'The dateline says March. Is that around the time he arrived in Goa?' Neville asked.

'I can't be sure, but maybe a bit before that? You see, Josh would never meet me before travelling out on an assignment. I'd only know when I received that card. It exasperated me, but I think he found it amusing to surprise me by writing from some exotic place. The last time I met him was in February, at a pub in Piccadilly.'

Neville got up and refreshed their drinks. It had grown dark outside but when he offered to switch on the lights, Shehnaz stopped him. Instead, she fetched a fat red candlestick from the windowsill and lit it. The cicadas had started their calling, and the candlelight threw long shadows on the veranda walls, producing an eerie effect, as if they were immersed in a séance around the table.

'And there was no further communication after that solitary card in March?' Neville asked.

'No, there was. But always tangential. Out of the blue, he'd WhatsApp a picture of a baked crab he was having for dinner. Or of a mango. We didn't speak that much on the phone, so it was through these stray messages I would gather that he was doing fine.'

Shehnaz hesitated, then asked, 'Weren't you close as siblings?'

'I know how it sounds, Shehnaz. Mum couldn't believe that we lived in the same city much of the year yet hardly met, even on weekends. We were close in our own way but led our own lives. What else can I say? Josh was a bit odd. When he was on a story, which was always the case, he would lose interest in anything else. Almost as if nothing in the world existed other than that. Even if he was sitting with you, he wouldn't be all there. I found that a bit off-putting, honestly. So, I just let him decide when he was keen to meet, and this arrangement suited us well. As kids, we were much closer.'

'How is your mother now?' Shehnaz asked. She detected a slight frown on Neville's face, but Mia hadn't heard her.

'Oh, there was another thing. I think he had a girlfriend here.'

'You mean he found one here?'

'I guess so. Since he didn't have one back in London, to the best of my knowledge. Though with Josh, you could never be sure.'

'What was her name?'

'I have no idea! I got one of those cryptic messages from him, saying there's love in the air or something equally vague. When I asked him about it, he clammed up. There was a picture with the message. Let me find it.'

Mia looked through her phone again. 'Here it is.' A shot of two beer mugs on a table. The sea in the foreground and a plastic table that seemed to belong to a beach shack, though no other details were visible. Only the glasses, with the message.

'And that's it?' Shehnaz asked.

When Mia nodded, she felt a surge of irritation inside her. She would have found such a brother absolutely infuriating. Perhaps sensing this, Mia said, 'He was this way only with me. Not with Mum. After every overseas assignment, he'd go home to Cornwall and spend a few days with her. Mum gave him his space but would never take that secretive shit. I hoped he would tell her about the girl on his return from Goa, but he never came back.'

'Obviously this girlfriend, whoever she was, hasn't made any effort to get in touch since that incident, right?' Neville asked.

'No.'

'Did you try to find out about her?'

'Mum did, when she came here last year, but the police seemed to know nothing about her. You see, for them it was always an accidental death, and they were reluctant to dedicate resources to dig deeper. At the time, there was a lot of hue and cry about the murder of a Finnish boy called Leo Jarvinen, and the last thing the police wanted was another suspicious death of a foreign tourist to hit the news.'

'How come we never heard of these cases, Neville?'

'Darling, we were in Birtola around that time, settled into our life of blissful ignorance. I don't know about you, but I didn't read the online papers every day. It didn't seem that important, somehow.'

Shehnaz smiled at him. She remembered; it was exactly as Neville had just described.

'I met Leo's mother, Ella, before I came to India. There was a gathering in Cheltenham, organized by Hannah Wright's mother. You know about that case, right? They contacted mum, but I went for it. Mum hardly ever leaves the house these days.'

At that moment, Agnes knocked on the drawing room door. 'I have laid out dinner, madam. It will get cold.'

They rose and followed Agnes back inside. There was quite a spread on the table; Agnes had made a special effort for their guest. Neville offered Mia a glass of beer, in case she found the food spicy, which she accepted. The food was delicious, and Mia made all the right noises, but Shehnaz could sense she was distracted. They refrained from speaking about Joshua at the table. Agnes was hovering nearby, and they could hear Martin pottering about in the kitchen. When the meal ended, they returned to the veranda. The candle had nearly burnt out and the street was quieter. Neville thought of offering Mia a post-prandial drink but decided against it. She had already had quite a bit, and he could also see she was beginning to fade.

'What's the plan for tomorrow then?' he asked.

'I wanted to go visit the guest house where Josh stayed – Rainbow Beach guest house in Anjuna. I want to see his room. He stayed there for about three months. You don't have to come, though.'

'I would like to.'

Neville left it there and Mia didn't protest. Shehnaz walked Mia back to her room before switching off the house lights. It was late and they decided to turn in as well. They had a long night coming up the next day, the party at Alicante.

As Shehnaz cleaned her face in front of the carved dressing table in their bedroom, she asked, 'Do you think the two murders could be connected?'

'You mean Leo and Josh's? It's possible. But how can we know what story Joshua was working on? And where did this girlfriend vanish? Over a year has passed, Shehnaz.' Neville shook his head.

Shehnaz rose from her chair and as she moved towards the bed, noticed a flicker of movement outside the window. She peered through the glass, then gestured to Neville to come over with a finger to her lips. They stood there by the window, captivated by a strange sight. By the caretaker's outhouse in the back garden, Martin was dancing. In the dim glow of the bulb outside their door, he moved gracefully in the light drizzle. Arms in the air, hips swaying in rhythm to some tune in his head, legs gliding back and forth. He was obviously drunk, but there was such natural elegance to his moves that Neville and Shehnaz watched in rapt admiration. Suddenly, Martin stopped and began to giggle uncontrollably, as if realizing the absurdity of his solitary dance. He was bent over in laughter when Agnes appeared at the door, sternly chiding him back to bed.

5

ANGELO LOBO SAT STARING FIXEDLY AT THE GLASS OF whisky in front of him. It was his fifth. A cigarette smouldered in the ashtray; peanuts scattered haphazardly around it on the table. He looked less like a powerful cabinet minister, more like a drunkard spoiling for a brawl. Occasionally, he lifted his gaze from his reverie to stare distractedly at the TV screen mounted on the wall.

'Francis!' he shouted. A young boy scampered in. 'Has Jakob returned?'

'Not yet, boss.'

'Motherfucker.'

Francis slinked away.

Angelo's attention returned to the newspaper. The page was folded to the same report DSP Alvares was reading earlier in the day. He drained his glass and called a number on his phone.

'Kamble, Lobo here. What's the situation?'

As Kamble answered, Angelo poured out another drink with his left hand. The ice bucket was empty, and he made a mess of trying to tip the cold water from the bucket into his glass.

'So, the CBI will take over the Jarvinen case. I see. And the other cases?'

'Well, you keep in touch with Alvares and that dickhead from Anjuna station. I don't want trouble, Kamble.'

Angelo slammed the phone down, his bloodshot eyes surveying the puddle spreading across the floor. A shadow fell on the table. It was his son, Jakob. He looked unsteady.

'You were looking for me?'

'Why aren't you looking straight at me, huh? What have you had?'

'None of your business. I do as I please with my own money.'

'I see. And who has to bail your ass out when you mess up white pussies, you bastard? Where is all this swagger then?'

Angelo picked up the newspaper and flung it at his son's face, snarling, 'Now listen to me, you fucker. Lie low for the next month or so. I don't want to hear a squeak about you until this thing blows over. There's enough shit to handle already.'

Jakob turned and walked away in a huff. Just then, a woman swept into the room, her hair wild and eyes burning. She wagged a finger at Angelo, who didn't appear particularly perturbed at the appearance of his wife. 'Judgement day is coming. You will all get what you deserve. No one will be spared. You wicked men! All of you will burn in hell.' She spat on the ground before disappearing into the dark corridor.

Francis returned, clutching an ice tray. 'Boss, shall I get something to eat?'

'What? No, not yet. Francis, do know where Cheltenham is?'

Francis shook his head.

'No? I do. Hell! It is in hell.'

6

IT TURNED OUT TO BE A CLEAR MORNING. MIA'S ROOM lay still as Neville and Shehnaz stood on the veranda, ready to set out for their morning walk. They decided to leave Mia undisturbed, letting her sleep off the jet lag. As they stepped out, Shehnaz glanced up at the sky.

'It promises to be a scorcher,' she remarked. 'I wonder what time Mia has in mind for the Anjuna visit.'

'Let her wake up first,' Neville replied.

From the other side, Vineet Shroff approached briskly, his Labrador – dashingly named Romeo – in tow. Another member of the Assagaon set – an architect.

'Hey, Neville. Morning, Shehnaz,' Vineet greeted them, his vest drenched with sweat. 'Quite sticky out here, isn't it?'

'It's either rain or sweat, take your pick,' Neville quipped with a smile.

Shehnaz patted Romeo on the head. 'We'll see you tonight at the mansion,' she said as Vineet headed off, a knowing smile lingering on his lips.

'I am convinced he's gay,' Shehnaz said under her breath.

'Perhaps,' Neville replied. 'He's certainly more personable than our other neighbours.'

The road curved gently as they turned onto an avenue parallel to theirs. It was humid.

'What are you thinking, Neville?' Shehnaz inquired.

'What? Oh, I was wondering if Mia is going to make much headway with her search. Returning empty-handed is one thing; I just hope she doesn't put herself in harm's way.'

'You think that's possible?'

'Why not? When there's so much at stake, people can become dangerous, you know that,' Neville replied solemnly. 'With all this publicity – PMO, CBI, a string of unsolved cases and a politician with a nasty reputation … I don't know. Just have a bad feeling about it.'

'You should tell her that.'

'She is unlikely to listen, Shehnaz. Put yourself in her shoes. She needs closure, of some kind, to be able to get on with her life. There's her mother, too.'

'Yes, her mum sounds clinically depressed. Maybe Mia feels she owes it to her to find out who did this to Joshua.'

'If I am to be of any help, I need to first talk to someone who knows the local scene inside out – one of those fact junkies who know everyone's business,' Neville mused. 'Every place has one of those, you know the kind I mean?'

'What if Satish Kalia were to suddenly appear from across the street?'

Satish Kalia, the Delhi Crime Branch officer who had assisted Neville in clearing up the Birtola case. They made an unlikely but effective duo.

'The things you think of, Shehnaz.'

'Why, you did end up getting along with him eventually, though initially he did strike me as a bit of a boor. Maybe that's what you are missing, Neville – a man in uniform to do the legwork, leaving you to do the thinking.'

Neville didn't contest this.

A woman selling jasmine garlands stood on the roadside. They had met her before, and Shehnaz picked out three.

'I'm not carrying money with me, Malti. Come home and take it later in the day?'

Malti shook her head with a wide grin, as if it didn't matter.

Upon returning home, they found Mia sitting on the veranda, holding a cup in her hand. She looked slightly dazed.

'Good morning, Mia. Here, some fragrant flowers to start your day with. You can wrap them on your wrist, like this,' Shehnaz offered, demonstrating.

Mia lifted her wrist to smell them. 'Amazing! I love them. Thank you so much. Did you go for a walk? I would have loved to join.'

'Tomorrow, you're welcome to come along. Slept alright?' Neville asked.

'Oh, yes. All those delicious things you fed me,' Mia replied with a smile.

'Feel up to an excursion or would you rather take it easy today?'

Mia stood up immediately. 'No, no. I must go to the guest house. Let me quickly go shower; I'll be ready in a jiffy.' She was about to dart off inside, but the puzzled faces of her hosts made her pause.

'I mean, whenever you're ready, of course. I'm so sorry, I don't mean to rush you. You've just got back from your walk.'

'That's alright. Anyway, it's only half past seven now. I don't think we can knock on anyone's door in Goa before ten.'

Once they had all had their baths and enjoyed a hearty breakfast of poi and akuri, Neville turned to Mia. 'This Rainbow Beach guest house – how did Joshua come across it? I tried looking it up online but couldn't find anything. It isn't listed on any of the booking sites.'

'That's odd. We might need to ask around once we reach the area,' Mia replied.

They left instructions for lunch with Martin, who appeared distinctly hung over, and got into the car. On reaching Anjuna, they asked a shop owner who pointed to two houses across a paddy field.

'The yellow house belongs to the writer, and the purple one next to it is what you're looking for,' the shop owner pointed out.

'A writer?' Shehnaz asked, intrigued.

'Naresh Sardesai, madam. Famous writer of Goa. Now with round-the-clock police protection.'

Shehnaz appeared bemused. 'A man in Josh's mould – speaking in riddles.'

Neville parked the car by the side of the field, and they walked down a raised mud path between two waterlogged fields. Under the bright sunlight, the greenery shimmered with neon-like intensity.

'It's refreshing to see open fields in a city. How come there are so few houses?' Mia wondered aloud.

'Farmland, protected from development by regulations. Doesn't stop them from trying though. This is one of the state's major scams – to grease palms and get the land use norms changed, enabling construction of buildings,' Neville explained. 'But these places are safe for now.'

They arrived at the purple house, where a jaded-looking man in bermudas and a singlet stood by a mini truck. He held a pair of pliers in his hand. There was no signage anywhere indicating that it was a commercial establishment.

Neville walked up and addressed the man, 'We are looking for the Rainbow Beach guest house.'

'This is it, but no longer a guest house. Since last December,' the man replied.

'Oh, I see. I'm Neville Wadia, and this is my wife Shehnaz. We live in Assagaon.'

A woman appeared at the doorway of the house, dressed in a crumpled nightie, her hair dishevelled, looking like she had just got out of bed. Shehnaz took a step towards her and caught a strong whiff of feni, a smell she recognized.

'Hello, you must be the owners of the guest house. Sorry about this unannounced visit, but this is Mia Davies from London, sister of Joshua Davies who stayed here last year.'

Shehnaz needn't have added the last bit, as the woman's face had transformed at the mention of Mia's name. She had known.

'There's nothing more we can say about the boy. We have said all we had to say to the police and,' the husband said, turning to Mia, 'to your mother as well.'

The woman raised a hand to stop her husband. 'Please come in.' She stood aside to let them enter. The reek of hooch was pronounced as they passed her. In the seconds they took to adjust their vision to the room's interiors, the woman stepped swiftly to the cot and placed something behind it. She pointed to a set of blue plastic chairs piled up in one corner. Neville pulled out three, and the woman sat down heavily on her bed, speaking in a very low voice, as if she had no energy.

'I am Jennifer Pinto. That is Roy outside. We used to run the place as a guest house until last year. There are a couple of rooms upstairs which were rented out, mostly to foreigners. It was good income during the season. We stopped after the incident. It wasn't worth the trouble.'

'How long did Joshua stay here?' Mia asked. Jennifer had no difficulty following her Cornish accent. She was used to foreigners, Shehnaz thought.

'I think he started staying here from the beginning of March. Till ...'

'You mentioned two rooms. Were there other guests while he was here?' Mia probed.

'Occasionally, but not often. April and May are the hot months; we don't get many tourists. Perhaps one or two guests for a couple of days, if that.'

Neville was happy to let Mia do the talking. She had a clear, logical mind. 'Did you guys get along with Joshua?' she pressed on.

Jennifer looked surprised at the question. 'Yes. We'd meet briefly in the morning when I brought him his tea and breakfast. After that, he'd be gone all day. He had his own key and used the back staircase to his room. Often, we wouldn't know when he returned.'

'Did Joshua ever talk about what kind of work he was doing here?'

'No,' Jennifer replied curtly.

'Did he have any visitors?' There was a moment's hesitation, which Neville didn't miss.

'There was a girl who came by sometimes. We saw her leaving the house a few times.'

'Do you remember her name?' Mia asked.

'I think it was Eva.'

'Eva what?'

'No idea. We never spoke. Sometimes, your brother left instructions with us to pass on a message if she came by when he wasn't around. That's how I know.'

'Was she British?'

'American I think, but I'm not sure.'

'Did you tell mum, my mother, about Eva when she visited?'

'No.'

'Why?'

'She never asked.'

Neville raised an unobtrusive finger, signalling that he wanted to ask the next question. 'Do you remember the last time Eva visited Joshua here?'

Jennifer paused to think. 'A few days before the incident.'

'Few? As in one, two, three?'

'Perhaps two.'

'Right. And during his stay, did you ever overhear Joshua talking to Eva, or on the phone … in passing, which may have given you some idea about his interests, friends or line of work?'

'No. As I said, he was out much of the time. We have our own work to do on the fields. My husband has a hardware shop. When he does deliveries on his truck, I go and sit there.'

'When the police came to speak to you, after Joshua's death, did they inquire about any specific people? Whether he may have known them?' Neville asked.

Jennifer hesitated briefly. 'They asked if he knew the other boy who had died. If he had ever visited Joshua here.'

'The other boy? You mean Leo Jarvinen from Finland?' Mia interjected.

A mild nod of the head.

'And had he?'

'No, I told the police he didn't,' Jennifer confirmed. 'Why are you asking me all this again?'

Mia's voice rose slightly. 'Because of me. I cannot be at peace till I have some idea of what happened to Joshua. My mother is ill. We need to know, don't you see?'

Jennifer stared down at the floor.

'I am sorry,' Mia was quick to apologize. 'Is it possible to see the room Joshua stayed in? It must not be in use.'

Jennifer rose, retrieving a key from a metal box on a shelf and handing it to Mia. She motioned for them to follow. Outside, the day was bright and sweltering. Shehnaz felt sweat trickle down her back as they rounded the house to a back area where a winding iron staircase rose to the first floor. Jennifer pointed towards the right. 'It's the door marked "1" on the right-hand side. You can return the key to Roy on your way out.'

Their interview was concluded, Jennifer had shared all she knew. They walked up the stairs and entered the room. It was dim and musty. Neville found a switch that flooded the room with harsh white light. Its sparse furnishings gave it a monastic feel: a single cot against the wall on one corner, a writing table and chair, one makeshift wooden clothes-hanger. The walls were bare except for whitewash, and a single closed window let in scant light. Dust and mildew had settled on every surface, mould spreading on the window ledge. It looked more like a prison cell than a guest room. There was a door near the foot of the bed, the bathroom presumably. Neville walked up to the table to check if there was a drawer. There wasn't. Every part of the room was immediately visible to them. Even the mattress had been removed from the cot; it was bare.

Mia opened the window, revealing a view of trees and the yellow house where the author lived. Shehnaz heard her exhale softly, as if finding solace in the fact that her brother had at least this view to gaze out into. Out of habit, more than anything else, Neville pushed open the bathroom door. A rank odour drifted out. A washbasin, a tap in a corner, a shower. A tiny mirror on the wall above the basin in which Neville caught a reflection of Mia, one hand at her neck, face twisted in distaste. She turned away, standing near the cot for a minute, eyes shut. Then she abruptly left the room. From outside the door, they heard her shaky voice, 'I am done, Neville. I will wait downstairs, if you don't mind.'

There was nothing to be gained by staying on in that miserable room, and Shehnaz and Neville followed Mia, locking the door behind them. They walked back to the front yard, where Roy still stood beside his van. Neville handed him the key. 'Thank you. And sorry for disturbing you again.'

Roy shrugged nonchalantly.

'Did you have a lot of people coming around to ask questions after the incident?' Neville asked.

'Not many. The cops came, once or twice. Then they let us be. Some newspaper folks with cameras,' Roy replied.

'And what about Eva, the girl Jennifer mentioned? Did she ever return?'

'No.'

'Not even once?'

Roy shook his head.

Neville gestured at the house next door and asked, 'Do you guys meet him sometimes?'

'Naresh, you mean? Yes, Jennifer makes his dinner every evening and takes it over. Once he has eaten, she cleans up and leaves. If he needs something, he tells me, and I fetch it. There's no one else working for him. Us and the policeman, now,' Roy explained.

'Did Joshua know Naresh?' Mia queried.

'Yes. They were friends.'

'Friends?'

'OK, maybe not friends but sometimes he would go across and they would sit and chat.'

'I see. Well, thank you again. You have been very kind,' Mia said.

As they walked away, Roy offered, 'I am sorry about what happened to your brother.'

Mia nodded awkwardly.

A man in full police attire sat on a chair under a tree, at the gate of the yellow house. He stood up as they approached.

Neville introduced himself and showed him – a bit bashfully Shehnaz thought – his old Mumbai police ID.

'We are not here in an official capacity. I retired from the force a few years ago. This concerns the death of a young man who Mr Sardesai knew. Can we speak to him for a few minutes?'

The man stood at attention immediately. 'Sir, please wait here. Let me check with him. He doesn't meet too many people.'

'I understand. We will wait.'

The guard came back in a few moments and ushered them inside. Entering the house, their first impression was that of having walked into a public library, only less neatly arranged. Every corner of the large room was crammed with books. Shelves, almirahs, tables overflowing with them. In the middle of all that sat a skeletal figure. The thing that struck one immediately about Naresh Sardesai was his eyes – large, bulbous eyes that burned like a fire. It was as if his emaciated body was only a receptacle for that extraordinary vision, and the mind that nourished it. They knew they were in the presence of an exceptional man.

Shehnaz walked up to him and bending down, said, 'Mr Sardesai, we are so sorry to intrude like this. It's just that Mia has ...'

'Mia? Did you say Mia?' The strength in Naresh's voice surprised Shehnaz; she had expected no more than a hoarse whisper. Naresh gazed intently at Mia's face.

'You are Joshua's sister then? Come closer.'

Mia approached him, and Naresh clasped her hand in both of his. They were so frail that Mia feared they might crumble at the slightest squeeze. He sat silently for a moment, holding her hand, before speaking again.

'Please, sit down. I can't offer you anything to drink unless you ask Laxman to give Jennie a holler.'

'No, no, that's not necessary at all. We will only be here a few minutes. We came to see Joshua's room at the guest house and heard that you knew each other. So, we came by to see you,' Mia explained.

'Yes. And what are your names?'

Neville introduced himself and Shehnaz.

'Ah, you are Parsis? I had a Parsi friend in Bombay, a doctor. He lived on Malabar hill. They say Parsis go batty with age, but not my friend. Very sharp, till the end. He was a man of science. Anyway, so you have come to see where Joshua lived?'

'Yes, and to learn about the circumstances surrounding his death, if possible,' Mia added, hesitantly.

Naresh cocked his head. 'Justice. You want justice then. It's a curious notion, this justice. I often ponder its meaning. What does it feed in us? What is its price? What do you come seeking, Mia? Revenge? Closure?'

Shehnaz could see Mia's face flush slightly.

'I cannot frame it in such intellectual terms, sir. I cannot sleep, knowing that my kid brother was battered to death in another country. I cannot digest the fact that his brutal murder has been covered up as an accidental death and ... and the guilty are roaming scot-free. And I cannot bear to witness my mother slowly fading away day by day.'

If Naresh was taken aback by this outpouring, he showed no sign of it. He responded calmly, 'Of course, I understand. But, what if ... anyway, you have my deepest sympathies, Mia. I knew Joshua. He was a lovely boy. I feel terribly sad about him.'

This defused any resentment in Mia. She looked embarrassed.

'Joshua visited the first time, intrigued by the idea of a doddering octogenarian writer living under police protection. I told him that I found it even more odd than he did. They restricted me from going on my walks, do you know? That was the day my physical decline started; I can feel it.'

'What led to all this?' Neville asked.

'An author, a close friend, was murdered by right-wing fascists in Karnataka. You know who I am talking about. Apparently, I featured in their hit list too. So, the state, which otherwise does a commendable job of sheltering these thugs, took it upon itself to provide me with what they call "security". You see, it won't look good if I am bumped off in the heart of Goa. Else, they couldn't care less,' Naresh explained wryly.

'Have there been any direct threats?'

'Yes, that too. There's an outfit here called the HSS, the Hindu Shresthata Sangh – the name is enough to tell you what they are about – who have apparently issued threats in public gatherings. An outfit your brother was interested in.'

Mia shot Neville a glance before continuing. 'Did Joshua mention anything about him trying to find out more about them?'

'No. But he was curious. He wasn't familiar with my writing, so he was surprised they could see me as a threat, someone unknown to the wider world outside. I remember telling him that *was* the reason, the fact that I wrote in Konkani and reached ordinary people. These thugs don't care that much about intellectuals who write editorials in English dailies or novels for Western readers. Joshua struggled to comprehend that. I didn't blame him.'

'Did he ever speak about what he was doing in Goa?' Mia probed further.

'No. I asked him once, but he was evasive, and I never pressed again. If he wished to, he would have told me. He wanted to know about my work. I gave him the only book of mine which has been translated into English and he read it; well, too. The boy had a curiosity rarely seen today in people his age. He was always asking questions,' Naresh recalled, his eyes drifting into the distance, as if he was reminiscing those conversations. They lapsed into a silence.

'You are sure you don't want some tea?'

'Would you like some? Why don't I make some for all of us while you guys talk?' Shehnaz offered.

'That's very sweet of you. I know it is kind of rude, but you can forgive a touch of rudeness in an old man, can't you?' There was a hint of mischief in Naresh's smile.

'How do you take it? With milk and sugar?' Shehnaz asked, heading toward the kitchen.

'Just a few drops of milk, no sugar please. Thank you. You will find everything by the stove,' he replied before turning to Neville.

'I eat the same things every day. Cereal and milk in the morning, which I fix myself, some fruit around mid-day. The only cooked meal is what Jennie brings me early in the evening from her house. A little rice and something. That's enough.'

'So, what else did you and Joshua talk about?' Mia asked.

'Nothing in particular. Sometimes books, sometimes the sea, turtles, politics, anything really. It gave him something, it provided me with some stimuli. The time passed. What else is there, to anything?'

Shehnaz returned shortly with the cups. 'So, you are practically housebound?'

'Unfortunately, yes. But next week, I have an outing.' The mischievous glint in his eye had returned.

'Some national body wants to give me an award, one of those lifetime contribution things. They said they would come and give me the prize in this house. I declined; I had one condition, it would have to be a public event. You know, I detest these gatherings, but it will give me a chance to get out of the house, be driven to Panjim, speak to some friends, and most importantly, deliver a speech where I can ruffle the feathers of these fascists again. That will give me some pleasure.'

'Don't you fear for your life?' Mia asked, concerned.

'What life? This? I've had my life. I cannot write anymore; all that is over. My death – now that would be worth something, if it were at the hands of these villains.

It would create a stir, maybe thwart their progress for a while. *Something*. More than anything I could achieve sitting here, drinking tea made by my guests.'

They could see that Naresh was tiring out; his hand trembled as he held the teacup. Suddenly, he looked very old. Mia had noticed it too. She said, 'I feel so glad to have come here today and spoken to you. You are probably the last person Josh had any meaningful engagement with. That means a lot to me.'

Naresh's eyes grew sorrowful. 'I remember him very vividly today, as if he is in the room, putting my books back onto the shelf. I hope you find what you are looking for.'

They stood up, preparing to leave.

Neville asked, 'Is it alright if we drop in again sometime for a chat?'

'I will look forward to it. Would you like a copy of my book? If nothing else, it may tell you why they hate me so. There must be a few copies in the case there,' Naresh offered, pointing at a glass-paned bookcase.

'I would love to read it,' Shehnaz replied warmly, rising to pick up a copy. *Enemy*, it was titled; winner of the Sahitya Sammelan Award. She thanked Naresh.

'I wish I could write. Perhaps then, I would have some fear of losing my life. You see, I died the day I put down my pen. Goodbye, Mia. Bye, Shehnaz, Neville. You've reminded me of my friend Framroz after such a long time.'

They walked out into the sun. Each moved, in their own way.

In the car, a suffocating silence stretched until Mia broke it with a discordant note. 'Neville, do you think I should meet the investigating officers next? Mum met this police fellow, DSP Alvares. She said he was civil but totally non-committal. Though frankly, I don't know what to make of her assessment.'

'Why do you say that?' Shehnaz asked.

'You should have seen her then. Grief had turned her into a zombie. She would have landed up here, knocked on every door imploring them to search for the truth, and they would all have humoured her as the disconsolate parent, knowing full well she didn't possess the tenacity to pursue the matter beyond a point. I should have come with her, but she refused to let me. Maybe out of fear that I would also come to harm.'

Neville tapped his fingers fretfully. 'I was thinking about what you asked, Mia. You need to speak to someone who has the details of this case. But the investigating officers, like this Alvares, are the ones who pushed it under the carpet. Quite conceivable that they are protecting someone powerful. If so, you would only be alerting them of your presence, and designs, without getting any wiser. I must add that your mother's fears about you ... well, they're not entirely unfounded.'

A flicker of alarm darted across Shehnaz's eyes. 'What do you suggest then?'

'All of this would have been so much easier if I was in active service, Shehnaz,' Neville sighed. 'Let me figure out if there is a better way of approaching it. But Mia, I wouldn't rush into a meeting with the case investigators. It may be counterproductive. Did you follow the local media coverage of Joshua's case?'

Mia looked into her phone, evidently her store of all information and research pertaining to the case. 'Yes, I did; quite closely actually. The reporter who covered it initially, Leslie D'Monte, seemed to sense something was amiss. But he couldn't piece together enough to back that instinct. Then he dropped it. I am forwarding you his last couple of articles.'

'Yes, it is never easy, with the police and medical establishment stonewalling you. But he is someone we can benefit from meeting. Let me ask around. By the way, the second autopsy report, does the local media know of it yet?'

'I doubt it,' Mia said. 'Mum only shared it with the police, and it would hardly be in their interest to have the media get their hands on it. There have been no new reports about the case for months now, to the best of my knowledge.'

'Good. That's useful.'

Shehnaz appeared confused.

While they cleaned up and waited for lunch, Neville

glanced through the news articles Mia had forwarded. Eventually, he looked up and said, 'We have to meet this Leslie fellow. He was on to something.'

Mia extended her phone to Neville, showing him the information about the reporter. There wasn't much – just a basic work profile and links to recent articles. He wasn't an old hand. Neville typed a quick message.

'Have sent him a message. Let's see.'

As they were eating, Neville's phone buzzed.

'That was quick. Leslie says he is free tomorrow, and would be happy to meet us anytime in the first half of the day. He is across in Caranzalem, near Dona Paula.'

'Thank you, Neville. I know now what Peter meant. Had I been on my own, I'd be stuck with that damned inspector now, being fed some fresh cock-and-bull story. Do things usually move this fast here?'

Shehnaz laughed. 'Quite the opposite; nothing does. When a Goan does not want to do something, nothing can make him do it. No inducement is enough. Try calling a plumber in the middle of the afternoon. He'll flatly refuse. Offer him double the wage, he'll refuse again. It can be frustrating, but there's something to be said for it, too. Some things, like a siesta, are more important to them than money. That's refreshing, in this day and age.'

Martin entered with a refill of rice. 'Madam, this is just the reputation we Goans have. Actually, we are very hard-working. And why blame us? My father used to say that his cousins told him they enjoy a siesta even in Europe.'

Agnes, within earshot, walked up to the table. 'Cut out your drivel. Europe, hah. Have you ever been as far as Bombay? Madam is absolutely right. Nothing can happen to a lazy lot like us.'

Before Shehnaz could protest, Martin interjected, 'This is not fair, Agnes. Don't I go to the fish market at seven in the morning when you ask me? Is that during working hours? So, why crib if I sleep a bit after lunch? I'm there when you need me, am I not?'

Neville could see this was heading in a different direction. 'Martin, Martin. No one is blaming you. Don't take it personally. It was a general comment, that too not in a bad way. We have nothing against a siesta, honestly.'

Martin shot Agnes a triumphant look and walked away. She rolled her eyes and followed.

'It's good we're meeting the journalist tomorrow, but sooner or later we'll have to enlist the help of the local police. Let me ask people at the party tonight.'

'Oh yes, I meant to ask Mia. There's a gathering at a neighbour's this evening. Would you like to come?' Shehnaz asked.

'I don't think it would be very wise, Shehnaz,' Neville said.

'Why? We can take a house guest along, can't we?'

'I don't mean it like that, dear. The people who will be there like to talk. Mia will only become the subject of prurient gossip. Maybe her presence here should be better leveraged ...'

Shehnaz looked irritated, but Mia said, 'I see what Neville is saying. Besides I cannot imagine enjoying an evening being asked all kinds of questions about Josh. That too, by strangers. You guys go ahead.'

'We'll have a drink with you before heading out. I don't think we need to be there before half past eight. Right, Shehnaz?'

'Guess so. I am going to read for a bit, Naresh's book.'

'And don't feel bad if you happen to doze off. It'll make Martin's day,' Mia teased.

Shehnaz laughed out loudly. Neville gave Mia a grateful smile.

In her room, Mia sat wondering if she should call her mother. She felt listless. There was something soporific about the place, or maybe it was the food; she wasn't used to eating so much rice in the middle of the day. Mia wished there was a pool where she could swim, to shake off the lethargy. As she sat in this state, between stupor and slumber, loud thumping noises on the roof startled her, followed by a crashing sound right outside her window. Mia rushed to look, only to find two large langurs prowling around the hibiscus tree, their tails as long as lengths of rope. They turned to stare at her, nonchalant. One of them used a branch to pull itself up and with a quick move, plucked out one of the flowers. Sitting down on the ground, it then proceeded, with great care, to shred the petals to tiny pieces before looking up at Mia again, as if daring her to do something about it. This done, the two made whooping sounds and with elegant, loping movements climbed on to the jackfruit tree. There they sat, dangling their legs and staring around at the world, without a care. Nothing frisky about their manner; still, calm, composed. And very human. Though Mia wasn't sure they would take that as a compliment.

She returned to her bed and dialled her mum. The voice that answered was nearly alien – flat, containing no trace of emotion, curiosity or energy. Nothing. Mia gave her a quick update and asked if she had ever met Naresh Sardesai on her visits. She hadn't or couldn't recall. Reminding her about the visit to the clinic on Monday, Mia hung up, uncertain if her mother had even registered what she said. The decline was worsening. Mia resolved to spend a week with her in Cornwall upon returning from Goa, whenever that might be.

She returned to her phone and opened Joshua's autopsy report. Cutting through the preliminary jargon, the most significant finding was blunt force cranial trauma being the probable cause of death. There were multiple comminuted fractures on the back side of his skull, consistent with being struck with a heavy object, while standing. There were subsequent blows indicating he was struck again while lying down. In the examiner's conclusion, the injuries were almost certainly the result of an assault rather than a fall from height onto a hard surface, particularly since the blows were multiple, not singular. The drowning was postmortem, not the cause of death. Mia could picture it – Joshua being struck down by a blow to the head and a man hitting him repeatedly as he lay on the ground, smashing his skull in.

She tossed her phone on the bed, gripping her elbows to still their shaking. This was no inadvertent error by an inexperienced medic; it was a cover-up. Mia emailed the autopsy to Neville and sank back against pillows, suddenly overwhelmed with fatigue. In that moment, she understood why her mum had become this way.

7

MIA STIRRED AWAKE TO INSISTENT KNOCKING AT THE door. She remembered the langurs and turned towards the window, but darkness greeted her. How long had she been sleeping? Glancing at her phone, she saw it was past seven in the evening. Four hours had slipped by, she couldn't believe it. Opening the door, she found Shehnaz standing there, a cup of tea in her hand.

'So sorry to wake you up, but it's evening already. I thought it may be better if you got up now. Else sleeping at night …' Shehnaz trailed off.

'Of course. I didn't realize I'd drifted off. Must be the jet lag. Are you guys ready to head out?'

'No, no, not yet. We're in the sitting room. Take your time.' She gave Mia the tea and turned away.

After washing her face, Mia joined her hosts in the sitting room. It was the first time they had gathered indoors since her arrival, in the room adjacent to where they had their meals. The oyster shells on the windows shone like moonstones in the lamplight. Neville and

Shehnaz were dressed smartly, ready for an evening out. Neville wore an olive linen shirt with beige chinos, while Shehnaz had changed into a pale peach dress with a string of tiny pearls on her neck. Mia had noted earlier that they made a striking couple – Neville tall, lanky with a gaunt handsomeness, Shehnaz petite and graceful, her pretty face studded with bright, sparkling eyes; the kind people noticed immediately.

'Oh, how lovely you both look! And how shabby I must seem, walking around in this same shirt all day.'

'You look well rested. Come, sit. There may be mosquitos outside now; we'll go out in a bit.'

Mia took one of the armchairs.

'We are all set for tomorrow morning with Leslie. Ten thirty at Miramar. There is a cafe opposite the beach. Is that alright?' Neville asked.

'Of course. I should also call the owner of the rented apartment and tell her I will reach tomorrow. She must be wondering what happened.'

'Tomorrow? Why don't you go Monday morning?' Shehnaz offered.

Mia hesitated. 'I have already taken up most of your weekend. I thought, after the meeting tomorrow …'

'Weekend? Darling, what do you think we do on weekdays? Every day is a weekend for us. Of course, if you would rather be alone, that's perfectly fine.'

'No, no. It's wonderful to be here, but I shouldn't get too comfortable. Who knows how long I'll need to be in Goa.'

Shehnaz couldn't think of an immediate reply, but then Mia continued, 'Okay, I will go on Monday. And thanks, Shehnaz. This is all so very kind of you.'

'How about a drink before we set out?' Shehnaz suggested.

'Sure, if you have the time. I don't want to hold you up.'

'Hold us up for what? We will only go there and have another drink. Gin?'

Neville rose and fetched the drinks, handing one to Mia and another to Shehnaz.

'What is this?' she asked, peering at her glass.

'Feni. Why, did you want something else?'

'You could have asked once. I may have liked something else today,' Shehnaz replied tersely.

'Oh, I'm so sorry. Hang on, I will pour you something else. What would you like – gin or a whisky?'

'Let it be now.' She looked glum. Neville was confused.

After a pause, Shehnaz said, 'It's alright. I just wasn't sure they will have feni there, and I didn't want to mix drinks.'

Neville stood up decisively. 'You're right. Don't drink that. Let me pour you a glass of wine?'

'Thanks. Mia can have some of that wine with her dinner. I have asked Agnes to make her some pork chops.'

Neville welcomed the change in topic. 'I got the report you mailed, Mia. Very helpful. I'm hoping to make some progress with it once the new week begins.'

After they finished their drinks, Mia walked them out to the veranda.

'Please don't wait up for us,' Shehnaz called back as she latched the gate behind her. It was a pleasant evening, though the day had been hot. A gentle breeze rustled through the trees as they strolled down the slope toward Alicante.

'You OK, dear?' Neville asked Shehnaz.

'Yes, why do you ask?'

'Oh, nothing.' They continued walking. In a few minutes, they reached a line of cars parked along the road – sleek black cars with gleaming grilles, entirely incongruous with the leafy surroundings.

'Our neighbours drove down from their houses?' Neville looked amused. Before he could ring the bell, the door was flung open, and Ravi stood there in an outrageous maroon silk shirt that matched the red frames of his spectacles.

'Welcome, welcome! A little bird told me you have a charming young lady as a house guest. I was hoping you'd bring her along. Would've added a bit of colour to this gathering of oldies,' Ravi quipped with a sly grin.

'You do have your ear to the ground, Ravi. Unfortunately, our guest is jet-lagged, so you will have to make do with our inadequate company,' Shehnaz replied dryly.

'Not at all, not at all. You look lovely as always, Shehnaz.' Ravi bent to kiss her cheek, and they entered.

Not all the guests had arrived but the party was in full swing. The faces were familiar. Rajat Dhar who had moved from Mumbai the previous year with his glamorous wife Kusum, a former model, greeted them as he walked away from the bar with two glasses of wine. He offered Shehnaz one of the glasses.

'You were carrying it for someone, Rajat. Let me inspect the bar before choosing my drink.'

From a corner of the room, a low siren-like sound echoed – Anirudh Thapar mimicking a police siren to herald Neville's arrival.

'Attention! Achtung! The cop has entered the scene,' he proclaimed, theatrically. His wife Mini, sidled up to Shehnaz. 'What a buffoon he is, especially after a drink.'

Neville did a quick scan of the room to see who the promised person of his interest could be. Rajiv Monga, the exporter from Delhi, definitely wasn't the one, busy as he was sharing a smoke with Vineet in the veranda. Pravin Nair, who owned a popular restaurant down the road, was engaged in animated conversation with his wife Sarita. A young girl, maybe in her twenties, stood listening to Rajiv's wife Nimmi with a bored expression on her face. Other than the girl, Neville had met everyone else. Shehnaz arrived at his side.

'Same old, same old. I'm glad you asked Mia to stay back. When you get your whisky, will you get me a glass of red?'

'Who's the girl, Shehnaz?'

'I haven't seen her before, but she's probably Rajiv and Nimmi's daughter. I vaguely remember them mentioning one who lives in Delhi.'

Neville walked across to the bar, where Ravi stood, proudly contemplating the range on offer. 'Ravi, you mentioned there would be a guest I would know …'

'Ah! Correct. Should be reaching any moment. Let me not spoil the surprise, except to say that you will be delighted to meet him,' he replied cryptically.

Neville returned to the party. Rajiv had come in from the veranda and was saying, to no one in particular, 'I envy you guys, really. The air is different here. I keep telling Nimmi we should spend more time in Goa. It will do our lungs some real good, if nothing else,' having just chain-smoked two cigarettes outside.

'So, what's stopping you?' Rajat asked.

Rajiv gave him a frosty glance. 'Not all of us are as fortunate. We have businesses to run. There are responsibilities. Can't just up and leave.'

The young girl who had been sitting quietly, nursing a clear drink, spoke up, 'It's more important to have a house here. Right, dad? The Assagaon set. We *divide* our time between Goa and Delhi, you see. So, what if it's three weeks in a year?' Sarcasm dripped from every syllable she uttered, unusual in a girl her age.

'Rhea,' Nimmi chided gently.

Rajiv was about to retort when the doorbell rang, and Ravi hurried downstairs. All eyes turned towards the staircase as lively greetings echoed through the house and soon Ravi appeared, escorting a couple into the room. Neville and Shehnaz exchanged bemused glances. The man was former Mumbai Police Commissioner Rakesh Sharma, who Neville had worked directly under for several years; along with him was his wife Vimla, whom Neville and Shehnaz had met on many occasions. The commissioner seemed equally surprised, and delighted, to see them.

'Neville Wadia! My man!' Commissioner Sharma's voice boomed through the room as he strode towards Neville, enfolding him in a warm embrace. They stood nearly equal in stature, though the commissioner was broader. Everyone else stood watching this reunion, Ravi beaming proprietorially at their side.

'How long has it been, Neville? It's so good to see you again,' Commissioner Sharma beamed.

'And you look just the same. Just a few grey strands, which unlike us ladies, you are not allowed to hide,' Vimla piped in. Neville stooped to peck her cheek.

'And look at you Shehnaz, my dear! I heard you two ran off to the mountains. Whatever it is you are doing, it really suits you. You are glowing!'

Sensing the need to move things along after the initial pleasantries, Ravi cleared his throat. 'Let me introduce my guests. Rakesh *bhai* here was the Commissioner of the Mumbai police for many illustrious years – a true legend. And this is my dear cousin Vimla.'

'Legend, you say, Ravi? The only cop in this room worthy of that accolade, is your friend here. In all my years on the force, I have never known a sharper man. He cracked all the major cases while I often got the credit.'

'Now, that's not fair, sir,' Neville protested.

'Ah, yes, you got some of it too. How else did you become such a star – the celebrity policeman,' Sharma continued in the same effusive strain, his words laced with more than sheer professional admiration; perhaps he had not waited to arrive at the party for his first drink of the evening.

Shehnaz and Vimla smiled indulgently at each other.

Suddenly, everyone seemed to be staring at Neville. The commissioner's fulsome praise had imbued him with a star-like quality. And Sharma's account wasn't a wild exaggeration either; Neville's face would pop up quite regularly in the Mumbai papers. Yes, he was a policeman but in a city which worshipped the cult of celebrity; where eventually, all eminent people were ordained that aura.

Small clusters began to form, inevitable at a gathering of a dozen or more people. The two former policemen and their wives gathered near the bar, sipping their drinks. Rhea eyed them from one corner of the room. For the first time that evening, her gaze contained something other than derision.

'So, here for a vacation?' Vimla inquired.

'No, we live here now. Just down the road actually,' Shehnaz replied.

'Really? Weren't you in the hills somewhere ...'

'Yes, we shifted only a few months ago. What about you guys? Here for the weekend?'

'Yes. We leave Monday morning. Do you remember Chandok, Neville?' Rakesh asked.

'You mean, the crime branch chief?'

'The same chap. Small world, ours. Chandok and I were the same IPS batch. His brother Dilip is now the Director General of police, Goa. So, Dilip's younger daughter is getting married this weekend. Chandok has been complaining we haven't met for a long time and anyway, Vimla and I were missing one of our long driving trips. So, we thought why not drive to Goa, attend the wedding and then head down to Bangalore to see my sister.'

'You are still doing your driving trips?' Shehnaz sounded surprised.

'Not as often as we would like, Shehnaz. You see, not all of us are ageless like the two of you.'

'Ah, so Dilip Chandok is DGP of Goa now,' Neville commented distractedly.

'Yes, you guys must be around the same age, won't you? Maybe Dilip is a bit younger. Yes, he must be. Nice, jovial fellow; not surly, like his brother.'

Anirudh, the filmmaker, ambled towards them, introducing himself to Rakesh and Vimla.

'Do you like it here, Anirudh?' Shehnaz asked, handing Neville her glass for a refill.

'Oh, yes, I find it really stimulating. The company of so many interesting people, so varied.'

Rhea, who had silently sidled up, butted in. 'Stimulating? This feels like any South Delhi party if you ask me. These days, even the *lalas* have one or two 'arty' types over to bolster their intellectual credentials,' she smirked, finger quoting the intellectual bit. 'And the arty types will go anywhere for the free booze.'

The girl had been drinking steadily and looked like she was itching for an argument.

'You don't sound too enamoured,' quipped Vimla with a conspiratorial wink at Shehnaz, both rather enjoying this irreverent rant. Rhea's caustic sermons had reached other corners of the room.

Vineet called out, 'I hear you, Rhea but don't you agree that the city, any city, can be stifling after a point?'

Rhea's eyes narrowed. 'You aren't the architect, are you? The brains behind this abomination we call our home? Know what you remind me of? That novel *Old Filth*, where Filth is – Failed in London, Try Hong Kong.' Rhea doubled up in laughter and Shehnaz discreetly took her glass away, guiding her to a nearby chair.

Neville whispered to the commissioner, 'Rakesh, there's something I wanted to talk to you about. Would you mind stepping across to the veranda? It's rather private.'

Outside, Neville told Rakesh about Joshua's death and the circumstances leading to Mia's arrival at their house. When he finished, Rakesh asked, 'And you are looking into the matter?'

'Only as a concerned friend, Rakesh. But now that Dilip is the DGP, I was hoping …'

'Of course! It goes without saying. Neville, why don't you come along tomorrow with me and speak to him?'

'No, no. It's a wedding – it won't be appropriate. But if you could have a word with him, perhaps I could drop by with Mia next week and explain the situation.'

Before Neville could finish, Rakesh had whipped out his phone. 'Dilip? Listen, do you remember Neville Wadia from Bombay? What's that? Hah, I must tell him you said that. But there's a serious matter, regarding a murder in Goa, that he wants to speak to you about. Yes, yes, I told him the same but you know these anglicized Parsis, too proper. Anyway, I am giving him your number and asking him to call. Thanks a lot. I'm sure you will do all you can. Yes, Vimla and I will be there by noon tomorrow. See you then. Bye.'

Rakesh looked up from his phone with a mischievous grin. 'Dilip knows of you, of course. "Neville, the lady killer", he called you. Anyway, he's happy to meet you Monday morning at his office, if that suits you. Dilip is a solid chap; you can count on his help.'

'Thanks a lot, Rakesh. This is just what I needed – a way to get the police here to relook at the case. It is quite clear to me that there has been a cover-up.'

The conversation was interrupted as their host walked in with Rhea's father in tow. 'I apologize for my daughter's behaviour. I don't know what has come over her, but since arriving in Goa yesterday, she has been this way,' said Rajiv, looking genuinely contrite.

'Come on, Rajiv. What's a party if someone doesn't get a bit tipsy?' Rakesh offered, before turning back to Neville.

'And how is life, Neville? I must confess, I was taken aback when Holkar called to tell me that you had put in your papers. It's been what, three years now, or more? I had you down as Commissioner but then ...'

'Yes, Rakesh. I couldn't take it anymore. The last couple of cases took their toll on me.'

Rakesh peered worriedly at Neville's face. 'Everything alright now?'

'Yes, I am fine. The quieter life suits me,' Neville assured him.

'Certainly looks that way. And we are blessed to have our better halves, Neville. As one grows older, one realizes the huge debt one owes them. We would be nowhere without them; at least I can speak for myself.'

Neville smiled. He liked what he saw in front of him – a contented man in his seventies, warm-hearted and generous, devoid of any signs of bitterness or senility. Rakesh had never been intellectual or exceptionally talented, but always solid. A virtue that helped his ascent to the top of the ladder.

Their glasses empty, they walked back inside to rejoin the gathering. Kusum ran up to them and asked, breathlessly, 'Would you mind if I took a selfie with the two of you? Two top cops together, it would be a shame to miss the opportunity.'

Without waiting for an answer, she stood between them, leaning on Neville's arm and snapping several pictures, before prancing away.

'See, Dilip was right about you after all,' Rakesh nudged Neville with his elbow.

Rajiv, Nimmi and Rhea were leaving. The parents had the girl in their middle, and Nimmi held on to her arm. They looked thoroughly embarrassed, but Rhea, undeterred, was singing Lennon loudly on her way out. 'A brotherhood of man, imagine all the people living …' and when she came to the *woo-hoo* bit, she turned back to give a parting look towards Anirudh and Pravin before convulsing into fits of laughter. Nimmi dragged her away.

'I like her,' Shehnaz told Neville with a smile.

As food was served and conversation continued, the evening wore on, and by the time they finished their meal, it was nearing midnight. They exchanged goodbyes, and Neville and Shehnaz walked out with Rakesh and Vimla.

'I don't know when we will bump into you again, Neville, but you have my number. It would be wonderful to receive a call some time,' Rakesh said warmly.

'I promise. Have a safe drive down to Bangalore.'

Shehnaz and Vimla shared a hug, and then the Sharmas were off. The night air wasn't cool but not oppressive either, and Neville and Shehnaz enjoyed the short stroll back to their place. Shehnaz linked her arm into Neville's and asked, 'It was better than last time, don't you think?'

'What? Yes, certainly. Rakesh and Vimla's appearance was a pleasant surprise. It was good to see him. Though the star of the evening was young Rhea, no question.'

Shehnaz chuckled. 'Rakesh seems to have become fonder of you, over the years. I do remember him always being a champion of yours but ...'

'Perhaps it is age. One mellows. But you're right, he's always been generous. And he played straight and fair, which is all you can ask for,' Neville reflected.

'It must feel nice to hear peers say such nice things, no?'

He smiled, uncertain if Shehnaz was only being wicked. But then, she surprised him by asking, 'Do you miss it sometimes?'

Neville didn't reply immediately. He was about to say no but somehow it seemed insincere. Instead, he asked, 'Do you mean if I miss the action of a police job?'

'No. I think you know what I am asking.'

'Why, do I look unhappy? Or restless?'

'No,' Shehnaz replied, taking care to choose her words well. 'The downtime has been good for you.

Yet, there was something in you when the Birtola investigation was on. It's not excitement, that's not the word … but a frisson of something. I could see it affect you, drain you yet also fulfil you in a way. Sorry, I am explaining this very badly.'

'No dear, I think you are doing rather well,' Neville said quietly. 'I won't say that it meant nothing. And yes, sometimes, after a few days of sitting on the veranda and looking at butterflies, I do feel myself longing to be part of some action. I realize how impractical it all sounds …'

Shehnaz shook her head. 'Why impractical? You got dragged into a case last year, and it looks like you are about to plunge into another soon … that's two in under a year, Neville!'

'But these are random coincidences. A tragedy befalls a neighbour; her former husband calls months later about a second cousin in need of help …'

'And if they weren't? What if the world that you left behind came calling, with the offer of picking your brains on cases they cannot wrap their heads around? Only occasionally?'

Neville turned and looked at Shehnaz. She had never tried to hide her disapproval at the prospect of him getting involved in any criminal investigations again, yet here she was, playing the devil's advocate. 'You mean a consultant investigator, something like that?'

'Maybe.'

'I doubt that such things really work, except on television. Besides you know me, I'm hardly the kind of guy who can sit at home and dole out armchair advice. I would need to meet the people involved and all that is never easy, as an outsider.'

'Hmm. You know better, of course, but in this country, reputation can supersede some of the issues you mention.'

Neville was taken aback by Shehnaz's clarity of thought. It really had worked out as she had just put it in the Birtola case, where the high profile of the victim had prompted the appointment of a senior officer from the Delhi Crime Branch to be in charge. Yet Neville's reputation, and track record with the Mumbai police, had led to a scenario where Satish Kalia, the case officer, had little hesitation in letting Neville lead the investigation, content to support him with the required police work. The results had been satisfactory.

'I am the first to dissuade you from getting involved in police work again. Yet, I realize how frustrating it can be to sit idly wasting an obvious talent. It hasn't happened yet, but it can make you restive, bitter,' Shehnaz said, her fingers clasping Neville's more tightly. 'I would never want that for you.'

'What you are talking about is the best of both worlds – a Goldilocks scenario, so to speak,' Neville asserted. 'I enjoy my retirement but when bored, dip my toes into a pool of challenging sleuth work. Real life rarely allows such leeway. You know that, dear.'

'Does it?' Shehnaz challenged. 'Depends on who is asking for the leeway, I think. If one has truly earned it, the world can bend backwards to make the accommodation you speak of. For successful men, at any rate.'

Neville decided it was prudent to steer away from the subject. 'Anyway, it was very handy to bump into Rakesh this way,' he said, proceeding to brief Shehnaz about Dilip Chandok.

'That's great, Neville. You were wondering how to enlist the support of the Goa police and this lands up on your plate. And the top dog, no less!'

'More than anything, I know that family. Chandok's brother may have faults, but he won't be a crook. Having just taken over as DGP, he wouldn't have had time to get his teeth into all these cases – though I can't imagine that the resolution of the long pending Hannah Wright case, so soon after his appointment, is mere chance.'

'Did you speak with him?'

'No, it's too late on a Saturday night; besides it's his daughter's wedding. Rakesh has lined up a meeting on Monday morning and before heading there, I'll send him Joshua's autopsy report. After that, we'll see how things unfold.'

The house was absolutely quiet when they reached. Neville opened the gate and walked ahead.

Shehnaz followed closely, her eyes darting from one side to another to spot any sign of movement in the undergrowth. A light flickered on in the veranda. As they neared the entrance, two large cars drove past their gate. There was a short toot – maybe a goodnight from one of the departing guests who had spotted them. Shehnaz saw the fancy tail-lights disappear around the bend, reminded of Rhea's earlier jibes.

'Once all this is sorted, Neville, we should spend a day driving around the Aldona area. The broker has been messaging about plots in Revora; he says it may be the next Aldona.'

'Already?'

8

SHEHNAZ WOKE TO THE MURMUR OF VOICES. SOFT sunlight streamed through the window beside the bed. Neville was still asleep, which was unusual; perhaps it was the late night. The voices came from the other window, at the back of the room. Shehnaz quietly slipped out of bed and tiptoed across. Agnes was giving Mia a tour of the garden.

'Bimbli,' she was saying, standing with a hand on her hip under the shade of the fluorescent pinnate leaves of the oddly multi-trunked tree with its yellowish-green, bumpy fruit. 'We sometimes use it in our fish curry. It's sour, but you can also eat it raw.'

'You know, I have seen these before, can't remember where. And these I recognize – Crossandras, aren't they?' Mia asked, pointing at the shrub with salmon-orange flowers.

'Yes, they grow easily here. You know, we used to have a lot more flowers in this village before the houses came up. Mostly marigolds, but also others. When I was a child, this was called *fulacho gav* – the village of flowers,' Agnes said wistfully.

Shehnaz joined them, smiling. 'Agnes, tell Mia about the Saint Cajetan's festival too.'

Agnes turned, her face lighting up. 'You just missed it, madam. It's held in the first week of August, at the church on the hilltop. Stalls with food, music. It's not a big tourist attraction, mostly for locals.'

'Sounds amazing, Agnes. Morning, Shehnaz. What time did you guys get back?'

'Late. Nearly one, I think. When did you turn in?'

'Oh, I had an early dinner, chatted a bit with Agnes and Martin and then packed my suitcase. I think I was asleep by half past ten or so. Was it nice, the party?'

'It was OK. But we did meet some interesting people. Neville will tell you when he is up. You have a morning meeting today, don't you?'

'Yes, with the journalist. Speaking of which, Shehnaz, weren't you a journalist too? I recall Peter mentioning something along those lines.'

Shehnaz chuckled. 'Feels like another life now, though it wasn't that far back actually. Yes, I spent nearly two decades at a newspaper. Then, when mum fell ill, I decided to quit.'

'Is that how you and Neville met?'

'You mean while following a crime story? No, it wasn't like that, though Neville did make headlines in his final years on the force. We met at a Parsi wedding in Bombay. He was quite a dashing young man, son of a famous bureaucrat – the most eligible bachelor in our circles. And since we Parsis still tend to marry within the community, it wouldn't have been wise to pass up on the prospect.'

Mia laughed out loud. Just then, Neville emerged from the room in his t-shirt and pyjamas.

'Morning. What's funny?'

'Morning, Neville. Shehnaz was regaling me with stories of your early days together.'

'Our early days? Well, that was many moons ago. Did she tell you about our fortuitous run-in with the commissioner last night?'

'Commissioner?'

Neville told Mia about their meeting with Rakesh Sharma.

'Maybe this is the break we've been waiting for,' Mia said, visibly brightening up.

'I certainly hope so.' Even as he spoke, Neville moved towards a nearby shrub, peering at it intently. Shehnaz pointed to the cluster of flowers on which rested the most exquisite butterfly Mia had ever seen. A jewel-like turquoise body with a dark border; it was majestic.

Neville watched it flutter away and remarked, 'The Malabar banded peacock. Appropriately named, don't you think?'

'It's a positive sign. Today will be a good day,' said Shehnaz as they returned inside.

Mia's suitcase awaited outside the room door. Neville checked the clock on the wall.

'The meeting is at half past ten; we've got time. Do you want us to drop your luggage off on the way? It's not a big detour.'

'Us?' Shehnaz asked.

'Yes, aren't you coming?'

'I thought the two of you ... won't it look odd if I tag along?'

'I don't think so. It's just an informal chat with a reporter, not a meeting with a police officer.'

'Alright then, I better get ready. We don't have that much time either,' Shehnaz said, rushing away with the eagerness of a child who had just been promised a picnic.

During breakfast, as Agnes served them, Shehnaz turned to her, 'Agnes, Mia madam is leaving today. She'll come visit us again, of course.'

'Oh, I see,' was all she said.

But at the gate, once Martin had placed her luggage in the boot, Agnes placed a reassuring hand on Mia's. 'Be careful, madam. This place is beautiful but can also be dangerous. Always keep that in mind.'

Even Martin assured, in an uncharacteristically sombre tone, 'You will find what you have come looking for.'

Mia looked moved, on the verge of tears, as Neville started the engine.

The drive was quiet. They followed the familiar road back towards Mia's flat, not far from the guest house. It stood within a small cluster of apartment blocks enclosed by a walled boundary. Beyond the enclosure, green fields stretched into the distance. Mia had called before setting out, and a middle-aged woman in a printed dress stood waiting at the gate. She walked up as Neville parked the car. 'Hello, I am Mary.'

Mia shook hands with her and introduced Neville and Shehnaz. Mary led them into her cheerful apartment. The curtains were drawn, and through the French windows at one end of the drawing room, they could glimpse the fields – a view that lifted one's spirits. The decor was functional, with light wood furniture and a modern kitchen.

'It's quite nice, Mia. Frankly, this rented apartment thing can be hit and miss. And you have security at the gate,' Shehnaz said, immediately regretting adding the last bit.

'It's not quite Sossegado, but I will manage.'

The drive to Miramar took longer. Mia remembered the Mandovi bridge and the yachts on the river. The surrounding hills looked spooky – creepers and climbers, grown thick with the rains, formed a vast unbroken canopy over the trees. In the sunlight, they appeared like an army of green monsters with their arms aloft, engaged in a macabre dance.

As they drove, Neville gave Mia a guided tour, pointing out some of the old Panjim houses, until they reached a roundabout from where a vast expanse of beach came into view. Neville parked and they stepped out. The sky was clouded over, and the first visitors were already beginning to trickle in; it was a Sunday morning in Goa, after all.

'Miramar,' Neville announced.

'So different from Vagator. Flat, no rocks,' observed Mia.

'Also, placid. In monsoon, it still shows signs of life, but in other months, the sea is as still as a pond. I somehow prefer the Bay of Bengal; it feels like a real sea,' Shehnaz remarked.

'That's the eastern coast of India, Mia. Places like Odisha, that you may have heard of. Lovely beaches,' Neville elaborated.

'And where are we meeting Leslie?' Mia inquired.

'Just across the road,' Neville pointed to a cafe with a distinctive red sign.

Despite having some spare time, they decided to head straight there. The moment they entered the cafe, a young man in his late thirties rose from his table and advanced towards them. He had an eager expression on his pleasant spectacled face and that odd thing, a short ponytail. It was easier to imagine him as a geeky engineer who played guitar in his spare time than an investigative reporter.

'Hello, sir. I am Leslie,' he said, in a deferential tone. Neville surmised the man had read about him in the papers or looked him up online.

'Hi Leslie. Thank you very much for meeting us on such short notice. This is Mia Davies, Joshua's sister. And this is Shehnaz, my wife.'

Leslie beamed at Shehnaz. 'Ma'am, big fan of your writing. Your weekend column – I always looked forward to it. May I ask why you stopped? Many people followed your work.'

Shehnaz looked amused. 'Really? I didn't know my pieces were read in Goa. Glad to hear, though.'

Leslie shook hands with Mia, and they settled at a corner table, from where they could see the sea. Leslie insisted on fetching the coffees. 'It's a privilege to meet both of you,' he said grandly.

Once they were settled, Neville broached the matter. 'Leslie, you know why Mia is here. You've been following the murders, and now with the verdict on the Hannah Wright case, we sense an opportunity. There was a second autopsy report, done in the UK, which we will send you. It proves, unequivocally, that Joshua was bludgeoned to death; it wasn't accidental.'

'Oh, that was quite clear to me,' Leslie nodded knowingly. 'You see, I was also covering the Leo Jarvinen murder at the time and the same happened there – both cover-ups. But then I had to back off.'

Leslie looked away briefly, a shadow crossing his face as if he had somehow let them down.

'Yes, I was following your reports from London but then they stopped suddenly. My first impression was that you had left the newspaper. Why did you stop?' Mia asked, in an accusing tone. On matters pertaining to the case, her manner could often be sharp – at odds with the sweet-natured person she was – Shehnaz observed.

Leslie hesitated.

'This stays between us, Leslie. I have an inkling of what you are about to tell us, and I assure you, it won't leave this room,' said Shehnaz.

'There was pressure on my editor, right from the top. Ministers, cops – I stopped filing the reports but poked around for a while, out of personal interest. They caught wind, and I was issued an ultimatum. After that, I gave up.'

'When you say cops, was it the investigating officer?' Neville inquired.

'He was part of it, but higher up too. DSP Alvares didn't mince words in warning me, but the orders to my editor may have come from the DGP himself. There's also a minister here called Angelo Lobo. Very powerful,' Leslie added.

'DGP? Not DGP Chandok, right?'

'No sir, he wasn't around then.'

Mia sat up.

'Leslie, it would be really helpful if you could walk us through your investigation from the beginning. Other than the police, who appear compromised, there's no one with a better first-hand grasp of the facts.'

Leslie took a long contemplative sip of his latte. 'Where do I start? It began with the autopsy report – it seemed fishy. DSP Alvares was adamant about not letting me get in touch with the doctor who conducted it. Frankly, I wasn't even sure that a qualified doctor had done it.'

'What do you mean, a doc hadn't done it? How is that possible?' Mia looked perplexed.

Leslie turned pleadingly in Neville's direction.

'Mia, autopsies in India aren't always the same thing as they may be in your country. It's not uncommon for recent medical graduates, with no experience in performing the procedure, to be tasked with investigating a corpse and filing a report. In some cases, even hospital interns have been known to handle them,' Neville explained.

'And while the sheer volume of cases to be handled in the system is the main reason, the police have often used this laxity in standards to their advantage,' Leslie added, in an apologetic tone, as if shouldering the blame.

'By tailoring reports to suit their needs?' Mia inquired in an acerbic tone.

'You could say that,' Neville confirmed.

'I sensed something was amiss because only a few months before Joshua, there was another death – Leo, as I mentioned – which followed a similar pattern. A rushed autopsy declaring that he had died of accidental injuries to the head. In that one though, I managed to reach the medic who had apparently done it; he wouldn't swear to it in court but told me off the record that he had practically signed off on a report handed to him by Alvares.'

'Did you write about it?' Shehnaz asked.

'No, I was about to when the embargo was slapped on these stories. But now, with Wright's conviction and the new autopsy on Jarvinen, the story's back and the tune has changed a bit. Others are reporting it – websites, national media. Why should we be the only ones with a gag?'

Mia shot a quick glance at Neville. He knew instinctively what was going through her head.

'If we gave you a copy of Joshua's second autopsy, would you want to file a fresh report on it?' he asked.

'Of course! It'd give me the perfect reason to start again, especially with his sister in Goa to chase the investigation. You know, I have already started testing the waters; earlier this month, I reported on a gathering of victims' families in Cheltenham. Grace Wright wrote to me about it.'

'Oh, did you? I was there at the meeting.'

'Really? Would you mind if I mentioned it in my report? That would be quite a scoop.'

'Sure. Anything that puts pressure on the administration to re-open the case,' Mia said.

'But no picture of Mia in the report, OK?' Shehnaz cautioned.

'Of course, ma'am. I won't.'

'You mentioned Angelo Lobo. Did you dig around to see what his connection to the case may have been?'

Leslie looked over his shoulder to check if there was anyone within earshot. 'Sir, that *is* the story. The moment I started asking questions about the Lobos, the doors slammed shut. I knew I was getting close. One thing is a fact: Joshua Davies knew Jakob Lobo well and had met him on numerous occasions.'

Leslie's eyes gleamed, the journalist emerging more clearly.

'Jakob? Angelo's son, right? What's his deal?'

'Fascinating character, sir. Not your typical minister's wayward son. Well, wayward he may be, but also educated, sharp. Qualified engineer and one of the brains behind the casino boom. But he has two weaknesses – recreational drugs and,' Leslie lowered his voice, 'women.'

'And the father?'

'Angelo? He is the classic goon. A land shark. Made millions scooping up agricultural land at low rates and getting land use laws changed for development. You know all this, sir. Goa has two main sources of money – land and mining. And now, you could add gambling. The big fish divvy it up. For the rest, there is tourism, which is slowly going down the drain.'

'Is it?' Shehnaz queried.

'Ask any resort owner or cabbie and he will tell you. Each season is worse than the one before. Indian tourists have discovered newer pastures and the foreigners, they are scared,' Leslie said, eyeing Mia.

Neville butted in, sounding a bit restless at Leslie's digression. 'To come back to Angelo, how did Joshua cross his path?'

'I cannot say for sure. I never met Joshua. When I started sniffing around later, I got two versions of him. One, he was a nosy parker; two, no one seemed to know much about him.'

Mia nodded; it was an accurate description of her brother.

'And what was he being nosy about?' she asked.

'Well, that's where it gets interesting. Apparently, he was quite curious about the new airport coming up in Mopa. And I have a feeling he was also looking into potential money laundering through the casinos. That might explain why he sought out Jakob's company.'

'I see. And is this speculation on your part, or you had something to go on?' Neville asked.

'The Mopa stuff I had from the horse's mouth. I've known the Anjuna station head for many years, Inspector

Rane. A low-level crook with a fondness for alcohol. After I was pulled off the story, I took him for a drink. He warned me I was treading dangerous waters, but not before he let slip that Joshua got what he had coming as he made the mistake of poking his nose into a game involving billions – Mopa, with Angelo Lobo as a key player. But as soon as Rane mentioned it, he clammed up and began warning me about dire consequences if I ever spoke about it. Anyway, I couldn't; I would have lost my job. His bosses were the ones who put the leash.'

'Did Rane mention Jakob at all?' Mia asked.

'No, that information I got from independent sources. The three of them were seen hanging out quite often, on the yachts.'

'Three? You mean Joshua, Jakob and Angelo?' Mia asked, though Neville could guess who the trio would have been.

'No. My mistake, I should have mentioned earlier. The girl involved – Eva – she is another big mystery. Rumour has it she was involved with Leo before getting close to Joshua. Now, I can't confirm if it was romantic, but Jakob, with his reputation, would undoubtedly have been interested.'

The air in the cafe had changed. Suddenly, everything appeared to be taking a different shape.

'Have you ever met this girl?'

'Only once, at a beach shack during my investigation. She left abruptly as soon as I approached her.'

'Can you describe her?' Mia asked. Shehnaz gave her a puzzled look.

'Young, white – likely American – with brown hair. Quite attractive, actually.'

'Do you think the police would have questioned her?' Mia wondered aloud.

'I know they did, after the Jarvinen murder. She may even have been a person of interest, but her alibi was iron clad. In the days around the murder, she was not even in the country. Apparently, she was in Sri Lanka. Once that was established, the police lost interest in her, and so did the media.'

'And after Joshua's death?'

'She vanished into thin air! No one saw her after that. Gone, just like that. I tried asking around but found nothing. No sightings, no records of her leaving the city. Hospitals and morgues turned up nothing. Eventually, I gave up trying to find her.'

'And the police?'

'They seemed uninterested. You see, the official version was that the death was accidental, and they could not be seen chasing a possible homicide. But to me, the total disinterest in her also suggested they knew who was behind the murder and saw no point in investigating a white tourist who had fled the scene.'

'Is that what happened you think? Do you think she fled because she was scared?' Mia asked.

'Seems likely. A foreigner facing police scrutiny might panic and run. It's easy enough to disappear in a country like ours. Hop on to a bus and head to Mumbai or Bangalore, and she could be anywhere in no time. How would one find out? Unless the CBI were to conduct a nationwide search or something like that; hardly worth the trouble.'

Neville surprised them with a question. 'Did the HSS ever figure in your investigations regarding Joshua or Leo?'

'HSS? The Hindu outfit? No, it didn't. Should it have?'

'No, just checking. So, in the last few months, you would have had no further interactions with this Inspector Rane, would you?'

'Nil. He won't return my calls anymore.'

'And the Lobos?'

Leslie shook his head with a wry smile.

'That would be asking for trouble, right?'

'What makes the Lobos so powerful? Politically, I mean,' Shehnaz inquired.

'Money wields power in Goa, ma'am. Our governments are fragile coalitions and ministers are routinely bought over with cash to make up the numbers. Someone like Angelo, with his crores, will naturally be close to the seat of power. Such people make the coalitions happen and in turn, governments look the other way with their nefarious activities. Even protect them, when necessary.'

'Were these the main lines of enquiry or did you explore other possibilities?' Mia asked.

'With Joshua, you mean?'

'Yes.'

'I covered the obvious haunts – popular pubs, trance bars and drug dens – places which usually turn up leads with deaths of tourists. But your brother wasn't that kind of white tourist. He wasn't into the drug scene or involved in some small-time racket with a local gang. That happens a lot too, but it was quite apparent to me that this case didn't fit that mould.'

'Leslie, do you suspect the Jarvinen and Joshua cases are linked in any way?'

'Sir, I tried my best to find a link, but aside from that girl, I couldn't establish any other connection. And to the best of my knowledge, Leo was dead by the time Joshua reached Goa.'

'Still doesn't rule out the possibility,' Mia muttered, absent-mindedly.

'Have you met the new DGP?' Neville redirected.

'Not personally yet, though I attended the first media briefing. He has a clean reputation, so far. He's not local, though I read that he served as a Superintendent here nearly twenty-five years ago. Came from the Intelligence Bureau. Why, are you planning to meet him?'

'Maybe,' Neville replied, before Mia could answer.

Leslie appeared on the verge of saying something but checked himself.

'Eva,' Shehnaz murmured, almost to herself. They were all thinking about her.

'Sir, do you have some time?'

'Why do you ask?'

'The only person who could tell you more about Eva is the owner of that shack where I saw her. Eva would hang there all the time; it's near Vagator. I could take you now, if you're free.'

Mia had begun rising from her seat but sat down again. Looking in Neville's direction, she proposed, 'Neville, it seems worth a visit?'

'Sure. Leslie, are you sure you have the time to ferry us around? It's your Sunday ...'

Leslie grinned widely. 'Come on, sir. When do I ever get a chance to hunt around with someone like you? Can't tell you how exciting this is,' he gushed before looking embarrassedly towards Mia, 'I mean, we must get to the bottom of this case. Any small way in which I can help ...'

'You already have, immensely; thank you. We'll take you up on your offer then. Eva does seem to be at the heart of our case.'

They left the cafe, Mia looking visibly wired. Outside, the day had brightened, drawing more people to the beach. The footpath was crammed with vendors selling balloons, trinkets and sun hats. Despite the hustle and bustle, the beach looked surprisingly clean from a distance.

'The plastic ban is still in effect, Leslie?'

'Yes, ma'am. That's one good thing we managed to get going here. You should have seen these beaches before the ban. Terrible.' Their friendly reporter didn't miss a chance to don the hat of local guide.

'Shall we take my car then? I can drop you back here once we are done,' Neville offered.

'Where are you putting up, sir?'

'Assagaon.'

'Oh, then it makes no sense for you to come back all this way from Vagator. I'll take my car, and we can meet outside the beach there. You know your way around these parts, I am guessing?'

'Yes. In that case, Shehnaz do you mind driving with Mia? I'll go with Leslie and pick his brain on the way,' Neville proposed.

'Sure.'

Leslie pointed to a red hatchback, and they approached it. He got in and opened the door for Neville. Inside, an acoustic guitar lay on the back seat.

'Part of a band?'

Leslie smiled, coyly. 'Of sorts, sir. On Sundays, a few of us get together and strum a few tunes; nothing serious.'

'There, we have ruined your Sunday gig.'

'No, no, not at all! Comes around every weekend, hardly a big miss,' Leslie assured him.

They drove on. Meanwhile, in the other car, Shehnaz adjusted the seat for her legs, much shorter than her husband's.

'Nice fellow, our Leslie,' Shehnaz commented.

'Yeah, and big admirer of yours, Shehnaz. I didn't realize you had such a fan following.'

'Hardly. But it's always good to hear that one's work is appreciated. Else, we are like satellites to our men – often even introduced as such, as if all we ever did in our lives was have the incredible fortune of cohabiting with our partners. Any glory is only reflected.'

Mia listened for any sign of bitterness in the way Shehnaz said this, and detecting none, agreed wholeheartedly. 'So true, though Neville doesn't strike me as a man who fits that mould. He's got a kind of old-fashioned gallantry about him, if you know what I mean.'

Shehnaz smiled. 'Useful meeting though, wouldn't you say? You would have known some of this but it's the first that I am beginning to get a hazy picture of what may have transpired.'

'Actually Shehnaz, much of it is news to me, too. All this stuff about the Lobos, Eva – I had no clue. Joshua was sniffing around for something, or several things. That could lead us to his killer,' Mia seemed to flinch from using that word.

'Neville's intuition is usually spot on with cold cases like this. The question is, how cooperative will the local cops be? If they are hostile, he may hit a wall,' Shehnaz mused.

'But if the top boss gives the green light, that could open doors, right?' Mia suggested optimistically.

'That's the hope.'

'I feel like kicking myself for not having landed up sooner. The trail wouldn't have gone totally cold. But then again, you guys wouldn't have been here last year, and I would have made no headway without your help.'

Shehnaz reached out and gently patted Mia's knee. 'Now you are thinking like me. I see good tidings in all these coincidences. You meeting us, bumping into the commissioner at the party, Leslie being so helpful, and even the arrest of Hannah Wright's killer at this juncture – sometimes things fall into place for a reason.'

Mia's face lit up; Shehnaz had articulated her very thoughts.

'What confuses me is that postcard from Josh about "love in the air". It is easier to imagine that he was using Eva's company to get close to Jakob. But if he was involved with her …'

'Let's see what the beach shack throws up. Did Joshua get involved with women easily?'

'Not really. He went without a steady partner for the longest time. I cannot say for certain that he didn't have relationships, but as I told you earlier, we weren't that plugged into each other's lives. I wish it was different now.'

The twinge of regret. Mia was no longer visibly grief-stricken, so much time had passed after all, yet Shehnaz sensed the lingering desolation, always lurking beneath the surface, a mere word or gesture away. She would appear fine and then suddenly have that distant look in her eyes. How could she not?

Shehnaz decided to break the silence with music. She pressed a button on the stereo and Fiona Apple's voice wafted out. 'If you don't have a date, celebrate,' she was crooning. Shehnaz couldn't recall when Neville and she had put that disc on, though she remembered that it was Clare who had introduced her to the artist, on one of their nippy evenings together in Birtola. She felt a tug in her heart.

'Sorry if this is intrusive, but do you have a partner, Mia?'

Mia took a few moments to respond. 'There is but I'm not entirely sure anymore, Shehnaz. Sorry, I don't mean to be evasive. His name is Jeremy; he works for Airbus. It's not him, the problem lies with me. I guess I need to sort things out in my head.'

The roads felt familiar to Mia now. Since her arrival, she had taken this route a few times and was slowly beginning to get a sense of the place. The fields appeared again, and she knew that they were close to their destination. Turning a corner, they spotted Neville's car slowing down. Shehnaz pulled their car alongside, and Neville gestured to a side of the street where they could park.

It was hot when they stepped out of the car. Shehnaz donned a wide-brimmed straw hat and handed a green one to Mia. 'Wear madam, else your skin will turn black soon,' she quipped, mimicking the voice of the vendor woman who had accosted them on their previous visit.

'It's this way,' Leslie announced, leading them down a narrow path lined with shops on both sides. Though open for business, the shopkeepers sat around listlessly, as if they didn't expect to sell anything. Shehnaz could smell the sea in the distance. The path opened onto a sandy stretch of beach, with a few makeshift shacks that appeared shut. This didn't deter Leslie as he walked up to one of them and shouted something through a tiny opening. There was a muffled reply from inside.

'Come, we need to go to their house, just over there. The shacks are closed during the monsoon,' Leslie explained.

They walked up a slope to a small house, painted lurid green on the outside. The door was open.

'Tony?' Leslie called out.

A thin, dark-skinned man emerged, clad in floppy shorts and a blue singlet. He smiled at Leslie.

'Tony, these are some friends who want to talk to you and Faye. Is she around?'

Tony disappeared briefly inside and returned with a young woman. She was emaciated and her bulbous eyes stood out prominently. Back home, Mia would have put her down as anorexic. She introduced herself softly, addressing Mia, 'Hi, I am Faye. How can I help you?'

Leslie was about to speak but Mia beat him to it. 'Hi Faye, my name is Mia. I've just arrived from London to look into the death of my brother. You may remember a young man named Joshua Davies who died last year, not very far from here?'

Mia pointed generally in the direction they had just arrived from, but she needn't have.

'He was your brother?' asked Faye, her face contorted with pain.

'We didn't know him,' Tony interjected quickly, perhaps sensing trouble.

'No, but you knew a friend of his. Eva.'

At this, Faye abruptly turned and retreated into the house. Tony raised a hand apologetically. 'Sorry, but Faye gets very upset at the mention of Eva's name.'

'Why? Did something bad happen to her?' Mia pressed.

Tony didn't answer. They waited outside the door in an awkward silence; seemingly, any information about the missing girl would come only from Faye. After a few minutes, she returned, her eyes red from crying.

'Eva was a friend. She and Leo would come often to our shack, have a few beers. Sometimes she came alone. Her visits became less frequent after Leo's death. Then she disappeared altogether.' Faye's gaze wandered into the distance.

'Faye, I know this is difficult for you, but Eva's disappearance could have a connection with Joshua's death. If you know anything at all ...' Neville prompted in a low voice.

She shook her head.

'Faye, please; I need your help,' Mia implored.

'She left without saying anything. I don't know what happened.'

As Faye began walking back inside, Mia moved to follow her, but Neville gently restrained her.

'Maybe we will come back later, she seems very upset now. Tony, sorry to have disturbed you. I hope you can understand,' he apologized.

Tony nodded. 'She cared about Eva and was very cut up when she left. Don't think she is hiding anything.'

Leslie shook Tony's hand, and they started walking back towards the cars. A few steps away, Shehnaz whispered, 'She knows something, Neville. Shouldn't we have pressed more?'

'No, Shehnaz. She isn't ready to come clean yet. We need to be patient. Come, it's been a long day, and we shouldn't hold up Leslie's lunch.'

Leslie looked at his watch and said, somewhat embarrassedly, 'Actually sir, I do have to be somewhere. If there is anything else I can do, just give me a call.'

'Thank you, Leslie. I can't overstate how helpful this meeting has been. We'll keep you posted on how things go, and please do reach out if anything surfaces at your end.'

'That goes without saying, sir. Just one last thing: I will write out a report tomorrow mentioning the new autopsy findings and the arrival of Joshua's sister in Goa. It should be in Tuesday's paper.'

Turning to Mia, he asked, 'Ma'am, your full name is Mia Davies?'

'Yes, and you can add that I don't intend to leave Goa till I get to the bottom of this,' Mia declared.

Leslie gave her a thumbs up and walked away.

It was nearly half past two, the blazing sun casting angular shadows resembling a slender stalk flanked by mushrooms – Neville and the two women with their wide brimmed hats. The beach lay deserted. It was siesta hour for the locals and too hot for tourists. Neville mentioned lunch, but no one seemed to be in the mood for a sit-down meal. Mia wanted to rest for a while, so they decided to drop her off on the way back home. It had been a long and draining morning.

At the apartment gate, despite her visibly droopy manner, Mia thanked them profusely.

'Call us, for anything. And hop across for a drink or meal, whenever you want, OK? No formalities,' Shehnaz offered warmly, giving Mia's hand a squeeze.

'I'll pick you up in the morning tomorrow, for the DGP's,' Neville called out before she disappeared into the compound.

As they drove off, Neville pre-empted Shehnaz's questions. 'No, Shehnaz, don't jump to conclusions.

It's too early; we've only been pointed in one direction. There may be many others.'

'You mean Joshua could have been pursuing more than one story?'

'Wouldn't you, in his shoes? For an investigative reporter this place must be like a buffet – every felony on offer, in plain sight. Take Joshua's case. He starts digging into the Lobo family, which alone offers two angles – the Mopa airport scam and money laundering through the casinos. Simultaneously, there are ongoing high-profile murder investigations, notably involving a former boyfriend of the girl he hangs out with. On top of that, he has befriended a writer targeted by extremist outfits, living under police protection in his own house. Forget a report; Joshua could have been writing a book!'

'Titled *Trouble in Paradise*, as he wrote in his card to Mia?'

'Why not?'

'One of these hunts would have led him into trouble. Leslie was categorical – Joshua wasn't the typical hippie sort who would get his head bashed in over a bar brawl or a drug deal gone wrong,' Shehnaz mused.

Neville sighed, 'All that sounds plausible, dear, but don't forget this is a closed case. Over a year has passed. Not only were the investigating officers bent on obfuscating all leads, but they also had ample time to clean up any evidence. Sure, we can suspend the officers now, but how does that help us? These cold cases, they can be notoriously difficult.'

'But then they went and caught that chap in the Hannah Wright case. He was convicted after ten years, right?'

'True,' Neville conceded. 'But reclaiming bits from the past is always tricky. You never know what to trust. Sometimes, your own instinct leads you astray.'

Just then, Neville's phone chimed. He slowed down to check the message, his eyebrows raised in surprise.

'What happened?'

'DGP Chandok. He has gone through the autopsy report I mailed him and has taken the liberty to call a Superintendent of Police to join us after our meeting tomorrow.'

'Isn't it his daughter's wedding lunch today?'

'Yes. Perhaps Rakesh is by his side, urging him on. You know what a bloodhound he can be,' Neville remarked.

'And for his blue-eyed boy, he will pull out every stop,' Shehnaz smiled impishly, poking Neville in the ribs.

9

MIA WAS JOLTED AWAKE BY THE SOUND OF HER PHONE. Disoriented and surrounded by darkness, she fumbled to figure where she was. The unfamiliar landscape outside added to the confusion, leaving her momentarily adrift. She reached for her phone – it was her mother, Olivia.

'Hi mum,' she managed to mumble.

On the other end, Olivia was howling. She had been trying frantically to reach Mia but her calls had gone unanswered. She had jumped to the most dire conclusions, and was in the throes of a full blown panic attack.

'Why won't you answer the damn phone? I have no way of knowing what is happening there,' she kept complaining, again and again.

Finally, Mia managed to pacify her with the promise of calling her every day – once in the morning and again before she went to bed.

When the call was over, Mia rose from the bed and stood by the window, feeling unsettled. Dark fields stretched ahead, with a few distant lights. The cacophony of cicadas, to Mia's ears, had the ring of a sinister chorus. Even the view, which seemed inviting in the day, now harboured an unnerving aura. Mia drew the curtains shut and flicked on a light.

She understood Olivia's panic all too well. Her young daughter, alone in a foreign land, unreachable, digging into the death of her son with his murderer still on the loose. Mia sent a reassuring message, promising she was safe and looked after.

Pouring herself a cup of tea, Mia settled onto the sofa. It was well past seven in the evening. She missed the Wadias, wishing Neville was around to fix her a drink. That reminded her – she had picked up two bottles from the Mumbai duty free, the gin still tucked away in her suitcase. The tea was insipid; she poured it out into the sink, replacing it with a shot of gin instead. Opening her laptop for the first time since her arrival, Mia found a cluttered inbox.

Amidst the messages, one stood out – Grace Wright's heartfelt note, wishing her luck in Goa and warning against lowering her guard; not to visit bars alone or to walk around unescorted late in the evening. Also listed were names of some local lawyers and journalists who had been of help to her over the years, in case Mia needed assistance. Mia would need to be patient and eventually, she would find justice, Grace assured. Nothing out of the ordinary, yet it immediately made Mia feel stronger. What a strange object the spirit was, she mused, also realizing what it was she missed about the Wadias; not the comfort of their home or their hospitality, it was their quiet assurance. Over the years, having met so many people touched by tragedy, perhaps it came to them naturally – to be able to impart a belief that all will be well again, that hardships will fade and the pain, diminish. It made her wonder if she should have brought her mum along with her. Maybe it wouldn't have been wise, she concluded.

Her thoughts turned inevitably to Joshua. The entire morning, hearing Leslie's account, she was flooded by memories of him. It almost felt as though he hadn't truly left – like unearthing some fact would bring him back as suddenly as he had departed. Mia remembered their last meeting at the pub which had ended in an argument. Josh had spent the entire evening poring over his phone, as usual, having no time for Mia's suggestion of bringing their mother to London for longer spells, so that she could divide her time between the two of them. Frustrated, she had snapped and shouted at him. Josh had walked out, leaving her alone. He did call later, on her birthday, to mend fences and Mia realized that must have been just before he came away to India. Now they would never be seated across a table again.

As a toddler, Josh had been besotted with her, following her around everywhere – even refusing to sleep unless Mia was lying next to him. Time eroded some of that clinginess, but they remained close, through their teenage years. Part of it may have been on account of their parents' unhappy marriage, obvious to both since their early years. Mia remembered her father as a reclusive, disengaged man with little interest in his wife or children. Olivia, frustrated with this loveless cohabitation, became distant herself, leaving the care of her son to his sister. Mia was only two years older but her attitude towards Joshua took on a maternal hue. Joshua depended on her till a certain age but rebelled when he felt Mia was trying to boss him around.

Once Mia left to study in London, distance crept in between them – a gap that was never bridged even after Joshua followed in her footsteps to the big city. This made Mia unhappy as she wanted to be close to her brother, more so after their father's passing. She believed a tighter-knit family would be a source of support to their mother through her twilight years. She knew Joshua cared deep down. His postcards from distant lands always filled her with joy – until that devastating call from Olivia, informing her that Joshua's lifeless body had been found on a Goan beach. How did one cope with something like that? Mia sat staring numbly at an image on her laptop – the two of them atop a wooden horse at a park in Cornwall. Little Joshua in front, clinging to Mia's hands wrapped around him from behind, his lips pressed to her linked palms.

Just a few miles away, in a more modest dwelling than Mia's, three figures sat hunched around a worn table. The room, dimly lit by a shaded lamp, featured blue walls bearing framed pictures of Jesus and Mary, a large wooden cross looming above the doorframe.

The woman wept quietly and the two men sat listlessly with their heads hung. The only sound in the room was the distant rhythm of lapping waves. The three appeared to be in the grip of a terrible tragedy, unable to shake off its weight from their weary shoulders.

10

THE RAIN BEGAN ITS PATTER BEFORE DAYBREAK, A welcome relief after days of sultry heat. Neville and Shehnaz had planned to start the day with their usual walk, but it was coming down quite heavily and they decided to forego it. Neville made a pot of tea and they sat with it, on the veranda.

'An important day for you guys,' Shehnaz remarked, cradling her cup.

'Yes, I do hope the meeting goes off well. A lot hinges on it.'

'It will be fine. You know, Neville, I was thinking of Mia last night in bed, wondering if she had a miserable evening alone in that flat. All that talk about Joshua through the day; must be hard on the girl.'

'I know. But maybe we should let Mia do this her way, Shehnaz. We have offered and she knows she is welcome. She is a spunky girl, she will find her way through this.'

'And Leslie mentioning her in his report?'

Neville paused, weighing the question. 'I know what you mean, but on balance, I felt that the pressure from that publicity, in the current mood, may work in Mia's favour. The new DGP might push for progress on high profile cases. Besides ...'

'Besides?'

'I don't see this being a long-drawn-out affair, Shehnaz. If the case is assigned to a new investigating officer, the line of enquiry is pretty straightforward. The autopsy report is in and other than that, there isn't any great physical or circumstantial evidence to be gathered. The list of suspects is fairly short and unless there is a fresh development, it will hinge on the testimonies. If no one cracks, it will be tough to prove anything. I know you will bring up the Hannah Wright case, but there the police had eyewitness accounts and solid physical evidence to match DNA.'

Shehnaz sighed. It wasn't usual for Neville to sound so disheartened, but she knew better than to think he was defeated. It was his way of winding himself up before the chase, of stacking the odds as if to gauge what he was up against. Shehnaz had seen it before. But something made her uncomfortable and she made a mental note of bringing up the issue of Mia's safety at another opportune time.

'Well, you better get ready then. First thing in the morning means ten, right?'

Neville managed a smile. 'I would have asked you to come, Shehnaz, but it might seem odd.'

'Oh, absolutely out of the question. Me, tagging along for a meeting with the DGP – preposterous.'

After a quiet breakfast, Neville set out. He turned to catch Shehnaz waving from the balcony and felt a pang of regret. Despite what she said, he knew how much she would have wanted to come along.

Mia was waiting at the gate of the compound, her face puffy. Neville pulled up beside her.

'Good morning, Mia. Hop in.'

'Morning. Wet start to the day.'

It had stopped pouring but the sky was overcast, and they could see that there would be more showers during the day. The fields looked fresh, and the air smelt clean.

'You had something to eat?' Neville asked.

'I had a granola bar and tea. I'll sort out breakfast later. Mary mentioned a lady who makes stuff in her home and brings it for guests.'

Traffic slowed their progress into Panjim, but soon they arrived at the imposing red and white colonial building housing the headquarters of the Goa police. The moment Neville mentioned his name at the gate, a uniformed constable saluted them and led them up the stairs to the DGP's office. The constable knocked on the door and held it open for them.

'JCP Wadia! What a pleasure.' An ample belly preceded the thickset man who advanced towards them with an extended hand. With a wide smile spreading on his fleshy, moustached face, Dilip Chandok looked like a genial cop.

'Neville, please. It's so kind of you to see us, DGP Chandok. I really appreciate it.'

'Well, if it's Neville, then it has to be Dilip too,' the DGP chuckled. 'And it's my great pleasure. I have heard so many good things about you from Rakesh bhai and even my own brother, who isn't exactly generous with his praise.'

He winked at Neville as he said this.

'Dilip, let me introduce Mia Davies. She arrived in Goa last week.'

They shook hands.

'Thank you, sir, for agreeing to meet me,' Mia said politely. 'And congratulations on your daughter's wedding.'

'Ah, thank you, thank you. Yes, I have been up to my ears with it over the last few days, but it's all done now. I have dispensed with my paternal duties and the bride and groom will soon be off to the South of France,' the DGP beamed. 'Enjoy it while it lasts, I told them!'

He bellowed with laughter.

'Please sit down. Coffee?'

Neville was about to decline but remembering Mia's frugal breakfast, accepted.

'At the outset, let me offer my sincere apologies, Ms Davies. I have looked at the British autopsy report and there can be no doubt that this was a botched-up investigation at our end. Now, I can tell you that I wasn't around when it happened but that isn't particularly helpful. I spoke to Commissioner Sharma, whose counsel I always take very seriously, about it yesterday, and we concurred that the case needs a fresh look. So, I have asked SP Kerkar to join us after our chat. One thing though, I hope you will keep all this to yourself for now. Eventually, we will see what is to be done about the DSP who was in charge of the case, but it doesn't help you or me if this becomes a public thing – a DSP reprimanded, new SP assigned the case and so on. Let's just get on with the job, OK?'

'Agreed,' Neville affirmed. 'Our interest is only in finding the truth, not in any blame mongering. And thank you, it is very generous of you to agree to transfer the case files to a new Superintendent. Kerkar, you said?'

'Yeah, Vishnu Kerkar. Solid fellow. Been around, knows everyone here and clean as a whistle; not the slightest sniff of corruption, ever. You will like him, Neville.'

Mia looked sideways at Neville, as if she had a question but wasn't sure if she should speak. He nodded subtly.

'Sir, we have been speaking to people who followed my brother's case with some interest. The general impression is that there may have been powerful people involved – politicians, businessmen,' Mia ventured cautiously.

Dilip sighed. 'I don't need you to tell me that, Ms Davies. I spent two years in Goa, back in '92–'93, and have some idea how things work here. That is why I picked Kerkar. You need someone with a spine to stand up to these goons. It still won't be easy but rest assured, we won't cower under any pressure. And you have Neville Wadia at your side, what could be better? Kerkar's utility is only in the uniform; without it, Neville may not be able to approach people directly.'

Neville shook his head, refuting the suggestion that the SP would only be an appendage.

'Thank you,' Mia whispered.

'It's my duty, young lady. Do you think I enjoy the reputation this force has earned for itself, internationally? And all this talk of handing over the tourist cases to the CBI, what does it imply? That we aren't competent enough to solve them ourselves, right? Which DGP can swallow that? The Jarvinen case is already with the CBI, but I am going to personally oversee this one now till it's closed.'

The DGP rapped his knuckles on the table, in a gesture that held determination and frustration in equal measure. Neville leaned back in his chair, feeling relieved. This was exactly what he had hoped to hear.

Glancing at his watch, the DGP motioned to summon SP Kerkar. A steel bell rang, and the same constable appeared promptly.

'Send Kerkar in,' Chandok instructed, as they took sips of their coffee.

'Awful, isn't it? Some things are impervious to change, among them the quality of beverages in public institutions. I didn't offer you tea, because Ms Davies would have swooned from the amount of sugar in it.'

Neville laughed, Mia wasn't sure if she should.

There was a knock on the door and a serious-looking man entered. He saluted the DGP. 'Come, Vishnu. Meet JCP Wadia. I don't need to tell you about him.'

Kerkar shook Neville's hand. 'Honoured, sir.'

'This is Mia Davies, Joshua Davies' sister,' Neville introduced.

'My condolences, ma'am.'

Mia thought it was an odd thing to say, more than a year after someone's death.

'Sit, Vishnu. I have told Neville that you have the case now. The correct procedure would be to call in the investigating officer – Alvares, isn't it – and debrief him, but you know as well as I do that it is going to be a waste of time. My suggestion would be to skip protocol for a day and meet the key people in question before Alvares can tip them off. Who knows, maybe you will get something if you catch them on the cold. After that, summon him here so that I can give him a piece of my mind. He will know better than to meddle, if he values his job. Sounds OK to you, Neville?'

'Perfect, Dilip,' Neville agreed. 'Time is of the essence and if we can get even twenty-four hours before news gets out that the case has been officially reassigned, it may help. SP Kerkar?'

'Sir, please call me Vishnu. Since you spoke to me yesterday, sir, I have looked at the case file and asked around. The basic facts I was aware of anyway. Sir, may I speak candidly?' he asked, casting a furtive glance in Mia's direction.

'Absolutely,' Chandok assured him. 'Everything discussed here stays between us, you don't need to worry.'

'Alvares is known to be close to the Lobos. Father, more than son,' Kerkar revealed. 'He owns acres in Pernem, lives in a house which, frankly, is way above what a cop's salary would permit. It's an open secret that he is on the take. The station officer in Anjuna, Rane, is his lackey. These were the two in charge of the case, as the body was found on Vagator beach. The victim was known to Jakob Lobo, and they were often seen together at his yachts. I think the obvious place to start would be with them.'

'Agreed,' Dilip nodded decisively but he could sense that there was something bothering Kerkar.

'If it is the prospect of pressure from the CM's office that is worrying you, don't even think about it. One phone call, and I will threaten to involve the PMO immediately. With the sensitivity of this case, who do you think will get their support? Anyway, let me handle all that. You have a free hand. Just help Neville get to the bottom of this. And quickly.'

Kerkar stood up. The hesitancy was gone, he looked all charged up. Turning to Neville, he said, 'Sir, I will wait in the meeting room downstairs, whenever you are ready. We will take it from there.'

He saluted Dilip again and strode out of the room with purpose.

'Looks like the man for the job,' Neville remarked.

'I told you you would like him. Also, Neville, don't forget, some of the officers here have been itching to have a go at these crooks. But they have been sheltered, in the past. I won't be the only one delighted if you can bring some of them to ground.'

'We'll take your leave then, Dilip. We have occupied enough of your time already.'

The DGP walked them to the door. 'You have my number, Neville. Anything you need, anytime, give me a ring. And when all this is cleared up, you and your wife must come home for a drink, OK? Geeta would be delighted to meet you.'

'Certainly. I look forward to it.'

'Thank you again,' Mia added sincerely.

'You are welcome, Ms Davies. And good luck.'

Downstairs, in the meeting room, Vishnu sat at the head of a table. Next to him was a young man who stood up eagerly as soon as they entered.

'Come, sir. This is Inspector Bosco, who will work with us on this. He has worked on cases involving the

Lobo family in the past and is familiar with the turf. Please, have a seat.'

Bosco pulled two chairs out for them to sit. Vishnu addressed Mia directly, 'Ma'am, if there's any information you have which may help us, this is the time to tell us. I have asked Bosco to figure out where Angelo and Jakob Lobo may be now. Once we are done here, I propose that we meet them today.'

'Separately, you mean?' Neville asked.

'Exactly,' Kerkar confirmed.

Mia cleared her throat, then spoke up, 'Other than the Lobos, the other possible line of interest could be the right-wing outfit, correct, Neville?'

'Correct. The first thing you ought to know, Vishnu, is that Joshua Davies was an investigative journalist. It's almost certain that he was in Goa working on a story. Now what that story, or stories, may have been we don't know yet; it would help us a great deal if we could find that out. Maybe it was a probe into the irregularities in the Mopa airport project, or alleged money laundering in Jakob Lobo's casinos. Or as Mia mentioned, it could even have been the activities of the right-wing outfit HSS as well.'

'Why HSS?' Kerkar inquired.

'Because Joshua had befriended the famous local writer Naresh Sardesai, who is under police protection, and from whom he would have learned about the activities of the organization, notably their alleged role in the recent murder of a prominent author.'

'Ah, I see.'

'Also, the Eva angle, Neville?' Mia prompted.

'I was just coming to that. Joshua had a friend or partner, Eva, who apparently was Leo Jarvinen's girlfriend before his death. And very mysteriously, she seems to have vanished without a trace since the time Joshua's body was found.'

'I know about this girl, sir, but my impression was that she was cleared in the Jarvinen case. I wasn't aware that she was close to Joshua; it's a strange coincidence.'

'It is and one which raises the possibility that Joshua was digging around for details on the Jarvinen murder. It would have been front page news here around the time he landed up in Goa.'

Bosco, who had been absorbing all this quietly, spoke up, 'It is possible that these cases are linked.'

'Absolutely,' Neville said.

Kerkar looked at Bosco. 'Any news on the Lobos?'

'Sir, Jakob Lobo will be in one of his two boats after lunch time. That's where he is every day. I am waiting for a confirmation that Angelo Lobo is in his office, but we can start driving in that direction.'

As they prepared to leave, Kerkar looked inquiringly at Mia. Neville got the hint. 'Mia, I don't think it is a good idea for you to accompany us to these meetings. I would rather they didn't see you, in person.'

'Oh, alright,' Mia acquiesced, though unable to hide

the disappointment on her face.

'These are not nice people, ma'am, best avoided,' Kerkar added.

'Of course, I understand.'

'Why don't you head back to Assagaon, Mia? I'll call Shehnaz and let her know; you'll get a full update on my return.'

'Sure. But ...' Mia started.

'Kerkar, can we go in my car to Lobo's office while your car drops Mia to Assagaon and meets us there?' Neville proposed, pre-empting Mia's query.

'Of course.'

On exiting the building, Mia departed in Kerkar's car. Bosco offered to drive them, but Neville opted to take the wheel. As they were getting in, Bosco looked up from his phone and said, 'Angelo is in the Porvorim office. As of now, at least.'

On the way, Bosco pointed out two boats on the river – the *Mandovi Queen*, a grand four-storied affair that could pass off as a modified European cruise liner and the *Mandovi Princess*, more modest in size but no less swish.

'Jakob's boats.'

'You mean he owns them?'

'Well, there are other investors, but he is the main guy; exact ownership of these casinos is always difficult to ascertain. Jakob is a minister's son, fingers can be pointed.'

'But it's all legal, right?' Neville probed.

'Yes, but always on the edge. And there is intermittent trouble. One political party swears to purge Goa of the curse of casinos before an election only to become its biggest champion after. There are frequent allegations of laundering and income tax raids. The business continues to flourish but there is an unease around it.'

'Have you ever been inside one of these?' Vishnu asked Neville.

'Never.'

Vishnu smiled. 'A surprise awaits you.'

Crossing the bridge, Neville asked, 'Bosco, why don't you give me a brief background of Angelo Lobo, before we meet him? It will be useful.'

Bosco needed only a minute to compose his thoughts. 'Mid-fifties. Four times cabinet minister; currently of tourism and development. No particular party loyalty, switches depending on which way the wind is blowing. Close to the present Chief Minister. Basically, a land shark. Dabbled in mining too but wasn't very successful and anyway, all that has been stopped now. His game is to acquire large tracts of land and to manipulate legislation for development. Sometimes, he will participate in the development, along with a builder, or flip the plot at a multiple of the price he paid for it. Very wealthy. Lives in a huge farmhouse in Nachinola with his wife – apparently, she has mental problems – and drives around in SUVs with armed bodyguards. Extensive criminal record – forced eviction of landowners, use of weapons, arson, forgery, assault and even murder.'

'Murder? I didn't know that, Bosco,' Kerkar sounded surprised.

'Sir, it was hushed up, not reported in the press. I picked it up from someone in Pernem. Do you recall that case last year where two Mopa farmers committed suicide because their land had been snatched for airport development?'

'Yes, but they drank poison, right?' Kerkar recalled.

'That's what was reported. According to the locals, one of them was beaten to death and poison poured down his throat. Angelo's name came up but was swiftly buried. Hush money changed hands, apparently.'

'Very illuminating, Bosco. Anything else?' Neville inquired.

'This again is hearsay, but there's friction between father and son. That doesn't stop young Lobo from enjoying political immunity by virtue of being his father's son. They live in the same farmhouse.'

'And any reason for this acrimony?'

'Angelo drinks like a fish but detests drugs. That's one racket he has always stayed shy of. And while Jakob may not be involved in drug running, he has a reputation of enjoying party drugs. There are also rumours of escort girls on his boats, but the police look the other way. Angelo may disapprove of his son's lifestyle, but he has his back. If there is trouble, daddy will bail him out;

everyone knows that.'

'Sounds like the Godfather,' quipped Neville.

Kerkar laughed. 'Except Angelo is no Brando, as you will see shortly. We have arrived.'

The car pulled up outside a fairly nondescript concrete office block. On the ground floor there was a pizzeria and an ice-cream parlour, and two floors on top had sliding windows that were shut. Bosco led the way up the stairs.

On the first floor, a board outside one of the entrances read innocuously: Lobo Estates Pvt Ltd. They pushed the glass door and walked in. A girl sat behind a reception desk reading something on her phone; on a bench by the wall sat a beefy security guard with a rifle balanced between his legs. Seeing the policemen, he stood up. 'Yes, sir?'

'Is Mr Lobo in? We have come to see him on a routine matter. Please give him my card, will you?' The guard took Kerkar's card and vanished behind the reception desk.

Within a minute, he returned and gestured for them to follow him. On the wooden plaque above Angelo's cabin were the ornately inscribed words: 'Angelo Lobo, Hon'ble minister, Government of Goa.' They knocked and entered.

The image Neville had conjured in his mind's eye on listening to Bosco's account wasn't far off the mark. A swarthy man in a spotless white shirt sat behind the desk. The first thing which struck one about the minister was his neck; a thick prize-fighter's neck, giving an impression of raw physical strength. Angelo Lobo was portly but solidly built. The hairless arm he extended towards them was like an ebony log. Kerkar walked up and shook it.

'Morning, Mr Lobo. Apologies we came without an appointment, but DGP Chandok thought it was urgent. I hope you don't mind if we take a few minutes,' Kerkar began diplomatically.

Lobo met Kerkar's gaze, as if unsure what to make of this visit. Without a smile, he pointed to the chairs in front of his desk. He didn't appear nervous, just mildly irritated.

'What is this about?' Lobo inquired curtly.

'You may have heard that the Leo Jarvinen murder case has just been handed over to the CBI. Well, we are re-opening the Joshua Davies case as well. This is Inspector Bosco D'souza and JCP Neville Wadia from Mumbai.'

'Mumbai?' Lobo raised an eyebrow.

'I have retired from the force, Mr Lobo. The victim's family is known to me and the DGP asked me to help SP Kerkar on the case.'

Lobo looked sceptical but didn't object.

'How do these cases concern me?' he demanded.

'I am not saying they do. We have only come to ask a few questions.'

Kerkar turned to Neville.

'Mr Lobo, did you ever meet Joshua Davies?' Neville asked.

'No,' Lobo replied tersely.

'Never?'

'I said no. Why, should I have?'

'Apparently, he was known to your son.'

Lobo made a face. 'So? My son and I lead independent lives. I have nothing to do with his friends. I have my ministry and my private businesses, and he runs his own venture. Who he meets, spends time with, is of no interest to me.'

'Joshua Davies was an investigative reporter working on a story about the second airport in Goa. We have reason to believe that he may have gotten in touch with you.'

Lobo's glare intensified. With each question, his temper seemed to rise a notch. 'Reason to believe? Meaning what? You have pictures of him with me? Recorded phone calls? What exactly are you suggesting?'

'No, we have none of this. However, since you are so closely associated with the airport, it is conceivable that he would have tried to get in touch. This is not an accusation; we only want to know if he did,' Neville clarified, calmly.

Lobo's tone softened a little. 'Many people try to get in touch with me. I don't meet most of them and cannot even remember the names of those I do. Work keeps me very busy. And what's the point of dragging up this airport again anyway; haven't you read the Supreme Court order?'

SP Kerkar spoke up, 'Yes, we are aware that the environmental clearance was suspended in March, but it wasn't so during the period we are referring to.'

The mention of the suspension seemed to enrage the minister. He sat up straight, wagging a finger at Kerkar. 'Environmental clearance, huh? Then what was the Prime Minister doing laying the foundation stone for the same airport? There ...'

Lobo pointed to a laminated photograph on the cabinet by the wall. The PM posing with a group of men in front of a development site, beaming into the camera.

'Is it me you see standing there?'

'But it is the Supreme Court ...'

'There can be no development in this country while we have something called this bloody Supreme Court, do you understand?' Angelo cut Kerkar off. 'All that's left is for these jokers to leave the courtroom and take to the streets carrying placards!'

They waited for him to pipe down.

'There are different points of view on this airport, Mr Lobo but we aren't here to debate that. Our only point is that Joshua Davies was collecting facts about it and may have contacted you. Did he?' Neville asked directly.

'He may have. Many journalists called last year, he may have been one of them. But I didn't meet him. Anyway, what does this have to do with his death?'

Lobo countered.

Bosco stirred in his chair. 'Mr Lobo, last year, two cases of suicide were reported from Mopa. Local farmers. No FIR was registered but were you familiar with any of them?'

Lobo looked at Bosco with eyes that questioned his audacity in asking him such a question. 'Mopa is not my constituency, nor a farmer suicide any business of mine. And young man, I don't know what you are implying, but you better be careful.'

'The suspension must have come as quite a setback, right?' Kerkar pressed on.

The minister's pique was rising, they could feel it. But Kerkar wasn't one to relent. 'So many hundreds of acres of land purchased; heard prices shot up ten-fold in the last two years, but now?'

Lobo had picked up a glass paperweight and was tossing it around in his palm, not without intent from the look of it.

'This meeting is over, SP Kerkar. Next time you wish to talk to me, call in advance. I am a minister of this government; don't forget that. DGPs come and go, sometimes before their time. Now, if you'll excuse me,' he said in a level enough voice, though there was no mistaking the menace in it.

They stood up.

'Thank you for your time,' Neville said tersely before walking out.

Outside, the police car had dropped Mia off and returned. They got into Neville's car and asked the driver to follow. It was a short drive back to the riverfront.

'What did you make of it, sir?' Kerkar asked.

'My bet is Joshua did contact him. Seemed quite apparent that Lobo knows of him, and not just from seeing his picture in the papers. But there's one thing, Kerkar. I understand the Mopa airport land runs into crores and that the game would have been hot around the middle of last year, but for a minister to murder a foreign national, I don't know. However, the farmer's death, now that's a more serious motive.'

Bosco shook his head, as if he disagreed with Neville's assessment. 'Sir, if I may say something, Angelo Lobo is a hot-headed man. He doesn't always do things after weighing the consequences. Once, he smashed a beer bottle on the head of a man in plain view of a dozen people. Under the influence, he is capable of anything.'

'Hmm. Good to know, Bosco. By the way, I am glad you brought up the farmer case with him. I may not have.'

'Let's see what the son has to say,' Kerkar said.

11

UPON REACHING PANJIM, KERKAR ASKED NEVILLE TO park near the jetty. They handed the keys to the police car driver and boarded one of the small ferries. Bosco requested to be taken to the *Mandovi Queen*.

'Let's try the big boat first,' he told Neville.

As the boat set off on its brief journey, Neville looked around. The setting was surreal. It was midday, and the river glistened like liquid silver under the sun. On one side, Panjim's bustling main street teemed with cars, while on the other, lush green hills with veins of red earth rose above the water. Amidst this landscape, large boats floated with a peculiar incongruity. Neville counted six of them, flanked by smaller private yachts – toys of the elite from Goa or Mumbai. His last memory of being at sea was when he and Shehnaz had taken a catamaran from the Gateway of India to Alibaug.

In a matter of minutes, they reached the imposing yacht, even more formidable up close, and ascended a gangway, at the end of which a formally dressed man stood waiting.

'Is Jakob here?' Kerkar asked brusquely, without any preamble.

The man looked unsure of what to say.

'Can we go in and see anyway?' Neville asked, but Kerkar was already striding purposefully towards the casino entrance. Pushing through the glass doors, they entered a room that resembled the opulent images of Las Vegas casino pits Neville had seen in movies, minus the crowds.

'Sir, please wait here. I will check on Mr Lobo and let you know in a moment,' blurted the casino official before running away in search of his boss.

The room was vast, spacious enough to fit at least three tennis courts. There was no natural light and, even at that hour, harsh ceiling lights and opulent chandeliers lent a kind of faux grandeur to it. Spread across the central portion of the room were card tables of varying sizes, bound in green leather. There were at least fifty or sixty of them. In some, sat serious-looking men nursing drinks and clutching cards.

'Poker?' Neville asked Kerkar.

'Or Teen Patti, what they call Indian flush.'

Dotting the outer periphery of the room were slot machines, mostly unoccupied. A young woman sat at one, pressing buttons somewhat disinterestedly, as if resigned to a fruitless outcome. Roulette tables and vertical wheels added to the eclectic mix. Attendants in waistcoats hovered nearby, and one approached

Neville only to back off, noticing the uniforms of his companions. The air-conditioning was cranked up high, making the room uncomfortably cold.

'Vishnu, has it always been like this? This could be any place in Macau or Vegas. Not that I've been to either, but this looks truly world-class. I remember seeing a gambling room in a hotel in Kathmandu many years ago – it was a dingy basement dive compared to this.'

'Sir, you haven't seen anything yet. There is an upper floor with live entertainment, bars, restaurants and of course, more tables, machines; it's like a mini city.'

There was almost a note of pride in the Superintendent's voice, the way he described it. Neville was thinking of taking a picture on his phone to show Shehnaz when a voice next to him said, 'Hello gentlemen, what can I do for you?'

They turned around to see a dark, suave man smiling at them. Jakob Lobo had his father's complexion but little else of his physical appearance. Dressed in a sharp, cream-coloured suit and pointed leather shoes that looked Italian, his gelled hair was combed back over a high forehead and gaunt face. His teeth looked unnaturally white against his dark skin, or maybe it was the artificial indoor light that produced this effect. He looked lithe and moved gracefully. There was another thing – Jakob exuded a kind of nervous energy, as if he was high on something, though not alcohol. They shook hands.

'Hello, I am SP Kerkar. This is JCP Neville Wadia

from Mumbai. And Bosco D'Souza.'

Jakob looked towards Bosco and said, 'Your face is familiar. We have met before, haven't we?'

'Yes, Mr Lobo.'

'I never forget a face. Will this take long, gentlemen? In that case, we better walk over to my office. The sight of uniformed policemen on a gambling floor can make our patrons nervous.'

He turned and led the way, before they had a chance to see another flash of those glittering teeth.

Jakob ushered them into a glass elevator, open on all sides. They rode up a floor, still marvelling at how capacious the vessel was.

The office was modest in comparison but stylish. A few monitors which presumably allowed the owner to keep an eye on the casino floor. An open laptop on a glass table, a drinks trolley with spirits of every conceivable kind and framed photographs of casinos from across the world adorning the dark red walls. Jakob invited them to sit and offered them coffee, which they declined.

'We are here to ask you a few questions about Joshua Davies,' Neville said, without beating around the bush.

Jakob looked amused. 'Really? I thought that was a closed chapter.'

Neville ignored the remark. 'You knew Joshua, didn't you?'

'Yes, I did.'

Neville waited.

'He came by the ship sometimes. We'd chat on the deck, share a smoke. He came a few times. Nice guy, I liked him.'

'Did he come to play?'

'No, I don't think he did. The floating casino intrigued him, and I guess he enjoyed my company.'

Jakob's demeanour was relaxed, almost as if he was savouring the banter. If there was any anxiety, he concealed it well.

'Oh, so you were friends?'

'Not really. I must have met him, what, half a dozen times in all? That doesn't make him a friend, does it? When he had nothing better to do, he'd come and shoot the breeze with me.'

'Did he usually come alone?'

A mild hesitation spread across Jakob's face. Neville noticed a slight tremor in the wrist that sported an elegant Rolex Yacht-Master.

'Perhaps he brought friends along. I don't remember too clearly. There are a lot of people who come to my ships, not always locals.' Jakob held Neville's gaze as he said this, a challenge glinting in his eyes.

'Of course. Leo Jarvinen would come too, wouldn't he?'

'Is it an offence to entertain foreigners in my casino?'

'Not at all, just odd that many of them end up dead, that too under suspicious circumstances,' Neville answered, his tone still even.

'Oh, is that what this is about?'

'So, who else would come along to shoot the breeze with you, Mr Lobo?'

Jakob didn't respond.

'How about an attractive young woman called Eva? Does the name ring a bell?'

Still no reply.

'Mr Lobo, numerous witnesses have seen the people I've mentioned in your company. It might be better for you to speak up. After all, we haven't accused you of anything. Yet.'

'Leo and Eva were friends. Both of them liked to play, Leo particularly. Baccarat or poker, low stakes. Usually, I don't join, but sometimes I did. They were known to the staff as friends and didn't need to buy minimum use coupons. It's good to have a few white players on the floor; it makes locals feel they are in Vegas,' Jakob said with a deadpan expression, having shed his genial smile.

'And then Leo died. Did Eva's visits stop after that?'

'For some time, yes. She started coming again, after a while.'

'On her own?'

'Yes, the first few visits. And then, with Joshua.'

'Were they partners?'

'Joshua and Eva? I'm not sure. I mean, it wasn't obvious. They hadn't known each other for too long, anyway.'

'Did Eva talk about Leo when she came later, alone?'

A faint smile ghosted across Jakob's lips but disappeared almost instantly. 'Eva got it into her head that something was fishy about Leo's death. She thought I could help her look into it. Not me directly, maybe, but using my father's influence to request the police.'

'And why did she think there was something suspicious? Did she ever tell you?'

'You see, the police questioned her repeatedly following her return from Colombo, almost as if they were trying to pin the blame on her. If it was an accidental death, why would they do that? That was Eva's logic. So, once she was cleared, she tried asking but the police clammed up.' Jakob gave Kerkar a pointed look.

'I see. And did you give her the assistance she sought from you?'

'I asked my dad and was told to lay off. In our position, it's not wise to get involved in such cases. I gave Eva the same advice – to let it go.'

'And it was she who brought Joshua along to the ship the first time?'

'Yes, she introduced me to Joshua.'

'Did you have any contact with Eva, after Joshua's death?'

Jakob seemed to stiffen in his chair, his fingers arranging the pens strewn on the table into a neat row.

'No.' Just that one word, which hung heavily between them.

'That's odd. Joshua and Eva would come and hang with you; Joshua dies, accidentally or otherwise, but Eva never returns, and you make no effort to reach her?' Neville asked in the same flat tone, as if he was inquiring after the weather.

There was no response.

'Did you call her? Try to find out where she was?'

The faintest of nods.

'And?'

'She was gone. Phone switched off, no word at all. She vanished.'

'Did you know where she lived?'

'I had an idea it was somewhere near Taleigao, but I never visited her there.'

'Didn't you worry that something may have happened to her?'

'No. I thought she may have gotten frightened and left Goa.'

'Frightened?'

'Well, first her boyfriend died and then the next guy she was hanging out with died too. It's certainly odd. Before the police could question her again, she must have upped and left. Not too difficult to imagine, is it?'

'When was the last time you saw her? Or them?'

'A few days before Joshua's death. Here.'

'And everything seemed normal?'

'Yes.'

There was a knock at the door. A young boy entered. He wasn't dressed formally like the attendants on the gambling floor. On seeing the policemen, he froze.

'Sorry, sir, I didn't realize ...'

'It's OK, Danny. What did you need?'

'The boys are waiting, sir.'

Jakob looked at his watch. 'Oh, it's time already? Ask them to wait, will you? I'll be down soon.'

Danny left.

'We have a daily meeting around this time. Routine check for the evening arrangements. That's when the action picks up,' Jakob explained.

'In your interactions with Joshua, did you get an idea of what he did for a living? Or what he was doing in Goa?'

'I think he mentioned a book, but I've no idea what it was about. I assumed it was a novel or something.'

'You said he was intrigued by the casino. Did he ask you a lot of questions about the gambling business?'

'Not particularly, just the usual stuff. A floating casino stokes the curiosity of most people.'

'Does your father come here?'

A shadow flitted across Jakob's eyes. 'No.'

Neville waited.

'He is a cabinet minister. Perhaps he thinks it wouldn't be right for him to be seen here.'

'Perhaps he thinks? You mean the subject has never come up in all these years? Don't you live in the same house?'

'What happens between me and my father is none of your business.'

Neville had been expecting this, at some point. In fact, he was surprised that Jakob Lobo had allowed the questioning to continue in this refrain, for so long. There was nothing directly linking him to the murder of Leo Jarvinen or Joshua Davies, and he would be perfectly within his rights to end the meeting. Neville's tone shifted to conciliatory. 'Quite so. I was only wondering if he disapproves of your involvement in the gambling business.'

'There is no reason to. It's perfectly legal and even supported by the state government. As Tourism Minister, he knows how big a role it plays in attracting tourists to Goa. In fact—'

Jakob was about to blurt out something but checked himself.

'In fact?' Neville nudged.

'It's nothing.'

'Perhaps Mr. Lobo was about to mention that his father has singled out casinos as a major thrust area for development around the new Mopa airport. A mini casino city, no less; tourists wouldn't even have to come all the way into town. All this was last year, of course. Before the freeze,' Bosco said, in his soft voice. Neville was beginning to like this boy.

Jakob shot a sharp glare to Bosco; now that face would certainly not be forgotten.

'I was about to say that it was my father who helped me with the initial capital for the boats.'

'I see. So, the differences are not over gambling. Mr Lobo, I've heard that elsewhere in the world, recreational drugs and paid escorts are very much a part of the casino landscape. People who come to gamble like to let their hair down. How is it in Goa?'

'Are you suggesting that we supply drugs and hookers? SP Kerkar would be able to tell you that these ships are monitored by them, fairly regularly.'

'No, I wasn't suggesting anything. Did Joshua or Eva have any interest in drugs?'

Jakob raised his eyebrows. 'You know, Mr …'

'Wadia.'

'Yes, Mr Wadia, I am beginning to dislike your line of questioning. I don't see what any of this has to do with me, and I am required by my team downstairs. So, perhaps you will excuse me?'

Jakob stood up. Kerkar looked at Neville, who nodded, and they rose as well.

'One last question, Mr Lobo. You wouldn't have a picture of Eva on your phone, would you? Even a selfie or something like that? This is such a stunning boat, I'm sure everyone wants to take a picture at some point.'

Bosco and Kerkar looked at Neville in surprise, but Jakob's reaction was a greater surprise. Without a murmur of protest, he peered into his phone and, after some swiping around, held out the handset towards Neville.

On the open deck of a yacht stood Jacob, flanked by a striking white couple. From images he'd seen online, Neville recognized the man as Leo Jarvinen. The woman was obviously Eva. The light on the water behind them, a glowing sunset, cast an ethereal glow on Eva's hair, which blew gently in the breeze. In this flattering golden light, she could have easily passed off as a glamorous film star. Leo and she made a handsome pair; Jakob in his impeccably tailored clothes, didn't look out of place either – as the couple's exotic Indian friend.

'Do you mind if I take a shot on my phone?'

'Feel free.'

Neville took his phone out and clicked a photo.

'What was her full name?'

'Eva's? Campbell. She was Eva Campbell.'

'Thank you, Mr Lobo. Allow me to compliment you on this yacht. I had no idea we had attained these levels in Goa.'

They shook hands and made their way towards the exit. Stepping onto the small boat that bobbed on the water, Neville turned for a last glimpse of the *Mandovi Queen*. On the deck stood the young boy, Danny, staring intently at them. His face looked vaguely familiar. As soon as their eyes met, Danny scurried back inside.

The police driver was waiting at the jetty. Collecting the car keys from him, Neville asked, 'Vishnu, hope you weren't offended I did all the questioning inside?'

Vishnu grinned warmly. 'What are you saying, sir? Just the one thing which struck me on our way out – DSP Alvares. Should we have mentioned him, just to see Lobo's reaction?'

'I thought about it, Vishnu. But I suspect that string is pulled by the older Lobo. Jakob may benefit from it, but the orders come from the top. In fact, I was going to suggest that you meet this Alvares once, perhaps in DGP Chandok's office. Best if I don't sit in for that.'

'Right, sir.'

'And, please call me Neville. Seriously. There is no loss of respect in calling one by his name,' Neville said, giving Vishnu's shoulder a reassuring pat.

'Bosco, can I ask you for a favour? I need to piece together the chronology in my head – Leo Jarvinen's death, the approximate date of Joshua's arrival in Goa, the day of his death, the last time anyone saw Eva or Joshua alive – you get the drift, right? Vishnu …'

'If Joshua was investigating a story, he would have spoken to potential sources. His investigations go deeper than a mere google search. We'll need to figure out who he may have been in touch with – journalists, cops, land lawyers, activists … we have to ask around. Someone will know something.'

They agreed to reconvene soon. Neville waved farewell and drove off, feeling a pang of hunger as it was well past lunchtime. There was a message on his phone from Shehnaz asking when he was likely to be back. He replied, informing her he was enroute from Panjim.

The drive took around half an hour and Shehnaz and Mia were already at the table when Neville reached; he washed up quickly and joined them.

'Sorry, I didn't realize that it had gotten so late. Hope you didn't wait too long for me?'

'Just started, tuck in,' Shehnaz said, gesturing to the spread of rice and fish curry.

'Enlightening morning, Mia. The new team you met briefly seems promising and we have established some clear lines of enquiry. It's only the start, but I am hopeful.'

'OK, finish your food first. Then you can tell us all about it,' Shehnaz said, but then she suddenly recalled something. 'Oh, before I forget, Neville, remember the felicitation Naresh Sardesai mentioned? That's this evening. 5:00 p.m. at the Centre of Arts and Culture in Panjim. I thought it would be interesting, Mia is keen to attend as well. But you've had a full day, if you would rather rest ...'

'Not at all. I will come with you. Intriguing man, Naresh, I quite liked him,' Neville replied.

Agnes had prepared caramel custard, which they enjoyed in the sitting room as Neville gave them an account of his meetings with the Lobos.

'So, it looks like Josh was on that story?' Shehnaz queried.

'He was certainly interested in them, but we shouldn't jump to conclusions. His arrival in Goa was not long after Leo Jarvinen's murder, and we know that he befriended Leo's former girlfriend. May not be a causal link but it is not impossible that he was investigating that case and it led him to the Lobos. Or it could also have been the new airport or the casinos, nothing to do with Leo.'

'Senior Lobo for the airport deals and junior for the casino angle, you mean?' Shehnaz asked.

'Possibly, or they could be related.'

'How?'

'There was a passing remark made by Jakob Lobo today about how his father helped him with the seed capital for the gambling boats. It got me thinking. Angelo Lobo deals in land, which would be throwing up tons of cash. A casino is a very handy way of legitimizing that black money into certifiable gambling profits.'

'What they call money laundering?'

'Yes. It's unclear which was Joshua's primary thrust of enquiry. It could all be interconnected.'

'But it's still the Lobos, right?' Shehnaz pressed.

'Not necessarily. Let's not forget what we heard from Naresh about his interest in the HSS,' Mia interjected.

'True, Mia. But we have just started digging. Kerkar and Bosco will explore all these angles and get back to us. Goa is a small place; we should turn up stuff pretty soon,' Neville assured.

'Somehow, this Eva seems to be at the heart of it all. You don't think Faye can tell us more about her?' Mia asked, tentatively.

'She might. But Faye strikes me as a sensitive girl; pressing too hard could shut her down. She has seen you now; let's give her a day or two to process it. I agree with you that she knows something and I am sure she will tell us too, without us having to subject her to undue pressure.'

Relief washed over Mia's face.

'But this talk of Eva reminds me, did Joshua's card about "love in the air" hint at a possible involvement with her?'

'I've thought a lot about it since yesterday, Neville. It is conjecture at best. And knowing how vague Joshua was, he could have been talking about something else altogether. Yet, you said that they used to visit the boat together.'

'They did but Jakob insists they weren't romantically involved. Though his account may be spurious,' Neville noted.

Mia sat up suddenly, as if she had been struck by a revelation. 'There's one thing, Neville. Leslie mentioned there was pressure on his editor from the very top. If it came from the CM's office, at the behest of the Lobos, it proves they were involved, right?'

'Probably, Mia, but we can't be *sure* that the nudge to the CM came from the Lobos. You were talking about the HSS earlier, and they have at least one very powerful patron in the government – an MGP minister who has earned the moniker of kingmaker. The government cannot crack down on these goons because of him. I do need to have another word with Naresh. Let's see if we can get a few minutes with him after the felicitation today.'

Back on board the *Mandovi Queen*, the staff meeting was over, and Jakob and Danny sat huddled together in the quiet of his cabin. The boy was in a state and Jakob was doing his best to pacify him. He poured Danny a measure of clear spirit into a glass and reached across to ruffle his hair. For good measure, he extracted a bunch of notes from his wallet, and stuffed them into Danny's shirt pocket. Taking that as a dismissal, the boy rose to leave, but Jakob hurried over to place a comforting arm around his shoulder. He seemed to murmur assurances in his ear, but Danny still looked every bit as disturbed as he slouched out with his head hung.

12

THERE WAS QUITE A CROWD OUTSIDE THE PANJIM auditorium, larger than could have been expected for the felicitation of a Konkani writer, even a very good one. The intrigue surrounding the death threat to Naresh Sardesai, and the consequent round-the-clock police protection, had added a frisson of excitement, drawing people eager to glimpse the man at the centre of the storm. Neville and Shehnaz watched with wry amusement as Naresh disembarked from a police car, greeted by exclamations from the crowd.

'Look, look, full state security, didn't I tell you?'

'Finally, they have started taking these threats seriously.'

'How frail he looks … who would want to harm such an old man?'

Naresh himself appeared bemused by all the fuss. At the entrance, he encountered Shehnaz and Neville.

'Ah, my Parsi friends.'

Neville shook the veined, trembling hand Naresh proffered.

'Can you believe this tamasha, Neville? You'd think there are mobs waiting to lynch me!'

They walked in together. The organizers came running to escort Naresh while Neville and Shehnaz broke away to join Mia, who had been holding their seats. The auditorium was already packed and the ones who had been hovering outside had to mill around the side walls of the hall, some even squatting on the steps of the aisle.

There was none of the characteristic delay, perhaps out of consideration for the writer's age. Naresh was helped up a short flight of stairs to a spartan stage; two chairs and a table with a vase of flowers. A lady greeted Naresh and garlanded him. He took one of the chairs, next to a gentleman who was from the organization honouring him. After the lady had introduced the host, he walked to the podium to read out a glowing tribute to Naresh and his illustrious career. Naresh sat still, with the same amused look on his face, not turning once towards the speaker, peering instead at the audience as if in search of a familiar face. When his speech ended, the man handed Naresh a plaque and invited him to say a few words.

Without moving from his seat, Naresh said, 'I hope you won't mind if I speak from here. My old knees won't allow me to stand for too long. But thank you all for coming today, even the three in saffron who skulk in that corner. I am happy they are here, if only to witness that I am not cowering under threats from their ilk.'

A rustle swept through the audience as heads turned towards the direction Naresh indicated. Sure enough, next to a police constable sat three men clad in saffron robes, their faces inscrutable.

'This morning, I thought about what I should share with you today. It's tedious to talk about my books; better you read them than hear me prattle on. Besides, I cannot speak for too long, I tire easily. So, I thought I would share two stories from my life.'

He paused, catching his breath, and took a sip of water from the glass before him. The audience hung on his every word. There was something magnetic about Naresh Sardesai.

'When I was a few weeks old, my mother fell gravely ill. She had a high fever, and the doctors were worried she may not pull through. She was in no position to breastfeed me in any case. There was a Christian lady in the neighbourhood who had recently had a child. The moment news of my mother's condition reached her, she came rushing and offered to breastfeed me till my mother recovered. My father had no choice but to accept. This lady continued to nourish me for days on end, sharing her milk between her own and the unknown fledgling she had taken under her wing. When my mother finally recovered, she came by to hand me over, said a prayer and left. We never saw her again. It was the generosity of a Christian woman that nourished this Hindu boy to health and life. And now they tell me that we don't belong together, that one of us is defiled by the other's presence. What am I expected to say? You tell me.'

The hall erupted into thunderous applause. It carried on for minutes, and eventually Naresh had to lift a frail hand to quieten them down. He resumed, his voice unwavering.

'I visited Tamil Nadu shortly after the devastating tsunami struck its shores. You have all seen images of the destruction, but what affected me was the sheer selfless spirit with which people helped each other. Caste, religion, status, gender – everything was forgotten; it didn't matter. Everyone reached out to save others, to console them. Even today, I hear that orphaned children there are being raised by men and women of different religions and castes, something quite unthinkable otherwise. I came away shattered from the scale of misery but also full of hope. I always think, why do we need a catastrophe – an earthquake, a flood, a tsunami – for people to be kind to each other? At other times, why do we become so small?'

Naresh's voice was fading, the exhaustion apparent, but he had a parting shot to deliver. 'I came here today not to collect a prize. At my age, these things mean little. I came out for a breath of fresh air and to share these stories with you. What is our life, after all, but a series of stories? We only need to be aware which ones to abide by, as our guiding lights through the journey. And to you, the saffron magi, I say – your threats don't frighten me. You can still my breath, but all your might is not enough to crush the spirit of this small man. You see, it is nourished by the same *other* that you despise.'

Naresh folded his hands together in a namaste. He was done. There was pin-drop silence in the hall, until someone stood up and began to clap. The applause spread, swelling to a roaring crescendo.

Neville turned to see if the saffron-robed men were there, but their seats were empty. Next to him, Shehnaz and Mia sat quietly, with solemn looks on their faces. As their row emptied, Shehnaz asked, 'You wanted to speak to him, Neville?'

'Yes, but he appeared spent. Not here. Maybe I will drop by tomorrow at some point.'

By the time they stepped out of the hall, the crowd had thinned. The sun had lost its bite, and they walked for a while on the footpath by the river, its leaden waters mirroring the heaviness they all felt inside. No one spoke.

Later that evening, well past midnight, two figures perched atop a jagged outcrop overlooking the desolate

Vagator beach. The sands lay undisturbed; the last of the visitors shooed off long ago by the coastguards. A half-drained bottle of liquor and a pair of tea glasses stood near their feet. The moon was quite full and the sea shimmered in the light. The waves advanced stealthily but relentlessly, one after the other. Like troubles.

One of them pointed a trembling finger in their direction, as if in accusation, or to stall their progress. The other poured from the bottle and passed on a glass to his companion. They drank silently, a forlorn air about them. Suddenly, everything seemed to be coming apart.

13

IT WAS TEN IN THE MORNING AND THREE MEN OCCUPIED a corner of a quaint tea shop in Ponda, huddled over the day's newspaper. They were members of the Ponda Yuva Sangh, a group of local youngsters with the laudable mandate of ensuring order, and upholding local customs and traditions. There were two articles of their interest in the paper: Naresh Sardesai's fiery speech at the felicitation in Panjim, and the other speculating the reopening of the investigation into the death of Welsh tourist Joshua Davies, prompted by new forensic findings. Apparently, his sister had arrived from London to expedite it. A photograph of the deceased accompanied the latter piece.

'It's the same guy,' exclaimed the youngest, animatedly.

'Of course, it is. He even told us his name, don't you remember?'

'Yes, but when exactly was this, Prakash? Seems like ages ago. And in all this time, no probe into his murder?' pondered another.

'Around this time last year, I would say. During the rains,' replied Prakash. 'The original autopsy said it was an accidental death and the case was closed. Now, new findings prove it was murder.'

'Well, we did warn him about this lot,' said the boy, turning his gaze to the innocuous-looking building in front, painted in white and yellow. A red flag bearing an image of an elephant fluttered on a metal trident atop its gate. The headquarters of the Hindu Shresthata Samiti and the scourge of Ponda, in the eyes of local residents. Ever since the HSS established its base in the area, they had stirred up trouble routinely. What the locals resented most was their self-appointed guardianship of the village of Ramnathi and meddling in long-held traditions; the burning of the Narkasur effigy a case in point. On their part, the Yuva Sangh resisted as much as it could, but the HSS evidently had political clout, leaving even the police cautious about ruffling its feathers. All kinds of rumours swirled around the clandestine activities within the ashram, a place forbidden to locals who could only seethe at the sight of saffron-clad sevaks moving in and out, cloaked in secrecy and an air of sinister purpose.

'He mentioned Naresh Sardesai, I remember clearly. And that writer they shot dead in Karnataka.'

'Was it proven?'

'What is ever proved, Mani? Forgot the Madgaon blasts? The accused were finally released, weren't they; yet, can there be any doubt who was behind that? I'm telling you, they're capable of anything. Just recently, I was reading that the police seized guns, bombs, god knows what else from one of their warehouses near Mumbai.'

'This Joshua, was he doing an exposé on the HSS, you think?'

'He must have been. Why else would he ask after Mahesh Talpade's whereabouts? Did he look like a devotee to you?'

'And then he turns up dead a few weeks later. Shouldn't we inform the police?'

'We must. But first, let's try and figure out the exact date when he visited us in Ponda; we can't be vague about these things. And before the cops, we should inform his sister.'

Just metres away, Mahesh Talpade, spokesperson of the HSS, stood by a window of the same white and yellow building, immersed in the folds of the newspaper. His shaved head and saffron robe evoked the image of an ascetic, yet the intensity of his hawk-like gaze and the curl at the corner of his mouth hinted at something more sinister. The intelligence in those piercing eyes was unmistakable, as was the malevolent quality that seemed to emanate from within. Intently he read, before looking up and gazing into the distance. He stared fixedly for a long time, as if to process the ramifications of what he had just learnt, before withdrawing his phone and making a call.

Michael Alvares parked his jeep in an empty slot outside the Panjim police station. He had been up drinking till late and his head throbbed. Leaning on the steering wheel, he fought off the nausea that lurked. The previous evening had been a nightmare. First, the call from Angelo Lobo and then the summons from SP Kerkar, to bring his ass down to the DGP's office first thing in the morning. If there was the slightest doubt about the purpose of that meeting, the damning headline on the front page of the morning paper had settled it. With some effort, he eased himself out of the seat to face the brutal day that loomed.

Kerkar was waiting for him in his office. The moment Alvares entered, he stood up.

'Morning, Michael. Let's go upstairs. The DGP is waiting for us.'

They walked up, Alvares breathlessly trailing Kerkar as he took the steps two at a time.

DGP Chandok was pacing behind his desk when the two policemen entered. Introductions were brief.

'Sir, I don't think you have met DSP Alvares,' Kerkar began.

The DGP waved them into the chairs across from him, but not before he had shot Alvares a withering stare.

'Alvares, I expect you've seen today's papers. The second autopsy report of Joshua Davies is with me. I will spare you the details but let's just say it is fairly conclusive – it was a homicide. So, perhaps you will enlighten us on why you were in such a tearing rush to brand it an accident and close the case last year?'

Alvares hadn't expected the DGP to beat around the bush, but this was more direct than he had feared. He offered the defence prepared on his way to the station.

'Sir, the original autopsy report indicated that the deceased had struck his head on rocks on the beach before losing consciousness and being swept away by the waves. There was no reason to suspect foul play. Any attempt to investigate would only have fanned the controversy raging at the time, surrounding other so-called suspicious deaths involving tourists. We chose to act decisively, in the interest of avoiding needless speculation.'

Chandok's eyes bore into Alvares'. 'Really? Kerkar, could you please meet this medical examiner who furnished such a convenient autopsy report? Was it even an examiner, or an attendant who was paid off?'

'Sir …' Alvares mumbled.

'Kerkar,' the DGP said, indicating that he should take over the questioning.

'Sir. Michael, how well do you know Angelo Lobo?'

Alvares stared down at the floor to compose himself. 'I've met him on a few occasions, sir. On the job.'

'Is that all?'

'Yes sir. Why do you ask?'

'Because we hear a lot of chatter about your proximity with the Lobo family. Some suggest that your promptness in closing the Davies case may have been at his behest.'

'Baseless gossip, I assure you, sir.'

'Joshua Davies' mother came down to Goa after his death. When she met you with a request to take another look at the case, why didn't you consider it? All she asked for was another post-mortem.'

'Sir, if we started re-opening cases at the request of every victim's family, how would we ever cope? Our workload ...'

'So, from the moment the autopsy report was furnished, you didn't do anything to pursue the matter any further. Nothing, is that right?' Chandok interrupted sharply.

Alvares didn't answer.

'We are reopening the case, Alvares. SP Kerkar will be the investigating officer. You will have nothing to do with it. In fact, it would be a good idea for you to go on leave for a while. And before that, if there is anything you wish to tell us about Joshua Davies or the disappearance of Eva Campbell, now is the time.'

Alvares didn't utter a squeak.

'You can go, Michael. I will call and speak to you later,' Kerkar said.

'And if word about this gets back to the Lobos, I will know where it came from. And you will have made things even more difficult for yourself. Keep that in mind,' the DGP barked.

Alvares saluted the senior officers and left the room.

'What could we have expected? A confession?' Chandok muttered to himself. 'Alvares is a smart fellow. He knows his best play is to remain silent and pretend that it was an honest mistake. It's up to us, to prove otherwise.'

Kerkar nodded. 'Indeed, sir. And the last thing Alvares would want is to burn his bridges with Lobo. He knows how vicious his benefactor can be. Anyway, our team is already in motion; we met with Jakob Lobo and his father yesterday. Bosco's unit is on the ground. I'll provide a progress report in a few days.'

'Thanks, Kerkar. And keep Neville updated, won't you?'

'Of course. That goes without saying.'

When Neville got off the phone with Kerkar, Shehnaz arrived with their mid-morning coffee. Taking his cup, he mentioned casually, 'Josh and Mia are in the papers this morning, apparently. We should take a look.'

'Oh, let me see where the damn paper is. Maybe with Agnes; I should retrieve it before she wraps it around a papaya. And we must get into the habit of reading these Goa papers, Neville.'

'You think so?' asked Neville, wryly.

Shehnaz chuckled, heading towards the kitchen.

Returning with the paper in her hand, she spread it out on the table. 'Here. Familiar faces on the front page.'

They read the piece, almost feeling Leslie's palpable relief, even relish, at being able to report on the story again.

'Maybe I should put Bosco and Leslie in touch. They may be able to help each other,' Neville thought aloud.

Shehnaz read the report on Naresh with greater interest. 'Neville, shall we drive over to Anjuna after coffee and visit our writer?'

'You've rather taken to him, haven't you?'

'Oh, I was reading his book last night. Not the best translation but the writing is incredibly powerful. Yesterday, though, listening to him speak, I sensed …'

'What?'

'Sounds awful saying it, but I felt he is fading. We may not have him much longer.'

'I know what you mean, dear. Come, let's go see him. You want to pick Mia up on the way?'

'No, let her be. We won't be there long, anyway.'

Neville changed out of his tracks, and they drove out. Shehnaz loved these days, which began suddenly, unplanned, on a whim.

Laxman sat at his appointed place outside the gate of the Sardesai residence. He smiled welcomingly at Neville and Shehnaz as they walked up. 'Morning Laxman, your sir is in the newspaper today, did you see?' Neville asked.

Laxman perked up. 'Yes, Jenny showed me in the morning.'

'You sit here all day, Laxman. Don't you read, walk about? Must get boring, no?'

'Yes, ma'am. From seven in the morning till seven in the evening, until Pramod takes over. Twelve hours of squatting here. Sir has given us this old Walkman and his box of cassettes to pass the time. Sometimes Roy comes by for a chat. Time passes,' Laxman explained, almost philosophically. 'When I first started, the days felt endless. Now, it's routine.'

'And in all this time, there has never been any incident?'

Laxman laughed. 'Not even a stray dog enters these premises. I can put my legs up and sleep all day – it won't matter.'

'You are probably right. But just the sight of a uniformed man at the gate is a deterrent. Everyone knows the house is guarded,' Neville said, giving Laxman an avuncular pat on the shoulder before they entered.

Jennifer had spotted them through the glass panes and opened the door. She greeted them. 'Sir isn't feeling too well today. He is quite tired.'

'Oh.'

'Who is it, Jenny?' A feeble voice floated up from inside.

Jennifer stepped back so Naresh could see them from his reclining chair. He did look worn out.

'Oh, the Bombaiwallahs. Come in, come in.'

'We won't disturb you today, Naresh. You should rest.'

'Yes, I do feel exhausted. Venturing out after such a long time yesterday ... I didn't expect it would tire me out so much.'

Shehnaz walked up to his chair. 'You were wonderful yesterday, Naresh. Everyone in the audience was deeply moved. Even if it was tiring, it was worth it.'

'You think so? Then I am glad I went.' A flicker of a smile.

Jennifer came and stood beside Shehnaz. 'I think he should shift to his bed now and sleep, don't you?'

'You are right. Is there a doctor on call, Jennifer?' Neville inquired.

'There is, but sir doesn't like to see him,' she replied softly.

Turning to Neville, Naresh spoke with effort, 'I don't have the energy today, but won't you come by once tomorrow? I had something to tell you.'

But even the effort of saying a few words was too much and his head lolled to one side. Shehnaz exchanged a worried glance with Jennifer, and together they helped Naresh up from his chair, virtually carrying him to his bedroom.

'If he gets worse, promise you'll call the doctor, even if he protests?'

Jennifer nodded grimly. Neville and Shehnaz quietly left the house.

'He is like a bird, you know, Neville. Practically weightless.'

At the gate, Laxman sat on his stool with earphones on, looking very much like a local DJ. They waved at him and drove off.

Mia lounged in her apartment, the morning unfolding lazily around her. Awoken at eight by the cheerful arrival of Lisa, the breakfast lady, and Katie, the effervescent cleaner, Mia found herself basking in their infectious energy. As Katie swept and mopped the floor, humming a tune as if it was the most enjoyable of chores, Lisa rattled off the items she could prepare at home and bring across for her. She had to describe the dishes as Mia had never heard of poha, upma, poi or sannas and Lisa didn't have words like chapped rice and semolina in her vocabulary. Mia settled on poha, which apparently had already been prepared and only needed to be fetched.

Both women spoke English and they were curious about Mia. She decided to be reticent, and deflected questions about her real purpose in Goa, asking them instead about their lives. The unhurried morning passed in a haze of chatter, breakfast, tea and after they left,

Mia decided to take it easy. She unpacked her suitcase and began arranging her belongings into the unfamiliar place.

She had downloaded books on her Kindle before arriving but didn't feel like reading. This made her wonder how long she would need to stay in Goa, how her days would pass. After all, she could hardly expect the Wadias to keep her company every day or to turn up at the police station for regular updates. She would have to get used to being at a loose end. Patience was the key, as Grace had written.

Around midday, Mia summoned Santosh, one of Mary's recommended drivers, opting to venture into Panjim for lunch by the river. On Santosh's recommendation, she ate a Goan meal at the Ritz Cafe, and enjoyed it thoroughly. Outside, it was humid but bearable under the shade of sprawling trees. As she strolled along, Mia identified copper pods, mango and rain trees, but not many others she walked under, making her wish Agnes was by her side. Ambling around, she reached the police building they had visited the previous day and imagined SP Kerkar hard at work inside, investigating her brother's case. Turning to the river, she could see the imperious *Mandovi Queen*, its form blazing in the sunlight. Joshua had been there. He would have walked down that very promenade, perhaps even eaten at the Ritz. As she strolled on, a surreal sensation washed over her, her heart skipping a beat as a young white man crossed the road from the other side. She paused to compose herself, then sought refuge in a nearby cafe, ordering a cappuccino. It was past ten in Cornwall and she sent her mother a message. The reply was almost immediate: 'I dreamt of you last night, darling. Stay safe.'

There were messages from Shehnaz, checking on her. Mia wondered if they would keep in touch once she returned to London. It often seemed that way when parting from people but the connection didn't always endure.

Panjim struck Mia as markedly different from Anjuna, even Assagaon. It was more of a town with some quaint streets and houses, dotted within an unexceptional urban sprawl. Goa itself, she thought, was part city, part village, not entirely one or the other but somewhere in between, as if it hadn't quite figured out what it wanted to be. The afternoon drifted by in such contemplations.

Around five, she called Santosh, asking him to take her to Vagator beach. There, she ran into the same women who had tried to sell her their wares the other day. They recognized her, or pretended to. This time, she bought a shell necklace from one of them and the woman even fastened the clasp behind her neck. Mia walked up to the rocks and sat there watching, till the sun began to set on the horizon. It was very peaceful. When the light started to fade, she rose and walked back to the car and asked to be driven home, feeling a calm she hadn't experienced on her previous visit to the beach. On reaching, she let Santosh go, asking him to call her in the morning for instructions. He seemed like a nice chap, not particularly talkative as some tourist car drivers could be, and Mia decided to keep the car on throughout her stay.

Back in the apartment, she switched all the lights on and poured herself a drink. She opened her mail and read Grace's note again. Leslie's name was listed among her contacts, along with a Panjim lawyer, Braganza, apparently a walking encyclopaedia on Goa. Mia made a note of the number.

Sipping her gin, Mia scanned the list of Anjuna eateries Mary had taped to the fridge door, selecting one with 'five min walk' scribbled next to it. It was only half past seven, but she didn't want to be walking around alone too late. At the gate, the security guard pointed to a lit billboard advertising a beer that promised to be the 'king of good times'. The shack was barely a hundred metres away. She strolled alongside a field, the gentle evening breeze brushing her skin.

The restaurant was mostly empty, perhaps it was still too early for the local diners. A young boy approached, handing her a menu. Mia settled into a seat and ordered a plate of squid and one of those beers. She drew a few glances, but a white tourist was hardly a novelty in this town. For an unpretentious shack, the food was surprisingly good, if somewhat spicy. Mia washed it down with the beer, paid her bill and stepped out.

The road was dimly lit and eerily quiet, punctuated only by the occasional bike zipping past. The sodium light at the complex gate glowed softly, the guard a shadow behind the glass window. As Mia walked briskly in the direction of her apartment, an inexplicable unease crept over her. Halfway there, the low growl of an approaching vehicle made her turn. A black SUV glided past the restaurant at a slow pace. She quickened her steps. The car edged closer and then, with a sickening screech, it began to accelerate.

Her heart raced. She scrambled for the edge of the road, intending to let it pass, but the SUV swerved violently, aiming straight at her. Realizing it was deliberate, Mia leaped, but it was too late; the car's front grille, a chrome maw, caught her ankle, sending her spinning into the field. The brakes screeched to a halt.

Left sprawled in the mud, Mia's breath came in ragged gasps. From the corner of her eye, she saw the car reversing slowly towards her. A primal sense of terror gripped her. Then, from the distance, came urgent voices, growing louder. Men sprinted from the restaurant, shouting and waving in Mia's direction. The SUV halted, then sped off down the road, its engine roaring as it fled into darkness.

14

WITH THE PASSING OF THE IMMEDIATE DANGER, MIA became acutely aware of a searing pain shooting up her right leg. She bit her lip to stifle sobs that threatened to overwhelm her. The men reached and gently pulled her out from the mud. Mia tried to stand but found she could not put weight on her foot. She looked down to inspect the damage. Her dress was blackened with mud, knees torn and bleeding, both her elbows badly bruised. A man offered her a handkerchief and pointed to her lip. She wiped it, revealing a smear of blood and dirt. Mia began to shake, prompting the men to lower her back to the ground, unnerved by her trembling.

The security guard, having seen the commotion, came running.

'Should we take her to a hospital?' he asked.

'Not the police station first? This wasn't an accident.'

Mia gestured to the guard to bend down and showed him Neville's number on her phone.

'Call him, now,' she whispered.

The guard complied, needing little explanation from Neville. The mere mention of Mia's name, the incident and the location were enough. He was on his way.

More men arrived on the scene, and a woman from the nearby restaurant joined them. She poured water on Mia's arms and legs, washing away the dirt from where the skin had peeled off. The ankle had started swelling up and Mia knew that something was seriously wrong there. She told the lady that a friend was on his way and would take her to a clinic, thanked the men for running to her rescue and even attempted a smile to let them know it wasn't too bad. One of the men, agitated, spoke up. 'I was on my way out and saw exactly what happened. The car was driving straight and then suddenly turned towards her! There was no other vehicle on the road. And they weren't done – the car started to reverse. Only on seeing us did it speed away.'

Mia looked at him and nodded. She reached down to feel her ankle with a finger but a current of pain passed through her at the slightest touch. She sat there, with the woman sweetly holding her hand, until there was the sound of a motor heralding Neville's arrival.

Neville and Shehnaz ran towards her. 'Oh my God, Mia! Are you badly hurt?' Shehnaz blurted, placing a palm on her cheek.

Mia pointed to the injured ankle.

'We need to get you to a doctor immediately. Can you try putting your weight on the other foot, Mia?' Neville asked as they stooped to raise her to a standing position. With their support, she limped to the car, and somehow managed to get into the back seat with Shehnaz's assistance. Neville spoke to the bystanders for a minute, taking down the number of the man who had witnessed the attack, before starting the car. He called Kerkar quickly to brief him about the incident.

'Where's the nearest clinic, Neville?'

'There's one near the petrol pump. It's called St Antony or something like that.'

Within five minutes, they reached the place. Neville dashed inside, returning with two nurses who brought a stretcher and carried Mia inside. Inside, the doctor assessed her injuries. 'We'll take an X-ray of the ankle and dress the wounds,' he said.

While they waited outside, Shehnaz's voice quivered as she asked, 'What happened?'

'From what I gathered from an eyewitness, an SUV tried to run her down. He was quite categorical. We will hear Mia's version soon. The car pushed her off the road and apparently even started to reverse in her direction, before the locals came running.'

Shehnaz gasped; her hand went up to cover her mouth. 'I had a bad feeling the moment Leslie said he would mention her in his report.'

Neville reached out to hold her hand. 'But how did they find out so soon? Barely a day has passed ...'

The doctor emerged, signalling for them to come in. Pointing to the X-ray plates, he explained, 'The right fibula has a fracture. It's a thin crack and shouldn't require surgery, but we'll see once the swelling subsides. A ligament may be torn, as there is some hemarthrosis – blood in the joint. I am giving her some painkillers and putting a preliminary bandage cast on. Tomorrow, you will need to bring her back for a proper weight-bearing cast. She is not to put any weight on the injured leg tonight.'

'And other than the ankle?'

'Oh, the rest of the wounds are superficial. We have dressed them; they are only scrapes. Her right elbow had a deeper gash. What exactly happened?'

Neville narrated the incident, and the doctor grimaced.

'She got off light then. These SUVs are brutes; a second later and she may have shattered her hip. I expect you will make a police report?'

'Of course. Can we shift her, doctor?'

'Yes, she seems calm enough. Someone will be with her tonight?'

'Yes, we will.'

The nurses helped Mia into the car. As Neville settled up at the clinic, Mia said, 'I have insurance, Shehnaz.'

'We'll see about that later, Mia,' she replied, trying not to sound too stern.

'Do we need to go to the station now?'

'SP Kerkar is on his way to our house. I think we should head there. Kerkar can take Mia's verbal report, and she can visit the station tomorrow. That should be alright.'

'Is it hurting, Mia?' Shehnaz asked.

'It's OK, I will be fine.'

Kerkar's jeep was waiting outside the gate when they arrived. He walked up as soon as they parked. 'Let's speak inside.'

Agnes and Martin had rushed out upon seeing them. They helped Mia hop on one foot up to the house. Inside, they settled her onto a sofa, propping her up with pillows and elevating her injured leg on a low footrest.

'What happened, madam? Accident?' Agnes cried out.

Shehnaz simply raised a palm, indicating she would explain later.

'Can I get her something?' Agnes asked, eager to help.

'Some chamomile maybe? Mia?' Shehnaz offered, though the idea of refreshments after such an ordeal struck her as distinctly odd.

'That would be nice, thank you,' Mia accepted, politely.

Neville and Kerkar pulled their chairs close to Mia and sat down.

'Whenever you feel up to it, it would be good to hear what happened from your own lips,' Neville said.

Mia described her evening in detail, from the moment she stepped out of the house for dinner, pausing intermittently to sip from her cup.

When she was done, Kerkar confirmed, 'And you are absolutely sure that the car's approach towards you was deliberate, not an accidental skid.'

'One hundred percent. It was moving at a slow speed, there were no other vehicles to avoid and the road wasn't wet. It accelerated only from around a few yards away. It would have rammed into me, had I not fallen into the field.'

'And you saw the car reversing?'

'Yes, and there was another witness.'

'Was the SUV black or could it have been any dark colour?'

Mia hesitated. 'I think it was black but I really can't be sure. The street was not very well-lit, and it all happened in a blur.'

Kerkar sat back. He seemed satisfied with Mia's account. He nodded to Neville, and they walked onto the veranda, closing the door behind them.

'It's an attempt, Vishnu. We cannot be sure if it was meant to scare her off or the intention was more violent.'

'Agree. It's the reversing of the car which I am not sure about. Was it to check if enough damage had been done or …'

'To finish the job?'

'Hmm.'

'Well, if we had any doubts that Joshua's killer is on the loose, this should put that to rest. An assault, whether to frighten or kill, within twenty-four hours of her presence being reported, is quite telling.'

Kerkar remained silent, his expression pensive. 'I am wondering if my meeting with Alvares in the morning may have set this off.'

'But her address?'

Kerkar shrugged.

'So will she stay with you now? Should I arrange for a constable?'

'No, I don't think that will be necessary. We'll bring her to the station tomorrow, once the cast is done at the clinic. And yes, she'll stay here with us. Anyway, I don't think she will be moving around much over the next few days.'

'Right. I'll be off then, Neville. I am very worried. I didn't want to alarm the girl any further, but this is serious. Anything could have happened today. We need to move fast, before something truly dire occurs.'

Neville nodded grimly. 'Anyway, I am meeting Bosco first thing tomorrow. We spoke briefly, and he sounded excited. I think he is onto something. Let's see.'

Kerkar got into his car and drove off. Inside the drawing room, Mia sat looking like a roughed-up doll, surrounded by the two attentive women. The cut on her lip and the spreading bruise on the forehead gave her a battered look, and the scrapes on her knee seemed even angrier against her flawless white skin.

'One thing is settled. You are not moving from here. The Anjuna pad experiment is over,' Shehnaz said in a matronly tone.

'I have to inform Mary,' Mia mumbled.

'This was probably meant to scare you off, Mia. If these guys were professionals, you wouldn't be sitting here sipping tea now. Something like this would be enough for a visitor to pack her bags and leave.'

'Maybe I would too, if you guys were not around. It was my first thought once the car sped away, I don't mind admitting.'

'Naturally. I think we can all do with a drink,' Neville proposed.

'But Mia …' Agnes protested.

'Oh, those are painkillers. A little brandy won't kill her. Right, Mia?'

'Even if it did, I don't care. I will have the drink, Neville.'

15

THEY SLEPT FITFULLY THAT NIGHT. SHEHNAZ HAD offered to sleep next to Mia, but Mia insisted that she would be fine alone. Once they had tucked her in, Neville and Shehnaz retired to their room and sat up in bed for a long time. Not that many words were exchanged, but they were just too wired to fall asleep easily.

'Things are escalating faster than I had anticipated. I should meet that girl soon,' Neville muttered, more to himself than to Shehnaz.

It was late by the time they finally fell asleep, and Shehnaz was still deep in slumber when Neville's phone rang in the morning. She woke up with a start as Neville stirred next to her. He turned to his side and took the call. It was only half past seven.

He mumbled a good morning and immediately, his expression changed. When he said, 'I will be there soon,' Shehnaz knew something was wrong. Neville reached out to hold her hand before speaking.

'It's Naresh. He was found dead in his bed.'

'Oh my god.'

'Kerkar called. He is there. I need to leave.'

'Kerkar? Why is he ...' Shehnaz's voice trailed off as realization dawned.

'They aren't sure yet, but it may not have been a natural death.'

Neville got out of the bed and headed to the bathroom. Shehnaz remained seated in the exact same place, looking stricken, as he emerged a few minutes later, fully dressed. Neville walked up to her and held her close for a moment.

'You should go,' Shehnaz whispered.

The roads were deserted, and Neville drove fast. On reaching, he was greeted by a line of police cars and an ambulance parked outside the house. The DGP's car was also there. Two uniformed policemen stopped Neville at the entrance, but Laxman intervened to usher him inside. Neville headed towards the familiar entrance before he heard Kerkar's voice calling out to him. 'This way, Neville.'

Neville followed the voice to a side door that opened directly into the master bedroom, where he beheld Naresh Sardesai lying on his bed, hands folded across his chest, a picture of calm repose. DGP Chandok, Jennifer, a medical examiner and another police constable stood around the bed with solemn expressions. The room filled him with a chill that even the sharp Konkan sun could do nothing to dispel.

Chandok acknowledged Neville with a nod, and Kerkar cleared his throat. 'Jennifer, the neighbour who doubled up as housekeeper, came in at her usual time, seven o'clock, to bring Mr Sardesai his morning tea but the main door was shut. Normally, he'd have it open for her to enter. Thinking he had overslept, she circled around to knock on the window but found a glass pane missing on the door. That is when she ran to Pramod,' Kerkar pointed to the other constable, 'and alerted him. Together, they returned to find the bedroom door unlocked. They tried to wake Mr Sardesai, but his body was cold. Jennifer called the doctor immediately and Pramod notified the station. That's when I informed DGP sir and we arrived here, just a few minutes ago.'

Neville turned to examine the door. It was one of those double paned ones where the bottom halves were wooden, and the top halves had four square glass panes each. The top corner glass square in one of the doors was missing, with only a thin border remaining. It had been cut out neatly. Next to the glass was the vertical door latch, which had presumably been opened to gain entry into the room.

Neville turned to Jennifer. 'This door was always kept locked at night?'

'Yes, sir,' Pramod interjected. 'Once Jennifer is done at night, she calls me on her way home and I come and check that the doors are locked from inside. Standard procedure since Laxman and I started guarding the house.

Last night was no exception; both doors were locked from inside. The curtains were drawn in this room.'

'And do you stay by the gate or patrol around the house at night?' Neville inquired.

Pramod glanced uncomfortably towards Kerkar. 'I do rounds, sir. Last night too, I walked around the house late at night and everything was as it always is. From the window, I could see sir sleeping inside.'

'What time would that have been, Pramod?'

'Sir, it's hard to say exactly, but maybe close to eleven.'

That guilty look, again.

'Before or after eleven, you would say?'

'Maybe just before.'

'So, shortly after dinner you took a stroll around the house, and everything seemed fine. Correct?' There was no apparent hint of reproach in Neville's voice, however damning his message may have been.

Pramod nodded slightly, averting his gaze.

'There was obviously no missing glass.'

'I didn't see it sir.'

'No. Wouldn't have been easy to spot against those grey curtains anyway. Unless you were looking for it.'

Neville faced Jennifer. 'What time did you leave the house last night?'

'Just before nine. I remember being back home in time for the 9:00 p.m. serial Roy and I watch every evening.'

'Right. And Naresh closed the doors behind you? He wasn't too well when we came by yesterday.'

'Yes, but he felt better after sleeping in the afternoon. He had his dinner at the table and then latched the main door when I left. I offered to come a bit later than usual in the morning but he said no.'

'And you called Pramod?'

'Yes. He came and checked the doors.'

'And this morning, when you came around to the bedroom side, was the door ajar?'

Jennifer paused before answering. 'The glass was missing, I spotted it right away. The door was not wide open but sometimes you can tell if it isn't fully latched. It felt ... loose.'

Neville nodded. He knew what Jennifer meant.

'Were the curtains drawn?'

'Yes.'

'Pramod, can you corroborate that the curtains were drawn?'

'Yes sir. We couldn't see inside. In fact, we knocked on the window to wake sir up, but he didn't respond. That's when we went in.'

'And you found him exactly like this? Did you change his position at all to make him more comfortable? Please think carefully.'

Jennifer and Pramod nodded in unison.

'Did Naresh take anything to sleep at night?'

'Yes. I gave him his usual sleeping pill and a cup of

milk every night before leaving.' Jennifer pointed to a cup on the bedside table. It was empty.

'Can I see the strip?' the medical examiner, who had been introduced as Doctor More, asked.

Jennifer opened a drawer on the bedside table and extracted a fold. The doctor took a look and passed it to Neville.

He looked up and said, 'Jennifer, would you and Pramod mind waiting outside for a bit?'

Once they left, Neville turned to the doctor. 'Doctor, I know you cannot be precise but what are your first thoughts about time of death?'

The examiner had obviously been expecting this. 'I would say he has been dead for at least six hours, judging by the rigor. And no more than nine. I will be able to narrow it down further on examination.'

'So, if the body was discovered at seven, that puts it between ten and one. But, if Pramod says he did a round at eleven, maybe eleven and one then.'

'Yes, that sounds about right, for now.'

'And any early indications of the cause?'

The doctor cast a nervous glance at the DGP.

'I know how tricky these assessments can be, doctor. Anything before the post-mortem is at best an educated guess. Even so, if there are any tell-tale signs ...' Neville prompted.

'There are a few things,' the doctor indicated to them to move closer to the body. He shone a tiny torch onto Naresh's face. They saw it immediately, very faint signs of bruising around the nostrils and mouth, almost imperceptible without close inspection. Using a gloved finger, the doctor pulled down Naresh's lower lip, revealing tiny red marks, where his teeth may have pressed into the inner flesh. The doctor withdrew.

'There are red marks around the eye, and they appear bloodshot. An examination of the inner organs will be needed to substantiate this, but my guess is death by asphyxiation. If you pushed me further, I would say it looks like he was suffocated with a pillow. The slight facial bruises point to that. We will look for traces of fibre in his respiratory tract.'

'You are right, doctor. I have seen such a case before, but the bruises there were more prominent.'

'Yes, but for older people, you would expect the bruising to be faint. The eye marks and the lip laceration are significant indicators. Now, asphyxia in the elderly can also cause cardiac arrest. So, the immediate cause of death could well have been that. But the post-mortem will provide more clarity.'

'Can it be done today, doctor?' asked DGP Chandok, in a tone that was more directive than query.

'Yes. As soon as the body has been moved. I should be able to confirm by evening.'

'Thanks.'

'Vishnu, did you see anything else that was unusual, on arriving at the scene?'

Kerkar led them outside, pointing to a narrow alley paved with square cement tiles. The path led all the way to the front, alongside the wall demarcating the boundary between the plots belonging to Naresh and the Pintos. On the other side of the wall were fields bordering Jennifer's house. What had Kerkar interested were footprints on the tiles, appearing to be from grooved rubber soles, the kind seen in hiking shoes or gum boots. The prints, size nine or ten, led to the wall but didn't continue all the way to the front entrance.

'The same marks are there in the mud on the other side of the wall, leading up to the road.'

'So, the intruder likely entered from the main road, along the edge of the field, and scaled the wall into the compound?'

'It's likely. The front gate has a guard.'

'Yes, and this approach, late at night, would have been a safe one, unless the guard was on his rounds. There wouldn't have been any sound of breaking glass either. This was a neat glass cutter and rubber suction cup removal. Standard intruder procedure.'

'Not a petty thief then, sir.'

'Hmm, hard to say, Vishnu. You can order both items online these days; even a child can use them.'

Upon returning to the room, DGP Chandok, who had been listening to the exchanges between Neville and Kerkar, spoke up with a vexed look on his face.

'The press will have a field day with this. Just what we needed. Heaven knows why he had to go and give that damn speech.'

Neville stared fixedly at Naresh's body, with more in his gaze than the mere scrutiny of a detective.

'What are you thinking, Neville?'

'It seems a bit odd. The attack on Mia last night and then this. Things are moving too fast.'

'You think there could be a connection?'

'It's possible, but …'

'Kerkar, try and keep that business out of the media, will you? Anyway, we have this on our hands,' Chandok said, not trying to hide his irritation. He waved distractedly at the two of them and walked away in the direction of his car.

The examiner was hovering outside the door with two medics, ready to move the body. As they shifted the body, Neville and Kerkar walked towards the gate, where Pramod and Laxman stood sullenly.

'Show me your phone, Laxman,' Neville requested.

Laxman handed it over, looking alarmed.

'Pramod, can you call his number once?'

Looking baffled, he complied. The phone rang loudly, playing a devotional song.

'Good. Now walk to the bedroom door, Laxman. Go on.'

Once Laxman reached the door, Neville asked Pramod to call the number again. They heard the ringtone, but it was a distant, muffled sound.

'Pramod, I am going to ask something which you shouldn't feel is an indictment of any sort. But it is very important to know the facts. Last night, around midnight, were you listening to the Walkman?'

Pramod didn't have to reply, his face gave away the answer. He hung his head. 'Sir, I put the chair in the middle of the gate, right here. If anyone entered, I would surely notice.'

Kerkar sighed. He could see what had transpired. Pramod would have had his dinner, taken a round and then settled down with the Walkman. There's no way he would have picked up the sound of careful footsteps.

Roy had arrived on the scene and Neville approached him.

'What time did you go to sleep last night, Roy?'

'I don't know exactly, around ten, half past ten maybe.'

'And you didn't hear any unusual noises at night?'

'Noises? No, nothing. Except Jenny's snoring. Both of us sleep like logs after a bit of feni.'

Jennifer stood sniffling by his side.

'Maybe I should've slept here on the sofa last night. It had crossed my mind once,' she mumbled.

'Jenny, this isn't your fault. There is a cop stationed here for that purpose,' Roy said sharply.

At this, Pramod winced and looked away.

'Sorry man, I didn't mean it like that,' said Roy, raising a hand to him in apology.

With little to gain from the scene, Neville started towards his car, Kerkar beside him. They paused where the boundary wall of Naresh's house ended and turned towards the field. A few metres ahead, Neville squatted down to spot a line of the same footprints they saw on the tiles outside the bedroom door running alongside the wall, all the way up to the point where the concrete road met the field.

'There may have been a bike or a cycle waiting here,' Kerkar suggested.

Neville nodded thoughtfully. 'Vishnu, did you happen to meet anyone from the HSS around the time of those death threats that surfaced last year?'

'Not directly sir, but SP Gomes might have. They have a spokesperson called Mahesh Talpade who fields queries from the police or media,' Kerkar replied. 'Why? Did you want to talk to them?'

'Let's wait for the post-mortem, but tomorrow morning it may be a good idea to pay this man a visit.'

'You think they would attempt something like this right after a provocative speech directed at them? Not even wait a few days?'

'Quite right. That's one way of looking at it. But if they wanted to send a signal, that such a brazen and defiant stance would not be tolerated, there wasn't any better way to achieve that. As long as it can't be pinned on them. From what I hear, they aren't exactly shy of violence.'

'Shy? They are like any terrorist outfit. If they sported beards in place of their robes, that's what they would be called.'

Neville shook Kerkar's hand. 'I'll swing by the station with Mia later. Perhaps we'll have more answers after the post-mortem. See you.'

Kerkar trudged back to the house. A new vehicle had just arrived and a young woman with a vaguely familiar face stepped out. The media had already got a whiff of the incident.

—

Neville arrived home to find the two women sitting quietly on the veranda: Mia, with her unsightly bruises and bandaged leg, looking ruffled while Shehnaz appeared stricken. He pulled up a chair next to them.

'How are you feeling, Mia?'

'I'm OK, just a bit drowsy. There's not much feeling in the leg unless I put it down.'

'Try not to do that. Let me grab something to eat and then we can hop across to the clinic for the cast.' Neville turned towards Shehnaz, 'Naresh died around midnight. The autopsy will confirm it, but it looks like he was suffocated with a pillow. There was a break-in.'

Shehnaz didn't say anything, just nodded faintly, as if she had expected to hear this.

Mia, visibly shaken, asked, 'What a terrible thing to happen. Do you think it was … the speech, Neville?'

'Well, they would appear to be the obvious suspects. Too obvious perhaps, but often the obvious is true.'

'The poor man ... how frail he looked yesterday. Would probably have gone soon, anyway,' Shehnaz murmured, as a tear trickled down her cheek.

They sat in silence for a while till Agnes arrived to ask about breakfast. Helping Mia over to the table, they settled in. She broke the silence again. 'Neville, do you think the attack on me and Naresh's death could somehow be connected?'

'I've been thinking about it too, Mia. It's not inconceivable. If Josh had been investigating the HSS, and if Naresh knew something he had uncovered ...' Neville trailed off.

'And you think Mia's arrival on the scene raised fears that a renewed thrust into Joshua's case would unearth buried secrets?' Shehnaz filled in.

'Yes, but what are these secrets that Naresh chose not to divulge for a year after Josh's death, which now warrant a near fatal warning to Mia and a murder? Or is it just a coincidence?'

'How did Jennifer take the news?'

'She is shocked, naturally.'

'Death haunts those houses,' Shehnaz said, with a mild shiver, almost sounding like a clairvoyant.

Agnes came in with breakfast, though with none of her usual morning cheer. Shehnaz had informed her about Naresh's passing, if not the manner of death.

Laying the bowls down on the table, she said softly, 'You know madam, I knew the story that's in the paper today, about the Christian lady who nursed him as a newborn child. She was a close friend of my grandmother. When I was a little girl, she came to our home and my granny told me about it, in front of her. She was very old, but I remember her laughing and asking me if I wouldn't do the same if a little boy was in need. I was so young then, but I said of course I would. I remembered her today after a long time.'

Shehnaz sat with her head bowed. Agnes went behind her chair and began to knead her shoulders. 'He was a brave man. I remember how he railed against these fanatical Hindu groups when the grave desecrations began in Goa. No one, even from our own community, protested more angrily.'

Shehnaz began crying, and even Mia's eyes turned glassy. 'He won't be forgotten easily in these parts,' Agnes said, and walked away. The food remained largely untouched on the table. They had only met the writer fleetingly, but Neville knew how deeply affected Shehnaz was by his death.

He poured himself some coffee and called the clinic. The doctor who had attended to Mia was out on a call, but they asked him to bring her over around midday.

'You know Shehnaz, I was thinking that once the ankle is fixed up, why don't I just shift to a proper hotel? I will be totally safe there and can just order room service.'

'Why, you aren't feeling comfortable here?'

'Of course, I am comfortable. But the thought of you two being saddled indefinitely with an injured person at home is making me feel very awkward. Really,' Mia replied earnestly.

Neville turned towards her with a serious expression. 'Mia, I must insist. After last night's incident, I wouldn't want you to be on your own in this city. Till …'

His voice trailed off, and Shehnaz noted the hesitation. She knew what Neville was thinking – that the odds of finding Joshua's killer had just become worse after the incident with Naresh. To pin it on a known suspect, after so much time had passed, was difficult enough but to go after an organization with hundreds of members would be near impossible.

'Neville, will the same police team be investigating Naresh's case?' she asked.

'I doubt it. Kerkar says there is an SP Gomes who was in charge of looking into the activities of the HSS. Since that is the obvious starting place for this investigation, he may lead the probe. However, I have asked Kerkar if we can meet the HSS rep tomorrow. I don't think it will be a problem, seeing how the cases may be related.'

'But Neville, are you sure about this?'

'Yes, why … oh, you mean would it be putting ourselves in danger? No, I will only be tagging along with a Superintendent of Police,' Neville tried brushing it off, though Shehnaz remained unconvinced.

'You are no longer on the force, Neville. There's no immunity from the uniform any longer; I hope you realize that.'

'God, what have I dragged you all into?' Mia exclaimed, in a desperate voice.

It was an uneasy moment. In a way, Mia was right and even Shehnaz could not come up with anything promptly to counter that notion of hers. She merely said, 'Come, let's eat something. Starving won't help any of us.'

The morning weighed heavily on everyone. Mia was handicapped by her injury but even Neville and Shehnaz felt leaden-footed. After breakfast, Shehnaz walked into their bedroom to find Neville at the window, staring outside. When she silently joined him, he murmured, 'Cyrus. I can't stop thinking about him today.'

Shehnaz wrapped her arms around Neville's back.

'Baby,' she whispered.

It was a name Neville hardly ever uttered, that of his departed brother. A young man in the prime of his life – successful, outgoing, with a child-like disposition, always brimming with energy. Then, after a sudden heart attack at the age of forty-five, he was gone within minutes, just like that. He was three years younger, and Neville adored him. Shehnaz knew it was a wound he carried inside him and would forever. It had even crossed her mind the moment Mia arrived – that all this time spent with a girl who had lost her brother might bring that painful memory to surface. Instead, it was the sight of a lifeless old man lying in his own bed that had brought it all rushing back. Cyrus, draped in a white sheet, lying on that hospital bed; Neville's father standing by the bed, his face crumpled. A man who had always had the strength to weather every adversity, but this. He never recovered from the blow and died a year later.

Every time Shehnaz went to Neville's Kalbadevi house after that, she was assailed by an image of the three men – senior Wadia with his two sons – eagerly waiting at the table like hungry children, to be served by her. Cyrus had never married and remained in the house where he was born. A year of bliss, a lifetime of bickering, he would often quip in explanation. Thus, when Neville's mother passed away, it had fallen to Shehnaz to ensure that everything functioned smoothly in that household of men. But in the matter of a year, everyone was gone, and the house lay empty, a shell of memories. They eventually decided to rent it out.

Everyone perceived Neville as strong, much like his father, and in a way he was. Yet, on nights he clung to her or stood by the window with a hollow look in his eyes, whispering his brother's name, Shehnaz knew he was not. No one was. It was only an illusion.

At noon, Neville drove Mia to the clinic where they encased her ankle in a formidable cast. A walking stick with a round base was provided, along with advice to bear weight on her good leg in the days ahead. The elbow wound was dressed again. The doctor asked Neville privately if Mia was showing any visible signs of anxiety or panic, to which he replied in the negative. Once they were done, Neville inquired if Mia felt up to the drive to the police station, and she agreed immediately. They headed towards Panjim instead of Anjuna, Neville opting to avoid Inspector Rane, who had previously suppressed Joshua's investigation. He needed to meet Superintendent Kerkar anyway.

Neville had called ahead and found Kerkar waiting at the entrance.

'How are you coping, Ms Davies?'

'I'm OK, Superintendent Kerkar. Thank you,' Mia replied, hobbling up the three steps into the building. They entered Kerkar's room, where Mia's statement was typed out and signed.

Once that was out of the way, Neville asked, 'Has the PM report come in?'

'Not yet, but it should at any moment. They are doing it on priority. Also, word has spread very fast. Apparently, two men belonging to some saffron group – not HSS – were roughed up in the South,' Kerkar updated.

'Has anything new turned up in our investigation?' Mia asked hesitantly.

'Well, Bosco is going to give us all a full report tomorrow afternoon. He has been busy, and I expect he will have valuable information. I spoke to the Crime

Branch officer who has taken over the Jarvinen case and he sent across a copy of the new autopsy. Traces of drugs in his blood, MDMA. I will share it with you, Neville. But please keep yourself free tomorrow for Bosco's report, okay?'

'Weren't we planning to meet the HSS spokesperson tomorrow morning?' Neville asked.

'Yes, that's in Ponda. SP Gomes has set it up for us. In fact, I told him you would be coming by today and he was very keen to meet you. His office is right across the corridor.'

'Of course. I have many questions for him, too. Mia, would you mind waiting here for a few minutes?'

'Not at all. Please take your time.'

They stepped out into the corridor and Kerkar knocked on a door with a nameplate that read M. GOMES, SUPERINTENDENT OF POLICE. Gomes stood up as soon as they entered. 'Please come in. It's a pleasure to meet you, sir. Heard a lot about you from my father.'

Neville looked at him in surprise.

'He was an IPS officer too and retired as Additional Commissioner of the Pune Police. You may not remember but the two of you met,' Gomes explained.

Neville tried to recall an ACP Gomes from Pune but couldn't readily summon up a face. 'I am so sorry, but I cannot seem to remember. But if he said so, we must have met.'

'Yes. He always said you are the kind of officer I should try to become, when I joined the IPS. So, when

Kerkar said you were coming ... I hope you don't mind.'

'Not at all. On the contrary, I have some questions for you about the HSS, if you have some time.'

'Of course, sir. I've informed Talpade to expect you at ten tomorrow morning. I could have asked him to come here as well, after what happened today, but Kerkar mentioned you may want to see their headquarters.'

'Indeed. This Talpade, is he just a PR guy or more than that?' Neville queried.

'Definitely more. Spokesperson is just a way of saying he is authorized to speak on their behalf, in the absence of their founder Doctorji who is no longer actively involved in the day-to-day running of the organization. In fact, my impression is that Talpade is the de facto boss now.'

'I see. Kerkar said you met him a few times last year. What did you gather about them?'

'Honestly sir, it wasn't our case. The Maharashtra police had evidence linking the HSS to at least two high profile murder cases of prominent regional writers. One of the detained members had Naresh Sardesai's name in his diary alongside the two victims, making them suspect that he was next on their target list. The Maharashtra police suggested that we place his house under protection and restrict his movements. Naturally, we were happy to oblige. Yet ...'

Kerkar spoke up, 'Actually, the initial security level was higher but then a year passed and there was no escalation. Gomes met the HSS guys who categorically denied any involvement and generally, the perceived threat of violence against these writers seemed to have ebbed. It clearly had not.'

'So, you will investigate the HSS as key suspects again, I presume,' Neville pressed Gomes.

'Just waiting for the autopsy report to act, sir. We have leads on individuals who were potentially involved.'

'You are convinced they're capable of something like this?'

'Absolutely, sir. Consider the evidence – a recent anti-terror raid uncovered truckloads of explosives and detonation devices in their warehouse a few months ago. And the raid in Panvel threw up boxes and boxes of drugs. Heaven knows what they are up to, but this is no peaceful organization, religious or political,' Gomes asserted.

'I'm surprised they haven't been banned.'

Gomes and Kerkar exchanged a glance. 'What can one say, sir? They have their protectors. In our own state, we have Jayant Satwalekar, the minister, who is rumoured to be a closet member of the Sangh and a big admirer of Doctorji. His wife is a sadhak at the ashram. But even the home ministry has dragged its feet, saying they don't have enough evidence to ban them outright. Our problem is that of all places, they have chosen to build their nest here.'

Neville sighed, shaking his head. 'Well, keep us informed. We can't be sure but there is a possibility that it may be linked to an old case that Vishnu is looking into.'

'I'm aware. Don't worry, sir, whatever turns up, I will keep Kerkar informed.'

As they were about to leave, a young uniformed officer knocked on the door. 'Sir, Doctor More is trying to reach you. He says it's important.'

'Oh, must be the autopsy.' Gomes looked at his phone, 'Yes, there is a missed call.'

Gomes called back and put the handset on speaker, on the table between them. The doctor's narration was clear and lucid. 'SP Gomes, it is what I had suspected from the initial physical signs. The petechial haemorrhages in the lungs are consistent with the red splotches in the eye. That, along with the high level of carbon dioxide in the blood, points to asphyxiation. We even found trace evidence of fibres around the mouth and nostrils, identical to the pillow that he was resting on. It's fairly clear-cut to me. The victim was suffocated with a pillow in his bed. We found Alprazolam in his bloodstream but not an overdose; nothing to suggest he was sedated. There was no foreign tissue under his fingernails, indicating an absence of any major struggle or resistance. Just some mild bruising around the wrists which may indicate that his hands were pinned down, but tough to say with certainty. The time of death would have been between twelve and one at night. You can extend that by half an hour on either side to be sure. I will mail you the formal report soon but thought I would give you the gist, in the interest of saving time.'

Gomes thanked the doctor and ended the call. If there had been any doubt, now there was none. Naresh Sardesai didn't die peacefully in his sleep.

On the way back, Mia asked Neville, 'You know, I was thinking, shouldn't we meet that girl Faye at the shack once more?'

The question threw Neville for a bit. He had been so overwrought since Naresh's sudden death that other matters had receded to the background. But for Mia, her single-minded focus remained uncovering the truth about Joshua. Anything else, however grievous, was a distraction. Neville understood her urgency and stamped out the mild irritation with which he had received Mia's suggestion.

'Yes, Mia, maybe tomorrow. I have it in mind. Let's speak to Bosco before that and get the facts straight, about Joshua's last few days, particularly. It's still hazy to me.'

16

NEVILLE WOKE EARLY THE NEXT MORNING. THE listlessness of the previous day was gone and he felt clear-headed. This wasn't new for Neville – sometimes a jolt was necessary to dispel the inertia. The events of the previous day, sad as they were, had the effect of reawakening his instincts, blood coursing inside him again, almost as if by muscle memory. Once a cop, he thought to himself.

Their meeting with Mahesh Talpade in Ponda was at ten, an encounter he wasn't particularly looking forward to. He would rather be in the meeting room at the police station in Panjim, being brought up to speed by Bosco. Neville had a feeling that would settle the thoughts swirling in his head, give them shape. It was impossible to move ahead without that clarity. The truth was, this investigation had been very uncomfortable for him, so far. This business of reaching back into the past and retrieving pieces of the puzzle was a bit like walking blindfolded. No one seemed to have known the victim well during his time in Goa, and those who might have, were long gone from the scene. The danger of proceeding like this was that they could dart off in the direction of any lead which seemed promising, without weighing it against other possibilities. He needed a better grip. It would still be difficult, but at least he would have a fair shot at the case. The case – yes, that was how Neville had to start seeing it. Mia staying with them, while pleasant, had somehow made it feel different. It interfered with Neville's ability to compartmentalize, to think clearly. The lines were blurred, and it wasn't helping.

Quietly slipping into his tracks, Neville tiptoed out of the room, careful not to wake Shehnaz. He fetched a rolled yoga mat and stepped out onto the veranda. As he eased into the first dog pose of the day, a stray caustic remark from Rhea at the party about the advent of Croatian yoginis in Goa crossed his mind, bringing a faint smile to his lips.

'Good morning, smiling yogi,' Shehnaz called from the doorway, radiant in her orange kaftan and sleep-nourished skin.

'Oh, morning! Didn't think you were up. Why, you are a sight for sore eyes this morning.'

'And you seem chirpier since I saw you last,' Shehnaz replied, walking up to Neville and burying her face in his chest, circling her arms around his waist. Neville drew her closer and there they stood, enveloped in the humid warmth of the day and their abiding affection, undimmed by all these years. If Neville had needed a tonic to shed the pent-up heaviness that had accumulated, this was it. Shehnaz's touch had always held this healing quality for him. During the darkest and most trying times, when he battled demons in his head, it was her warmth, her murmurs in his ear, her ever-reassuring eyes that saw him through. Neville silently counted his blessings before they parted from their tender embrace.

The morning flowed swiftly thereafter. Neville showered, had breakfast and just as he had settled down with a cup of tea with Shehnaz, Kerkar's car arrived outside their gate. Shehnaz pulled a face as Neville rose to leave.

'I'd better get going. It's a long drive down to Ponda. Bye, dear. Guess I will see you only in the evening now. I'll call in between.' He gave Shehnaz's shoulder a squeeze and headed out.

'Morning, Neville. I came a few minutes early on purpose. There may be demonstrations, about Naresh, in parts of the city today. We may be held up.'

'This early?'

'Maybe not, but they could time it such that it doesn't interfere with the afternoon siesta. It's Goa.'

Neville laughed.

'There's a lead. SP Gomes' team received a call last evening from someone named Prakash Ajgaonkar from the Ponda Yuva Sangh. Apparently, Joshua had visited

Ponda in June last year, just days before his death. He met Prakash and his friends and had lots of questions about the HSS and Mahesh Talpade. They believe he would have met Mahesh. Prakash read about Joshua's new autopsy in the paper and decided to reach out,' Kerkar explained.

'Oh. And did you speak to this Prakash yourself?'

'No. But I sent him a message this morning. He said he would be happy to see us there. At a tea shop right opposite the ashram entrance.'

They made good time and within half an hour had crossed the bridge and turned onto the highway towards South Goa. Neville remembered his early trips to Goa with Shehnaz, shortly after they had got married. How they would often opt for the South in winter, to avoid the mad rush of the Northern beaches. The Southern coastal belt didn't have the frenetic energy of an Anjuna or Baga, or as many dining options then, but it had a quiet charm which they found settling. A few times they had even ventured further south to Karwar, where the cliffs jutted out on to the sea.

'Is the South still quieter than the North, Vishnu?'

'Not as much as it used to be. With all the new five-star hotels, it has lost some of its quaintness. You remember the famous Bourne movie which was shot in Palolem? That really put it on the tourist map. It's still different, but not in the way you may remember it. When were you last there, by the way?'

'Oh, must be twenty years ago.'

Kerkar chuckled. 'In twenty years, what doesn't change, Neville?'

Kerkar's apprehension about hold-ups turned out to be unfounded and soon they could see road signs pointing towards Ponda. It was a relief to drive past long stretches of areca nut plantations which hadn't yet come under the builder's axe. The driver navigated confidently, sparing them the need to ask for directions as they approached the HSS headquarters. Neville spotted the tea shop as soon as he stepped out of the car. Two young men stood outside, looking expectantly in their direction.

'Prakash?' Kerkar called out.

One of the men smiled and walked up to them. They shook hands.

'Shall we sit inside, sir?' Prakash suggested.

'I don't mind. My morning tea was interrupted by your early arrival, Vishnu,' Neville said with a smile.

They settled on two weathered benches, facing each other, as the shopkeeper poured tea expertly from a height, from his much-dented saucepan into small steel glasses.

'So, you met Joshua here last year. Can you be precise about the date?' Neville began.

'No, but it was the latter half of June. The rains had just begun, I remember that.'

'Was it a chance encounter? As in, did he just run into you guys at the shop and start talking?'

'No sir, he knew about the Yuva Sangh. He came to the shop and was asking around, so the shopkeeper sent a boy to fetch one of us. He seemed to know quite a bit about us and of course, them,' he said, pointing to the building opposite.

'I see. What did he say about himself? Why did he want to know so much about the HSS?'

'I think he mentioned he was writing about them or making a film – something like that.'

'Writing,' Prakash's companion spoke up.

'What specifically did he want to know?'

'He seemed to know enough already. He asked us if we knew anyone inside the campus, someone we could put him on to. Also, what locals like us thought went on inside – who we saw going in, coming out; stuff like that. He had heard that they weren't exactly popular in the area and wanted to know why.'

'What made you call the police station yesterday?' Kerkar asked.

The two boys looked at each other. 'We saw his picture in the paper. The report said there was no doubt that he had been murdered. And then we heard about Naresh Sardesai. So, we thought ...'

'Did Joshua mention Sardesai at all when you met?'

'Yes, he did. Once we got talking, he said he was convinced the HSS was behind the murder of the other authors. He seemed to know Sardesai personally and feared that the threat to his life was very real.'

'And yesterday, when you heard of Sardesai's death, you thought that Joshua was right, about his intuition?' Neville inferred.

'We had warned him even then. These guys are very dangerous. Of course, you are from the police and know much more about it. But we have also seen how easily they can use force when required. The robes are only a fake mask.'

'Are you sure he met Mahesh Talpade?' Neville asked.

'I think so. He spoke to the security at the gate. Generally, visitors are not allowed inside but then he was ...' Prakash didn't spell it out, but Neville knew what he had been about to say. Being white-skinned made Joshua a different kind of visitor.

'But you didn't stay long enough to see him entering the campus?'

'No.'

'And you never saw him again?'

'No. We knew he died, of course. His death was reported in the papers last year.'

They finished their tea and got up. The boys insisted on paying for it.

Neville thanked them and as they walked out, couldn't resist a final question. 'How did Joshua seem, when he sat here with you?'

'Excited,' Prakash's reply was instant.

Neville patted him on the shoulder, and they proceeded towards the building gate. The security guard was expecting them and directed them to enter through a smaller side entrance.

The campus turned out to be deceptively large – one couldn't get a sense of its spread from outside the boundary walls. From the front courtyard, the central building itself resembled a large municipal school, but a passageway snaked along the boundary wall, and they caught a glimpse of more blocks spread throughout the enclave. Neville wondered who funded all this. Climbing up the stairs into the main building, they observed men and women in saffron attire walking around purposefully. The guard stopped outside a room and knocked. A middle-aged man stepped out, adorned in the same saffron robe, with a sandalwood mark on his forehead. Folding his hands in a greeting, he said, 'Namaskar. Welcome to our ashram. Please, come in.'

Inside, it could have been a corporate office. A laptop was open on Talpade's glass-topped desk. The decor was modern – shelves with books, a television set, the only nod to religious activity being a large, framed photograph of a monk-like figure. Neville guessed it was that of the founder.

'I know what brings you here,' Mahesh Talpade began with a faint smile on his face, as if he was reluctantly turning down a wedding invitation. 'It is unfortunate that every time there is violence against an intellectual figure in this state, we become the obvious suspects. So, let me repeat what I told your colleague, officer Gomes – the HSS categorically denies any involvement in the tragic death of Mr Naresh Sardesai. We may have disagreed with his views, but that is no cause for murder.'

'Your men were at the felicitation ceremony in Panjim the day before.'

'Yes, I asked them to go. We like to hear the views of our adversaries and critics. It helps in clarifying our own convictions.'

'We hear Mr Sardesai's name was in the diary of the man arrested in the case of the other murdered writers.'

A sneer appeared on Talpade's face.

'Whoever that individual may be, he has no affiliation with our organization. This is one thing we have to admit, sir. There are many in this country who wish to follow our path but, in their zeal, they choose a method that is more radical than what we advocate. Neither can we stop them, nor should we be held responsible for their actions.' The words slipped effortlessly off Talpade's lips, with practiced ease. As if he had uttered them before.

'You will be meeting SP Gomes later to discuss all this, but I have a different question for you, Mr Talpade. Do you remember meeting a man named Joshua Davies last year?' Neville asked directly.

Talpade was a cool customer yet couldn't hide the slight flicker of alarm that flashed in his eyes as he heard the name. He was too smart to deny it though.

'Yes, I read about him in the papers. Sad, how these young men come here from far and wide only to meet their deaths. He came to see me last year. Usually, I don't speak to visitors, unless they are from the media or have some official reason,' he waved in their direction, 'but there is a lot of interest in the Western world about the surge of Hindu nationalism in India. I thought he may have come for some such thing.'

'And, he hadn't?'

'No, he had. But strangely, he seemed to believe that we were seen as a threat by people in the state. I don't know who put that idea in his head,' Talpade scoffed.

'How long was he here?' Neville asked.

'Oh, a couple of hours, no more.'

'Did he meet other members of the ashram?'

'No, we don't allow that. He sat in this room and once I had answered his questions, he left.'

'Did you ask him to leave?'

Talpade's indulgent smile returned. 'A lot of people think we are a rude and hostile bunch, judging perhaps by the fact that entry is forbidden to outsiders. But we aren't really. The privacy is necessary to preserve the sanctity of our work. And our meditations.'

'Can you tell us the date of his visit?'

'I keep a diary on my computer. If you will give me a minute,' Talpade said, turning to his laptop. After a moment, he looked up. 'Tuesday, June 19th. Mr Joshua Davies from the UK.'

'Did he get in touch again?'

'No.'

'Did he appear to be in the possession of facts about your organization that are not known to the public?' Neville pressed.

'The HSS is an open book, Inspector. We have nothing to hide. What knowledge could you be talking about?' Talpade countered smoothly.

Neville held his silence.

'What goes on inside this campus?' Kerkar asked.

'Why, your men have been here before. I find the speculation in the media about us quite amusing, to be honest. A den of drugs and sex, members walking around in a hypnotized trance – it's all Hollywood inspired fiction. In reality we are a sect of people engaged in talks, discussions and prayers, along the path outlined by Doctorji,' Talpade responded, his eyes half-closed in reverence as he invoked the venerable founder's name.

'Sometime last year did you have any visitors by the name of Eva Campbell or Leo Jarvinen?' Neville inquired.

A frown creased Talpade's brow. 'Jarvinen? Wasn't he the tourist who died? Why would he have come here? I am quite sure he didn't, certainly not to meet me.'

'And Ms Campbell?'

'That name is not known to me. Another foreigner? There are very few tourists who enter our gates and I have a good memory for names.'

There was really not much more to ask. They could sit around and keep asking these questions and Mahesh Talpade would keep deflecting them, all day. Nothing would come of it. The truth was they had nothing on the HSS linking them to the murder of either Joshua Davies or Naresh Sardesai, except for the tourist's visit here and a motive in the writer's case. Neville nodded at Kerkar and stood up.

'Well then, Mr Talpade, we won't keep you any longer. I imagine SP Gomes will have more questions for you. Thank you for your time.'

'Anytime, sir. We are always happy to cooperate.'

They exited the room. Kerkar was taken aback at the pace at which Neville strode out of the campus, not even pausing to look around as he had imagined he would, out of sheer interest. Instead, he walked directly to the gate and towards their car, prompting Kerkar to almost jog to keep up.

The car retraced the road back to the highway as the two of them sat silently in the car. Neville stared out of the window with a stony face, visibly not interested in any communication. Only when they had driven for some fifteen minutes or so, did he say, 'If these are indeed the perpetrators, Vishnu, I won't get anywhere close to cracking the case. Gomes may have a better chance, but I have my doubts. You see, in Joshua's case, we have nothing. An autopsy showing he was murdered but other than that, not a shred of physical evidence linking anyone to the assault. A vague notion of him doing an investigative report which had unearthed something so damaging that he had to be silenced. Why? HSS members are behind bars on allegations of murders, hiding arms, carrying explosives ... what could Joshua have told us that we don't already know? This is a wild goose chase, Kerkar.'

Neville sounded angry, exasperated. Kerkar didn't know how to react. Meanwhile, the car had stopped moving. There was a pile-up on the road ahead. The driver cut the engine and stepped out. He walked forward, spoke to the drivers of the cars ahead and returned.

'Some rally is going on, sir,' he reported.

Eventually, they started moving in a crawl and soon came upon the reason for the hold-up. Near a roundabout, a large crowd of people had assembled. Hundreds of them, maybe even a thousand, walking silently, carrying pictures of Naresh Sardesai – a slightly younger version of him, mostly, before age had reduced him to the skeletal figure Neville had encountered. It was a silent march and despite the numbers there was no noise at all, not even honking from passing vehicles. A lane had been cleared for cars and they drove past the crowd. Neville could imagine Shehnaz walking there with them.

'Sorry for snapping that way, Vishnu. That bloody Talpade got on my nerves,' Neville said, his tone now softer.

'I understand. Let's see what Bosco has for us.'

At the mention of that, Neville seemed to relax, and they covered the rest of the journey talking about the serene beaches of South Goa.

17

THEY REACHED THE STATION AROUND NOON TO FIND Bosco eagerly awaiting them in the meeting room. He had scrawled out dates and names on the writing board mounted on the wall. As they took their seats, Neville glanced at Kerkar and asked, 'Should we ask Dilip to sit in?' and then seeing the apprehension on Bosco's face, he quickly added, 'Perhaps later. Let's see what we have first. OK, Bosco, the floor is yours.'

The young man seemed excited, nervous. 'The dates first, sir. Leo Jarvinen's body was discovered on 24th February last year. Joshua Davies arrived in Goa on 2nd March. Eva Campbell had been residing in Goa, on and off, since the winter of 2017. From the information we have, she left the country at least twice between November 2017 and June 2018, when she was last seen. Once for Kathmandu and once for Colombo. Joshua Davies' body was discovered on the 22nd of June.'

'22nd June. That's three days after his visit to Ponda,' remarked Neville, turning to Kerkar.

'You mean, the HSS headquarters there? Well, I also discovered that he attended the annual Hindu convention in Goa in April last year,' Bosco chipped in. 'Clearly, he was interested.'

'Anyway, please continue,' Neville urged, eager not to interrupt Bosco's train of thought.

'During the months of May and June, Joshua spoke to a number of lawyers, activists, journalists and environmentalists. It wasn't difficult to piece this together once I got to the first of them. His meetings were set up through references from the sources he started with and when I got a hang of the type he was seeking out, there were more hits than misses.'

'And what was he investigating?'

'Mopa and land grabs,' Bosco stated, pausing for effect. He waited for this to sink in before continuing. 'If Joshua was working on a major investigative piece in Goa, it was almost certainly with this angle. The people I met were quite amazed at the amount of information he had gathered in such a short period – regulations, land records, litigation, details of individual cases and even dirt on the key protagonists.'

'The Lobos included?' Neville asked.

'Yes, but not just them.'

'Meaning?'

'It appears he had tracked down Angelo Lobo's connections to people within the government and …'

'And?'

'Even our department, sir.'

Kerkar sighed. Bosco looked unsure if he had overstepped his brief.

Neville tried to deflect the awkwardness. 'We'll come to that in a moment. What did you dig up about Mopa?'

'Joshua went there, more than once,' Bosco explained. 'The villagers remembered him.'

'I wonder how he communicated with them. Everyone doesn't follow English here, do they?'

'No. The last time he visited, there was a local chap with him.'

'You mean, a translator?'

'They seemed to think he was a friend. Joshua managed to speak to the families of the farmers who had allegedly committed suicide. The daughter of one of the farmers told Joshua that her father was beaten to death.'

'How can you be sure of that?' Kerkar asked.

'Because Joshua mentioned it to Rachel Sequeira.'

'The environmentalist?'

'Yes sir. On the evening of 20th June. At her residence. On his return from Mopa earlier that day.'

Neville and Kerkar sat up in their seats.

'Ram Aroskar had reportedly consumed poison but Swati, his daughter, told Joshua that he was clubbed after he refused the final offer from the Lobos to sell his plot to them. Angelo Lobo visited their house after the incident and convinced Ram's wife to accept a financial settlement in return for keeping mum and parting with the plot on which they grew finger millets. With her husband gone, she figured the two of them – mother and daughter – would be easy meat for Lobo.'

'No police case was filed, right?'

'No. Swati wanted to, but her mother stopped her. She even begged her neighbours to be silent about it, keeping her family's safety in mind.'

'But Swati found a sympathetic ear in Joshua and opened up to him?' Neville surmised.

'Something like that.'

'Did Ms Sequeira say what Joshua was going to do with this information?'

'This part is unclear. She said he was very agitated when she met him. He had arrived at her doorstep in the evening without an appointment. And soon after that, he was found dead.'

'Ms Sequeira did not raise an alert?'

'She did find the timing suspicious but kept her own counsel when the autopsy indicated that it was an accidental death. The Lobos are a powerful family. Apparently though, she brought it up with the previous DGP at a party only to be told that the case was closed as there was no evidence of foul play.'

'And where is this young lady now?'

'Swati? Gone from Goa. The land is part of the development project, their small house demolished. No one has a number for them, though one of the neighbours said they may have gone to Satara.'

'That's understandable, isn't it?' Neville mused. 'So, the needle turns to senior Angelo now.'

Bosco looked unconvinced. 'Not sure about that, sir. His son is also in the frame.'

'How so?'

'The lawyers and journalists Joshua spoke to indicated that a significant part of the land around the new airport was to be used by casino groups to build integrated resorts. The total investment envisaged runs into hundreds of millions of dollars,' Bosco revealed.

'And Jakob Lobo was spearheading that initiative. Father gets the land organized, cashes in on the price arbitrage before handing over a chunk for the son to develop – a nice family operation. And you think Joshua Davies would have seen through this?' Neville asked.

'Exactly,' Bosco affirmed.

'Just one quick question before you continue, Bosco. Did any of the people you spoke to mention Naresh Sardesai?'

Bosco looked puzzled. 'No, sir. Why?'

'It's nothing. So, you were telling us about Jakob.'

'Yes, Jakob was a frequent visitor to Mopa. The villagers spotted him often, though never with his father. He usually came with other men.'

'Prospective partners, perhaps.'

'Someone from our side is exploring all that, sir. If companies had been registered, who the investors were, basically, how far into the game they had proceeded last year.'

Neville looked distracted. 'I see where you are going with this, Bosco, but Jakob's interest in capitalizing on the gambling opportunity in Mopa is not strictly illegal. The deals facilitated by his father may have been on favourable terms and that is a line worth delving into, but I am wondering if it is motive enough for murder. Did Eva Campbell's name come up anywhere?'

'No sir. I drew a blank there. In fact, the three missing links I intend to go after now are Eva, Swati and Joshua's local translator,' Bosco replied, before turning to Kerkar.

'Sir, I have taken the liberty of asking Inspector Barve to assist me. We need a few more hands on the case.'

'Sure, Bosco. Don't worry about that. We'll talk separately on the matter.' Then he remembered something.

'And you were saying something about Joshua having found links between Angelo Lobo and our department?'

'Sir ...'

'Don't worry, Bosco, you are telling me. I didn't hear it from you.'

'You know Dean Faleiro, right, sir?'

'Faleiro? The journalist? Is he still alive?'

Bosco smiled. 'Very much so. Old and a bit batty, but still remembers a lot. You will be amazed, the things he picks up. The old lawyers, they still get together at Faleiro's ancestral place in Salvador do Mundo for drinks and he hears all the local gossip. I heard from

Ms Sequeira that Joshua had met him. Faleiro told me about this company …'

Bosco hesitated. Neville had to intervene, 'Bosco, if you are afraid of consequences despite SP Kerkar's assurance, I can get DGP Chandok to personally …'

'No, no, not at all. It's just not nice to snitch about one of our own. So, there's a company called Sunrise Constructions, owned by Michael Alvares' wife and brother-in-law. According to Faleiro, it is a shell company but sums running into crores have been transferred to it from various Angelo Lobo firms, in return for fictitious construction services. That's not all. A two-acre plot near Morjim with a building permit was purchased by Mrs Alvares last year. You know what the market value of such a plot would be. I could verify the land ownership but not the transactions Mr Faleiro referred to, about Sunrise. It should not be very difficult though,' Bosco explained.

'I suspect Faleiro is correct. It's a good way to transfer the pay-offs. Cash gets cumbersome to shift beyond a point. Especially these days,' Neville observed.

'Sir, there's one other detail. Apparently, there was a policeman who visited the Aroskar household after the death,' Bosco added.

'You think it may have been Alvares?' Kerkar asked.

'No one mentioned a name, but …'

'It may have been, Vishnu,' Neville completed. 'Though it was a risk for him to have taken. To go outside his jurisdiction. But Angelo may have leaned on him to convey to the victim's wife that it would be no use knocking on police doors and that prudence lay in accepting Angelo's offer and clearing out. Coming from a uniformed cop, it would have added weight to the coercion.'

Bosco had stepped away from the drawing board. He seemed to have finished his report.

'Bosco, outstanding work. To dig all this up in a couple of days is terrific fieldwork. I am very impressed,' Neville said.

'Thank you, sir, but to be honest, it all fell into my lap. Faleiro asked me to meet someone, and that someone passed me on to someone else and by the time I met all of them, I had a much better picture of what Mr Davies may have been up to,' Bosco tried to make light of Neville's compliment but was visibly chuffed.

'There are still a few loose ends …'

'Indeed, and we won't keep you. Vishnu, if you don't have more work with Bosco, may I suggest that we let him go back to pursuing his leads. He can call as soon as he finds out more,' Neville suggested.

'Correct. Bosco, ask Barve and maybe even Nigel to join your team. I'll call them the moment I'm done here. Good luck. Keep me briefed,' Kerkar directed.

'Yes, sir.'

Bosco hurried off leaving Neville and Kerkar deep in thought. 'What do we do now, Neville?'

'Let's wait another day, Vishnu. We can confront Angelo and Jakob with what we have, but that, other than putting them on alert, won't achieve much. We still don't have enough on them, other than motive. Let your team dig around for another day.'

'I agree. I just worry that they might be watching us. Look how quickly they got onto Mia?'

'I know. But I have a hunch something will turn up. We are close.'

'Agreed. And Alvares,' Kerkar mentioned the name and no more. Neville understood how difficult it was, having been there before. When someone from your own fold betrays you.

'You will have to inform Dilip about him. You cannot keep it from him, but shall we do this tomorrow as well? We pull one string; the others get rattled too.'

'I'm just wondering what the extent of Michael's involvement may be.'

'I know what you mean, Vishnu. It's a lot easier to do many things in a uniform, and in a police vehicle. The amounts involved are significant. Policemen are also human. We expect some things to be beyond their moral scope, but nothing is, if the inducement or threat is big enough.'

'Quite a morning. Pulled from one direction to the other,' Kerkar said, shrugging off his pensive mood. 'Why did you ask Bosco about Naresh?'

'I can't explain, Vishnu. I have a vague feeling that he is linked somehow. It may appear, after hearing Bosco, that these are two discrete cases – the Lobos with Joshua and the HSS with Naresh – but I'm not entirely convinced,' Neville pondered.

'You think Joshua's killer may also be the one behind Naresh's death? Why, because Joshua shared something incriminating with Naresh? But even if that were true, why now, after one full year? Also, would Naresh have kept quiet after Joshua's death, if that was the case? He didn't scare easily.'

Neville smiled at Kerkar.

'The very questions I have been agonizing over, Vishnu, with no answer. But we are wiser now than we were yesterday and hopefully even more so, tomorrow. Let's stay optimistic. There's someone I need to speak to as well,' Neville said, rising.

'If you bump into Dilip, won't you tell him I said hello? I don't want to disturb him now. We'll speak in the evening then.'

Leslie's call caught Neville on his drive back. He probed, without being too intrusive, for more details about Naresh Sardesai's death. Neville thought it would be improper to divulge any. He requested Leslie to message him Faye's phone number and promised to meet up for a coffee soon. Distracted by the call, Neville missed the turnoff to Mapusa and realized it only when he had driven further down the Bombay–Goa highway. There were a hundred thoughts racing through his head and he wasn't sure he wanted to go back home and subject himself to Shehnaz and Mia's questions. Instead, he took a right turn from the highway and drove onto the Moira Road. Parking by a field, he sat still at the wheel, immersed in his thoughts.

Various fragments, with no apparent connection to the crime, occupied Neville's mind – a stray remark from the late writer, a face that had seemed familiar, a store he had passed on his drive, drug traces in Jarvinen's blood, something Shehnaz had said to him – all of which seemed to hold a significance that eluded his grasp for the moment. Despite the chaos, for the first time since Mia's arrival, Neville felt hopeful. Some of these hunches, he knew from experience, were part of a process, of his brain sifting through the information that was key to the solution. In time, it would all click, or so he hoped. He sat there by the field for a long time and then, on a whim, drove up further in the direction of Nachinola, barely a couple of kilometres down the road. On reaching, he slowed outside a tea shop to ask for directions to Angelo Lobo's house. The man pointed ahead and asked him to take the first right turn. Neville followed the instructions and in less than a minute arrived at a gate with an armed guard outside. A wall of exposed red laterite, ran along both sides of the gate. It looked like a large estate, nicely forested inside, with no house visible from the road. He turned the car around and drove back.

Back home, he gave the women a brief summary of what had transpired and retired to his room, saying he wished to be alone for a while. Shehnaz knew better than to protest. She sensed something was bothering Neville – it was that time in the case where he was close yet the final solution remained agonizingly elusive. Earlier in his career, it would drive him mad with frustration, sometimes even spill out into uncharacteristic outbursts. The years may have tempered all that, but not the simmering inside, she knew. The fact was that Neville could be very hard on himself; she only hoped he didn't doubt that his analytical edge had dulled with age, as someone of his disposition could be prone to believing. She briefly thought of comforting him, but held herself back for fear of being seen as patronizing. Neville was no child, though even intelligent men could often become childlike in their despair. Shehnaz was always there for him, and Neville knew that, but this was a bridge he needed to cross himself. And so, he had to be left alone.

From his lair, Neville emerged only as dusk settled, to dutifully pour them drinks. He sat with them but they could see that his mind was elsewhere. There wasn't much by way of conversation. Once or twice, when there was eye contact between them, Shehnaz thought she detected a glimmer of excitement there but later it looked like confusion.

Around eight, a call summoned Neville to the bedroom. When he came out, the atmosphere shifted perceptibly. There was a gleam in his eyes again, though he only said, 'I need to go out early tomorrow morning. Mia, at some point in the day, would you be up for a short drive? I know you shouldn't be moving around but I wouldn't ask if it wasn't necessary.'

'Of course,' Mia nodded, restraining her curiosity.

Quiet through dinner, Neville retired early to bed. When Shehnaz walked in later, she found him lying down with his eyes closed, the reading light switched off. But he had registered her presence and said, almost in his sleep, 'Jennifer and Roy had a young son, who died in a bike accident last year. No one mentioned it before.'

'What? A son? But how come …'

'Yes, dear. Bosco just discovered it. I'm as surprised.'

18

NEVILLE MET BOSCO OUTSIDE NARESH SARDESAI'S residence at half past eight in the morning, as planned the night before. Laxman, standing sentinel at the gate, greeted them.

'Morning, Laxman. You are still on duty here?'

'Yes, sir. A lot of media folks have been turning up to click pictures. SP *saab* wants me around until the attention dies down,' Laxman replied, still looking downcast.

'Any idea what will happen to the house?'

'No one from his family has come since the incident. I'm not sure he has a next of kin.'

'Take care then,' Neville said, before he and Bosco headed towards the Pinto residence next door.

'How come none of you knew about this accident?' Neville asked.

'Actually sir, I was at the Canacona station last year. A bike accident here in Anjuna wouldn't have come to my desk. So many of these happen all the time. DSP

Alvares and the Anjuna station head would have known of course, but there wasn't anything suspicious – just the date,' Bosco explained.

'21st June, you said. The day before Joshua's body was found. What was his name?'

'Xavier.' They had reached the house and could see Roy poking around for something in their metal scrapyard.

'Morning,' he said, not betraying any major surprise at their arrival at such an early hour.

'Is Jennifer up?'

He didn't need to answer as the door opened and Jennifer emerged, wearing a nightie. Her face was swollen and her eyes, puffy.

'Hi Jennifer, this is Inspector Bosco. Sorry to bother you so early, but we needed to ask you a few questions. We don't need to come in.'

'It's alright, I was making tea.' She walked back into the room. Neville and Bosco followed.

Once they had accepted the cups Jennifer handed them, Neville asked, 'Yesterday, I was told about your son's bike accident, Jennifer. The last time we came here with Joshua's sister, you didn't mention it. I had no idea.'

Jennifer sat quietly, staring out the window. Roy's voice drifted in from the doorway. 'What is there to mention, about such an incident? Everyone knew. We thought you did too. Jennifer doesn't talk about it.'

'Yes, I can understand that, Roy,' Neville said gently. 'There can be no greater tragedy for a parent. But, since it was so close to Joshua's death, would you mind if I asked you a few questions?'

Roy sat down beside his wife, with a resigned look on his face.

'What happened, exactly?' Neville could see the struggle in Roy's face, as he asked the question. Yet he had no option.

'They came from the police station and said there had been an accident. Asked me to come along and identify if the body was his – Xavier's.' Jennifer's face twisted in pain at the mention of the boy's name. She turned away from them.

'I went down and identified him, though it wasn't necessary. When they mentioned the bike number plate, I knew it had to be him.'

'Who came to inform you?' Neville asked.

'Inspector Rane from the Anjuna station.'

'Was it on the morning of 21st June?'

'Yes.'

'So, Xavier had not returned home the night before?'

'No.'

'Was this usual? Would he often not come back?'

'No, never. His phone was switched off. What could we do, he was a grown-up man. We decided to wait till the morning. But then, the Inspector came.'

'Was Joshua here in his room, when the police came?'

'Yes. He was asleep,' Jennifer answered. Her voice had changed. 'He came down just after Roy left with the Inspector. He was horrified when I told him what had happened.'

'And then?'

'Roy came back with the news. Joshua and I were waiting here. He left immediately.'

Neville sat still. Bosco glanced sideways and saw him staring down intently at the floor. The air in the room felt heavy. Finally, Neville looked up and asked, 'And did Joshua come back here after that?'

'No,' Jennifer replied.

'Did Eva come here that day?'

'No.'

'So, that was the last time you saw Joshua?'

Roy looked irritated. 'Yes, obviously. His body was found on the beach the next morning, right?'

'Right. Just being doubly sure. Did Xavier and Joshua know each other well?'

Again, a grimace on Jennifer's face. It was Roy who answered. 'Not to begin with. But later, they got to know each other.'

'Were they friends?'

'No, but sometimes Joshua would go out with Xavier on his bike.'

'Any idea where they went?'

'No.'

'You never asked?'

'They were two young men, roughly the same age. Xavier had a bike, which was handy.'

'It must have come up in conversation, surely?'

They could sense the tension, but Jennifer and Roy remained silent.

'What did Xavier do? In terms of work?' Neville questioned.

'Not much. He was a very bright boy. Did well in school, finished his graduation from a good university. I asked him to help with my hardware business, but he had no interest in it. For some time, he worked in a hotel but got bored of that.'

'Did you ask what he wanted to do?'

'He always said the same thing – that he wanted to do something interesting.'

'He was a good boy,' Jennifer's voice now sounded disembodied. Her eyes were welling up, a slight heaving in her shoulders. Roy put an arm around her, but she shrugged it off.

He stood up. 'I am terribly sorry to have brought this up again. We will leave now.'

Neville glanced once at Bosco before leaving the room. Roy came out with them.

At the roadhead, Neville asked, 'Did the media come around to ask about Xavier?'

Roy looked surprised. 'No. They came, but to ask about Joshua. Who cares about a local farm boy breaking his neck from a fall? He was buried and forgotten.'

Neville shook Roy's hand and bid him goodbye.

'The guys at Mopa didn't mention a name for the friend who accompanied Joshua there, did they?' Neville asked Bosco once they were in the car.

'The translator, you mean? No, sir. But it could very well have been Xavier, I think now.'

'Yes. Vishnu will meet us at the Anjuna station?'

'He has reached. Just got his message.'

They drove off. It was nine but the sun was already sharp. The rain had stopped over the last few days.

Kerkar stood outside his car. Bosco filled him in on their meeting as they approached the station building. Rane was waiting for them. A wiry, sun-browned man in his late forties, with a face resembling a squirrel. There was a shifty quality to him. On seeing Kerkar, he stood up and saluted.

'Morning, Rane. This is Inspector Bosco from HQ and Neville Wadia, former JCP, Mumbai police. As I told you on the phone, we have some questions about the bodies found in June last year.'

He turned to Bosco. 'Let's start with the body of Xavier Pinto, found on the morning of 21st June. What can you tell us about it?'

Rane didn't need to think before replying. 'Oh, the bike accident. We got a call from a local saying he had spotted a bike and a body lying in a grove not very far from here – one of those valley kind of depressions by the side of the road as you drive down from Mapusa. We went down immediately and found him. He was already dead. The bike was smashed; his neck broken, head caved in.'

'What time was this?'

'I can't be exact, but we must have arrived there around six or so. Early morning.'

'Was there a post-mortem?' Neville took over.

'Yes. There was a lot of alcohol and drugs in the blood. I had expected it.'

'We will need a copy of the PM report.'

'I'll find it, sir.'

'What was the cause of death?'

Rane looked confused. 'It was very clear. The boy was driving back late at night in a state of severe intoxication. He went off the road and into the trees. Because of the slope, the bike would have flipped. The boy's head ran into a tree with some force. He must have died on the spot. We see cases like this all the time. The examiner's report said the same thing.'

'And you went over to the boy's house to ask the parents to identify the body.'

'Yes.'

'Did you go personally?'

'Yes.'

'Do you remember meeting anyone other than the boy's parents there?'

Rane thought for a moment. 'No, I don't think so. It was quite early in the day.'

'You must have been aware that Xavier was friendly with Joshua Davies, whose body you found the very next day on the beach?'

They saw Rane stiffen. He averted his eyes and said, 'No sir. We knew that Mr Davies was staying there as a paying guest, till his death.'

'It didn't strike you as an odd coincidence that two young men, living in the same house, died one after the other, supposedly in accidents?'

Rane's face had turned a shade of red. He stammered, 'Sir, there was no doubt about the bike accident. He was driving drunk. The other one, we thought, was accidental but there may have been a mistake. There was nothing to … to connect the two.'

'Did you try to establish where Xavier was driving back drunk from?'

No answer.

'What kind of drugs were found in his blood?'

'Party drugs, sir. The PM will have the names.'

Neville glanced at Kerkar, didn't need to say anything else. 'Did DSP Alvares come to the station on the morning the body was found?' Kerkar asked.

There could be no mistaking the panic in Rane's eyes now. 'Why … he may have … I …' He gave up.

'He did, then. Did you call him? Why? This was a routine drunk driving accident in your area and the body had been identified, right?'

No reply again.

'Rane?' Kerkar raised his voice a notch.

'Sir, please speak to DSP Alvares about all this. I did my duty after being informed about the body. I know nothing else.'

Neville changed the subject. 'Inspector, you remember interrogating an American woman called Eva Campbell about the death of Leo Jarvinen, right?'

Rane looked pulverized, like a boxer staggering from a sequence of punches in quick succession. 'I ... I didn't. DSP Alvares did. I heard about it.'

'I see. And did you or DSP Alvares happen to see her around that time – the 21st and 22nd of June? At any point? Before or after the two bodies were found.'

'I don't think so, sir.'

'You don't think, or you didn't?'

'I didn't.'

'Did you meet Mr Angelo Lobo or his son Jakob right after the June incidents?' Neville asked pointedly.

Rane's eyes widened. 'I don't meet him, sir,' he blurted, shaking his head vehemently.

'*You* don't? Meaning what exactly, Inspector – that DSP Alvares is the one who does the meetings, not you?' Neville was quick to pounce.

'I didn't, I mean. Sorry,' Rane stammered.

'Rane, listen to me carefully now. Alvares is on leave. You are not to call him or the Lobos the moment we leave the station now. If they know about our meeting, we will know it came from you. This is not a request. Am I clear?' Kerkar snarled.

'Yes, sir.'

'And I want Xavier's autopsy report on my desk by afternoon.'

They left the room and walked out to the courtyard. Outside, Neville asked, 'Bosco, did you have any luck with that girl, Swati?'

'No, sir. Vanished without a trace. But I will get a report on Sunrise Constructions today.'

'Good. I have an errand to run. But I will stop at the station by late afternoon, if you guys are there. I have a hunch that things might move now.'

'I hope you are right,' said Kerkar, gloomily.

Neville waved and drove off.

19

WHEN HE REACHED HOME, SHEHNAZ AND MIA WERE already dressed, waiting eagerly on the veranda. Neville hadn't been very forthcoming about his venture and Shehnaz couldn't contain her curiosity.

'Did you meet Jennifer?'

'Yes, and the Inspector at Anjuna station. If you're ready, let's head out, shall we?'

'A cup of coffee?'

'No Shehnaz. There's no time to lose now,' Neville replied briskly.

Mia, now more accustomed to moving around with her cast, managed to get into the back seat without much difficulty. Neville typed out a quick message on his phone before starting the engine. As they drove, he recounted the morning meetings and Bosco's findings.

'We are going to meet Faye, right?'

'Yes. We have given her enough time to think about what she has to say. We cannot wait any longer. I should have met her yesterday.'

The drive was short, though it would have been even shorter had Neville not returned to fetch Mia and Shehnaz. They parked outside the green house, where Tony emerged, alerted by the sound of their arrival.

'Hi Tony. Did Faye get the message I sent earlier?'

'Yes. Come in.'

They entered the same sombre room where Faye sat on a couch, her legs tucked beneath her. She offered a weak smile and stared at Mia's cast.

'Please sit down,' she said to Mia.

'Faye, the last time we came here to ask about Eva, you were very upset, and I thought it better not to push you,' Neville began gently. 'I could see that you knew more than you let on. But now, over the last few days, new developments have taken place, and we need your help.'

Faye looked up at Tony, as if beseeching him to say something.

Mia spoke up. 'There was an attempt on my life too, Faye.'

'What?' Faye gasped.

Mia pointed to her leg. 'An SUV tried to run me over. Had I not jumped at the last moment, I would have been lying in a morgue now instead of nursing just a broken ankle.'

As Faye's expression changed to one of horror, Shehnaz turned to find Neville staring intently at the girl's face. And then, almost as if under a spell, he asked, 'Do you have a sibling, Faye?'

It was a simple enough question, but Faye looked stunned.

'Yes, a brother,' Tony answered for her.

'Are you twins, by any chance?'

Mia and Shehnaz exchanged puzzled looks. Faye's voice was barely a whisper. 'Yes.'

Neville sat back in his chair. A cloud seemed to have lifted from his eyes. Shehnaz recognized that look.

'His name is Danny, isn't it?'

Tony moved closer to his wife, holding her hand.

'I knew I had seen that face somewhere, just couldn't place it. For fraternal twins, it is a remarkable likeness. If you are wondering, Faye, I met him quite by accident at Jakob Lobo's office the other day. And now I have a better idea of what you may be able to tell us.'

Mia, who had had enough of this talking in riddles, cried out, 'Faye, please! These people need to be stopped. An old man was murdered in his sleep. They tried to silence me, that same evening. You have to tell us what you know.'

Tony whispered something to Faye, and she turned to look into his eyes. Neville decided to twist the screws. 'Tony, there is a reason I didn't come with SP Kerkar today, as I probably should have. The police will not ask you these questions so politely. The truth will come out, one way or another. If you and Danny cooperate, I promise you that I will do everything, within legal limits, to ensure that Danny doesn't come to harm.'

Faye looked like she believed Neville, but her fear was palpable. 'You don't know these people, sir. We cannot live in Goa after this. They will get to us, sooner or later.'

'No. There are ways to protect you,' Neville insisted, though his voice faltered. Shehnaz shot him a nervous glance, mindful of the shadows the past still cast on her husband.

'And if you do wish to relocate, I will help you. If you need money, it can be arranged. I mean it, really,' Mia butted in, sounding quite desperate.

Shehnaz rose and walked up to Faye, holding her hands. 'Faye, you want to protect your brother, right? We understand. But look at this girl sitting in front of you. Her brother was bludgeoned to death and left to drown in the sea. Her mother has become a walking corpse. Don't you attend church? So you know the difference between right and wrong. Sometimes, we have to be strong to walk on the right path. I know you are scared. But if your brother was not directly involved and the police have no reason to hold him, we will open the doors of our house in Bombay for you. You, Tony and Danny can stay there until you feel safe again. We'll help you in every way possible. It's a promise, OK?'

As Shehnaz spoke, Faye clung to her and began to howl. She muttered something but they couldn't make out what. Mia was about to rise, but Neville stopped her. When Faye's tears had subsided, she looked up at

Neville and said, 'I told Danny he has to speak up. We discussed it again the evening you came with Leslie. He agrees with me but just can't bring himself to do it. I will call him now.'

Tony handed her a phone, 'Ask him to come over right away.'

Neville looked hesitant. 'Faye, please try not to sound upset on the phone. There may be people around him, and you don't want to raise any alarms. Maybe say you are feeling very unwell, and Tony isn't home. Ask him to rush back.'

Faye nodded. She dialled Danny and relayed Neville's message. It wasn't entirely convincing, but to their relief, she said, 'He said he will leave immediately.'

'Shall I make some tea?' Tony offered.

'That's a good idea, Tony. We could all do with a cup,' Shehnaz said. Tony headed into the house.

Faye seemed more relaxed, perhaps relieved that the burden of whatever secret they carried was about to be shed.

'How long has Danny been working on the boats with Jakob?' Neville asked.

'Three years now,' Faye replied.

'And he loves his boss, doesn't he?'

Faye looked startled again. 'Yes. How did you …'

'I saw them together, very briefly, on the ship. The way he spoke to Danny, there was a certain affection.'

'He has been kind. That's another reason why Danny won't speak. He says he owes everything to Jakob.'

Loyalty – what a thing that was, Neville mused. How often had he seen it blur the line between right and wrong, the thirst for human kindness smothering every urgent appeal of conscience.

Tony returned with a tray of cups. 'I've been telling Faye and Danny that we should up and go. In fact, I don't think I will renew the lease on the shack this season. Business is just about OK and it isn't worth the price. Every time Danny comes home, it is the same talk all over again. We have to leave, or Faye will go mad.'

'But Danny doesn't want to?' Neville asked.

'Well, he earns quite a bit of money there, if you count the tips. But it isn't only that.'

'Yes. He thinks he is part of some glamorous world. And Jakob has cast a spell on him. Danny was always an underconfident boy … Jakob makes him feel better about himself,' Faye added.

'But he is torn, you said? He does have pangs of conscience?'

'He is my twin.'

They sipped from their cups and waited. Shehnaz wondered if Neville should try and extract as much information from Faye before Danny's arrival but knew that he was holding back for a reason. She trusted his judgement. The wait seemed interminable, and she could sense that Mia was getting impatient. They were so close.

A bike roared outside, and Danny barged into the house. He took one look at Neville, a moment for the recognition to click, and realized everything was over. The look he gave Faye was not of anger or even disappointment, but resignation. He must have known that this moment would arrive one day. He sat down heavily next to his sister.

'Hello, Danny. I am Neville. We met briefly at Jakob's cabin the other day.'

Danny nodded slightly, glancing at Mia.

'This is Mia Davies, Joshua's sister. The same Joshua you would have met on the *Mandovi Queen*. We are here to find out what happened on the nights of 20th and 21st June.' And then Neville resorted to a slight embellishment. 'We have an idea of what you will tell us, from your sister, but we want to hear it all from your lips.'

If Faye noticed this lie, she didn't protest. Danny remained silent.

'Danny, we are here to help. Tell me the truth and I will take you to the DGP and say that you are a vital witness to what took place. Unless, of course ...'

Danny looked up in horror. 'No. No, I didn't do anything. I swear on Faye's head.'

Faye reached out and held Danny's hand.

'I believe you, Danny. But you have to tell us what happened that night,' Neville insisted.

Danny turned to Faye, who gave an almost imperceptible nod. The language of twins, a little was enough. Neville gave him a few seconds, before asking, 'Let's start from the beginning, shall we? Do you remember when Joshua started coming to the boat?'

'No. But it was low season, so summer. Maybe April or May. Eva brought him along one day.'

It was just a simple statement, but relief coursed through the room. Shehnaz could almost physically feel Mia relax beside her. Faye and Tony exchanged a look. Only Neville remained unchanged, as if nothing had happened.

'Were Eva and Joshua seeing each other?' Neville probed.

'No, I don't think so. Joshua liked her, it was easy to see that. But Eva still hadn't gotten over Leo.'

'After Leo's death, Eva stopped coming for a while. Why did she come back?'

Danny looked down. 'I wasn't always with them. But I think she felt that something happened on that ship that may give her a clue to why Leo died, or how.'

'Did she think Jakob may have been behind it?'

'Oh, no. She trusted Jakob. When she came by with Joshua, Jakob would ask me to escort them to the *Princess*, where he took his best clients for private parties. Once or twice, I heard her ask about Leo.'

'Was Joshua curious about it too?'

'Yes.'

'And what would Jakob say?'

'Not much. He had no idea what happened. But Eva always prodded him to make inquiries. Jakob knows a lot of people.'

'So, Joshua and Eva came to the *Princess* on 20th of June?'

Danny gave Neville a strange look. 'No. Joshua wasn't there.'

'Eva came alone?'

Danny gulped, and Faye squeezed his hand. 'Xavier was there with her.'

A slight hint of movement in Neville. This was a surprise. 'So, Joshua would get Xavier along to the boat?'

'Not at first, but towards the end, Xavier would often be there with him. Jakob didn't mind. I knew Xavier, we were in the same class in school.'

Faye turned her face away from them.

'So, Eva and Xavier came together that evening, but Joshua wasn't there. Wasn't that unusual?'

'They were all supposed to come, but something urgent came up and Joshua said he'd join them later.'

Neville nodded, as if he had remembered something. 'And he never did?'

'No.'

Shehnaz looked at Mia. Her brow was furrowed.

'So, there were just the four of you on the *Mandovi Princess*: Jakob, Eva, Xavier and you. Is that right?' Neville said to himself, before lapsing into a brief silence. Then, he said, in a softer voice, 'Danny, I know it won't be easy for you to answer my next questions, but you must answer them with absolute honesty. And as clearly as you can remember them. OK?'

Faye murmured something to Danny while Tony patted his shoulder.

'What was everyone drinking that evening?' Neville resumed, in a far more formal tone.

Danny seemed surprised by the question. 'Eva always drank beer. Xavier was having a beer, too. He wasn't much of a drinker. In fact, he never drank till he started coming to the boat. There he started enjoying a pint or two. I don't drink.'

'And Jakob?'

A moment's hesitation, which Neville didn't miss. 'Maybe alcohol wasn't his thing?'

'Yes.'

'What then?'

'Coke.'

'Did he do it often?'

Danny nodded, avoiding Neville's eyes.

'What time in the evening was this?'

Mia looked irritated by these seemingly pointless questions, all this beating around the bush.

'Not late. Eva never stayed too late. Maybe seven or eight.'

'Did Eva join Jakob with the cocaine?'

'Maybe. Sometimes she did a line or two.'

'But not Xavier?'

Danny snorted. It was a strange sound, a laugh of ridicule or mockery. 'No, he was petrified of drugs. Didn't even smoke cigarettes.'

'Was there any talk about Joshua that evening? Like where he was, when he would join them?'

'I think he messaged Eva to say he'd be a bit late.'

'And she mentioned that to all of you?'

'Yes. I seem to remember it.'

'Did Jakob have a thing for Eva?'

Danny didn't answer immediately. He looked distinctly uncomfortable.

'You said you were with them whenever she came by to the boat. Surely you must have noticed. It isn't very difficult to spot something like that.'

'Yes,' Danny squirmed. 'His manner would change completely when she came. Even when she came with Leo earlier.'

'Right. Let's come back to that day. Did anyone appear drunk or high as the evening progressed?'

Danny buried his face in his hands. They had come to the difficult part. 'Yes,' came the muffled reply.

'Danny, you will need to describe exactly what happened,' urged Neville.

'I don't know what happened but it was all very sudden. Eva lay down on the settee, looking very drowsy. Maybe it was the coke; I'd never seen her like that before, ever. Even Xavier looked bombed. I asked him what it was, and he said he was feeling unwell. I took him to the bathroom.'

'And then?'

'When Xavier came out of the bathroom, he could barely stand. I had to practically carry him back to the room. But …' Danny dithered.

'But when you returned to the room, Jakob and Eva were not there, right?' Neville completed the sentence for him.

'Yes,' Danny's voice was barely audible.

'Are there private chambers on the yacht?'

Danny gave Faye a furtive glance. Her face was crinkled in disgust. 'Jakob has a small room. There are a couple of rooms with sofas that open up into beds.'

'I see. And Jakob and Eva were in one of those. Did you knock?'

'No, how could I?'

'So, you stayed with Xavier. Was he coherent?'

'He looked dazed. He kept asking about Eva, nodding off.'

'And then?'

'I heard noises from Jakob's room. Like a struggle, some shouting. I thought of knocking on the door but did not. Minutes later, the door opened and Jakob emerged, trembling. He looked like a mad man. He pointed to the room inside and mumbled something.'

'Was Xavier conscious then?'

'Yes. He just stared in a dazed way, as if he couldn't understand what was going on.'

'You went into the room?'

'Yes. Eva was lying on the bed, her clothes torn, head turned to one side. She looked asleep. Jakob returned and said, "She is dead", and collapsed onto the floor.'

'Did you check if she was indeed dead, as Jakob said?'

'No, I didn't touch her. I asked Jakob what had happened. He only said, "She spat in my face".'

'Those were his exact words, you remember?'

'Yes.'

'Think carefully now, Danny. You said her clothes were torn but did you see any other sign of injury? Was there any blood? Were her private parts exposed?'

They heard a sharp intake of breath. 'No, there was no blood. Only her shirt was torn open. There was no wound.' Danny's hand went up to his throat.

'Red marks there? Like she may have been strangulated?' Neville asked.

'Maybe. Yes,' Danny conceded.

'What did you do?'

'I asked Jakob if I should call an ambulance, but by then Jakob was losing it. He sat mumbling, rubbing his hands over his arms, as if he was very cold. Then he asked me to call his dad.'

'You knew Angelo Lobo?'

'No. I had only met him once. I used Jakob's phone to make the call. I informed Mr Lobo about the incident, that a woman was dead. He immediately asked who all were there in the boat. After I told him, he instructed me to shut the main door and not allow anyone inside. He promised to reach soon and specifically warned me not to let Xavier inside the room, asking me to stay with Jakob.'

Mia stirred in her seat. 'In all this time, did any phones ring? Eva's or Xavier's?'

'No, I don't think so. Or if they did, I didn't hear. The calls came later, after Mr Lobo's arrival.'

'And when did Angelo reach?' Neville took over again.

'Shortly after. I didn't check the time. He called Jakob's phone when he reached the yacht. I went down and let them in.'

'Them?'

'There were two men with him.'

'Did you recognize them?'

'No.'

'Would you, if you saw them again?' A shadow of fear passed over Danny's face. He didn't respond.

'What did the men do on reaching?'

'Mr Lobo saw Xavier, who had passed out by then, and asked about him. I told him who he was. He went into Jakob's room and shut the door. I could hear him shouting, from outside. Then he came out alone and asked me what had happened. I told him everything. He asked what Xavier had seen. I said he was with us in the room before Jakob took Eva inside,' Danny paused. 'Perhaps I shouldn't have.'

'Don't blame yourself, Danny. Anyone would have done the same thing, there,' Neville said softly. 'What happened next with the men?'

'Eva's phone rang inside the room. Mr Lobo rushed back to retrieve it. He showed me the phone – it was Joshua on the line – and asked me if I knew him; I mentioned that he was expected later that evening. Immediately after the call ended, there was a message beep. I can't be certain, but it may have been from Joshua. I saw Mr Lobo type a reply.'

'Hold on. Angelo replied from Eva's phone? You are sure about this?'

'Yes, sir. I later realized that he might have been telling Joshua not to come to the boat. Why else would Joshua not show up?'

Neville paused for a moment.

'Danny, I hope you are sure about what you are telling us. This is an extraordinary amount of detail to remember after so many months,' he said, sounding unconvinced.

Danny's reply was prompt. 'Sir, I think about that night all the time. I can't forget it, it's stuck in my head.'

'Right and was there any call on Xavier's phone?' asked Neville, moving on.

'No, as soon as Mr Lobo finished typing the message, he asked me to fetch Xavier's phone from his pocket.

He switched it off and placed it in his own pocket.'

'Did he speak to the men in your presence?'

'Yes, he instructed them to move the bodies, but not until later at night. There were too many people around.'

'He said bodies?'

'Yes. I didn't realize what it meant then. One of the men asked Mr Lobo if they should call Michael. It would be easier to shift them with his help, they said. I remember the name.'

'And did Angelo agree?'

'He went into one of the rooms and made calls. I could hear his voice but couldn't make out the details.'

'You didn't receive a call from Joshua, did you?' Mia asked.

'No. He didn't have my number.'

'How long did you sit there, waiting?'

'It felt very long, maybe until midnight. Then Mr Lobo received a message and went to the terrace to look down. When he returned, he signalled to the men. They entered the room and one of them brought Eva's body out. The other man lifted Xavier on his shoulder. Mr Lobo asked me how Xavier had reached the boat. When I told him, he asked for a description of the bike. They went downstairs with the bodies.'

'You remembered the bike number?'

'No, but it was a red Pulsar with a picture of Jesus on the fuel tank. Easy to identify.'

'Where was Jakob during this?'

'He came out of the room once the men had left. Mr Lobo asked him something – I think it may have been about me – because Jakob walked up and held my hand. He said, "I will deal with Danny. He is my guy."'

'Angelo was satisfied with that?'

'No. He grabbed me by the collar and warned that if I ever spoke about what had happened on the boat, me and my entire family would be killed. Then he turned to Jakob and told him to ensure that it never came to that, as it was his own neck on the line. Then he left.'

'And you had no idea where the bodies were taken? Eva and Xavier, I mean.'

'No, not then.'

'When did you find out?'

Danny blanched as he recounted, 'I learned about Xavier's bike accident the next day. I knew what must have happened. There was no way he would have even managed to start a bike in that condition.'

'And Eva?'

'I asked Jakob the next day. At first, he said the less I knew the better, but when I insisted, he said she had been taken to their farmhouse.'

A hush descended on the room. Neville asked Tony for some water. When he came back with a plastic bottle and glass, Neville poured some out and handed it to Danny. Danny drained the glass. Neville allowed him a minute to catch his breath before turning to Faye.

'When did you learn about all this, Faye?'

'The day after it happened. Danny might have wanted to keep quiet, but he cannot keep a secret from me. I knew immediately that something was terribly wrong.'

'And what was your advice?'

Tony answered, 'You are not a local, sir, so you won't know what Angelo Lobo is capable of. He would have carried out the threat he issued to Danny. It's his career, and his son's life at stake. We wouldn't have been surprised if Danny vanished mysteriously one day, to be honest. Faye lives in constant fear for his life, even today. What other choice did we really have?'

'And what did Jakob offer in return for your silence, Danny?'

Danny hung his head. 'I didn't take anything from him, I promise.'

'That's not what I asked.'

'He said he would buy me a restaurant to run on my own. Faye and Tony could manage it while I continued at the casino. That way, we would never have to worry about money. He said I would be secure for life.' He laughed one of those mirthful laughs again.

Mia was getting restless again. Sensing it, Shehnaz interjected, 'Danny, the next day when you met Jakob, surely the subject of Joshua came up?'

A lost look appeared on Danny's face. 'I asked him, but he didn't seem to know. I think he said he hadn't heard from him. And then he left.'

'Left?'

'Yes. Jakob left town. His father sent tickets, and he left the country that night – for Bangkok. He told me to lie low for a few days, take leave. Said he'd contact me when he returned.'

'How long was he gone?'

'About a week.'

'You are sure he left that very night?'

'Yes, he caught a night flight from Mumbai and left Goa by an early evening connection. He phoned from Bangkok a couple of days later to check if everything was fine.'

'Did you hear from his father again?'

Again, that film of fear clouded his eyes. 'Someone else called me. Not Mr Lobo. He warned me to not be seen around the casino till Jakob's return and to keep my mouth zipped, if I valued my life.'

Faye spoke up, 'A man visited our house that week with a small suitcase for Danny. It contained wads of notes. He told Danny it was a gift.'

'Not just that,' Tony added. 'He made it clear they knew where we lived.'

'I didn't touch a single rupee. We didn't even count them. I handed Jakob the suitcase the first time I met him after his return,' Danny insisted, still keen to assert that his silence had not been purchased.

'And while Jakob was away, and you were on leave, you read about Joshua's supposed accidental death in the newspapers, correct?'

Danny nodded grimly.

'You didn't think it was odd? All these people dying off one after the other? Eva, Xavier and then Joshua, who was supposed to be at the yacht that evening?'

Tony answered, 'I told them it was no accident. Angelo must have bribed the cops. No way could it have been a coincidence.'

'No, it wasn't. Within two days, the whole party was gone – Eva, Xavier, Joshua – and Leo before that. Danny, didn't you ask about Joshua later, at any point?'

This time Danny spoke forcefully. 'No, I did not. I did not want to discuss what had happened. What good would it have done me to know? What would I do, go to the police with it? No chance. All I could do was tell Faye and Tony that they had killed another man. That's it. So, I stopped asking. I went to the boats, did my job and pretended that nothing had happened. All the time, I thought the police would arrive at the boat any day, but no one did – till you guys showed up.'

Neville appeared unusually distracted. 'Danny, you are certain Angelo took both Eva's and Xavier's phones with him when he left the yacht that night?'

'Yes. I cleaned the rooms after they had left. There was nothing left behind.'

'Very well, thanks.'

Mia looked pleadingly in Neville's direction. They knew the fate of Eva and Xavier, but Joshua's remained a mystery. Unexpectedly, Neville stood up.

'Danny, you have to come to the station with me.'

'But, you said …' Faye protested.

'Faye, Danny witnessed at least one murder, probably two. It is important for him to give a complete statement to the investigating officers to avoid being charged as an accessory to the crimes. Besides, and I shouldn't need to tell you this, it is very important for his own safety at this point. All this sudden action would not have gone unreported to the Lobos. Danny left the boat and came away abruptly. It can't be difficult for them to piece together what may have happened.'

Tony and Faye looked alarmed.

'Danny will be safer in police detention. And Faye, you and Tony need to get away as well. Is there some place you can go, for a few days?'

Tony looked at Faye. 'Wendy's?'

'Guess so.'

'Faye has a cousin in Chicalim. We will go there.'

'Good, you should pack a case quickly. We will leave together.'

'Right now?' Faye asked incredulously.

'Yes, if they come looking, it won't be with an appointment.'

Tony hurried out of the room.

'Danny, can you please give me your phone?' Neville requested.

He looked surprised.

'Jakob may try to contact you and I wouldn't want you to speak to him.' Neville extended his hand. Danny passed his phone without demur.

Neville turned to Shehnaz and Mia. 'Come, we will wait in the car. Give them a few minutes. Danny, you can come in the car with us. Perhaps Tony and Faye can take the bike?'

'Tony has his bike. I'll be right there.'

As they walked out, Mia couldn't contain her urgency. 'Neville, do you believe that Danny truly knows nothing about Joshua?'

'I do. Danny has told us everything he knows. There is no reason for him to have held back that particular bit.'

'Jennifer told you that Joshua rushed out the moment he heard about Xavier's accident, right? He must have called Eva immediately, but the phone was with Angelo. Don't you think he would have rushed to the boat, to speak to Jakob?' Shehnaz asked.

'That would follow, would it not, Shehnaz? But according to Danny, Jakob was on his way out of the city. The question is, did Joshua manage to get across to him before that? And if he did ...'

Mia's agitation grew palpable. 'Neville, we must get hold of Jakob Lobo immediately.'

Neville sighed. 'Mia, calm down. I understand how you must be feeling, but we must proceed carefully. Now, the police will have to be involved. Shehnaz, you and Mia need to go back home after dropping us to Panjim.'

Mia was going to say something, but Shehnaz intervened. 'Mia, you must trust Neville. We have to let them do the job now. Neville will update us when he comes home in the evening. OK?'

There was a knock on the car window; Danny stood there, holding a duffel bag in hand. Neville waved at him to join Mia in the backseat. Meanwhile, Tony was putting a padlock on the door. Neville called out to him, 'I'll call on Faye's phone later. Not a word to anyone, OK?'

They drove off. Shehnaz tried to keep Danny's spirits up by asking about his childhood, where he grew up, but his replies were perfunctory and distant. He sat listlessly, looking morose; Shehnaz wondered if it was consternation for what lay ahead or perhaps regret over letting his boss down. Neville made a brief call to the station, speaking with Kerkar before they arrived in Panjim.

Outside the station, Neville requested Shehnaz to take the driver's seat. Danny turned to look warily towards the boats on the river, as he made his way towards the entrance. Shehnaz extended her hand out towards Neville and said softly, 'Good luck.'

'Thank you. I might be late. Stay at home today,' Neville responded, before disappearing into the station.

20

KERKAR AND BOSCO WERE WAITING IN THE MEETING room when Neville entered with Danny. They had the manner of expectant children, waiting for treats.

'This is Danny. By the way, I haven't even asked what your proper name is.'

'Daniel Gonsalves.'

'Right. And this is SP Kerkar and Inspector Bosco, heading the investigation into Joshua Davies' death and Eva Campbell's disappearance. Please, have a seat.'

'Vishnu, I spent the morning at Danny's place. I'll tell you later how I came to know of him, but Danny works closely with Jakob Lobo on the *Mandovi Queen*. He has just divulged everything that transpired on the night of 20th June last year – the evening Eva Campbell was murdered and possibly even Xavier Pinto.'

The two policemen listened in stunned silence as Neville narrated Danny's account. There were no questions till he stopped.

'Danny, you are sure Jakob Lobo told you that Eva's body was buried in the Nachinola farmhouse?' Kerkar asked.

'Yes. He even mentioned a caretaker who has been there since the house was built. I have forgotten his name but Jakob said he's a drunkard.'

'That shouldn't be difficult to find out,' Bosco said.

'The question is whether the body was shifted later,' Kerkar wondered aloud.

'It may have been, or not. If a body is lying under the ground, with no one the wiser, there may be a temptation not to mess with it,' Neville responded.

'How do you suggest we proceed, Neville? We may need a warrant, for searching the premises. I'll need to brief the DGP. Angelo Lobo is a minister,' Kerkar said cautiously.

'Indeed. Although the arrest of Jakob Lobo may not need a warrant from the magistrate. We have Danny's eyewitness account. For Angelo too, I should think, but it may be prudent to land up with a warrant. Let's consult Dilip. Bosco, will you stay here with Danny for a minute? Vishnu and I will return shortly.'

They found Dilip in his cabin and briefed him swiftly. If he was perturbed about the prospect of apprehending a cabinet minister, he showed no sign of it.

'After what you've told me, obtaining a search warrant won't be a problem. When were you planning to do it?' Dilip asked coolly.

'It has to be today, Dilip. The sooner, the better. Alvares is on leave, and we grilled Rane today. Danny left suddenly in the middle of a work day. Word would have reached the Lobos. We mustn't give them time to shift evidence. Assuming it is still there,' Neville emphasized.

'Right, let me get on the phone then. You guys get the teams ready.'

Neville appreciated how the DGP didn't waste time prevaricating. On the way down to the meeting room he suggested to Kerkar, 'I think it's best if we split into two teams, Vishnu. Bosco and I will head to the ship and you could take Barwe to the farmhouse?'

'You mean simultaneously?'

'Yes. Once Angelo sees the warrant, he will contact Jakob. Jakob needs to be with us when that happens.'

They re-entered the room. 'Bosco, can you call your guys and check where Angelo Lobo is at this moment? And if there is a way to send someone across to Nachinola to check discreetly about this caretaker. When our team reaches the site with the warrant, he can be shaken up first to see if he squeals.'

'Right, sir,' Bosco affirmed before leaving the room.

'Samuel,' Danny uttered suddenly.

'Samuel?'

'I just remembered. The caretaker's name is Samuel. I'm quite sure about that.'

Kerkar ran out, presumably to update Bosco about it.

'Will I be arrested, sir?' Danny asked apprehensively.

'No, but you'll be kept in a holding room for the next day or two, I imagine. Till the picture is clearer. This is the safest place for you now, Danny,' Neville reassured him.

Kerkar returned, and a policeman was summoned to escort Danny away and record his testimony in writing. Bosco returned shortly after, to report that Angelo Lobo was at his Porvorim office, and efforts were underway to locate Samuel.

'Shall we aim for 4:00 p.m., assuming we have a warrant by then?' Kerkar asked.

'Yes, while there is still light. You will need a bigger team. A small search party. Bosco and I can take a couple of uniformed officers with us. That should be enough for the boat.'

The next hour crawled by slowly. Sandwiches were brought from the canteen. Finally, there was a buzz of activity; the warrant had arrived. Jeeps were waiting outside, ready to leave. At the gate, Neville said, 'Good luck, Vishnu. Call me the moment you find something, OK?'

'Hope it goes off fine.' Kerkar left with a frown on his face.

Meanwhile, Bosco and Neville joined two other armed officers in a jeep and headed towards the jetty.

'We should hold off for a bit, Bosco. Don't want to reach too early. Let the other team get close to Nachinola, we will take the boat then,' Neville strategized as they drove.

About forty minutes later, Neville received a message from Kerkar. They were turning into Nachinola. He signalled to Bosco to get the boat ready, to take them across to the *Mandovi Queen*.

The gambling room was quite deserted when they arrived on deck, which suited Neville fine. Walking in with uniformed officers was bound to have created a stir. Jakob was in his room when they knocked. He didn't hide his surprise on seeing them.

'Oh, it's you again. Has anything happened?' Jakob asked, rising from his chair.

'Yes, Mr Lobo. We need to have a chat. About the events that took place aboard the *Mandovi Princess* on the evening of 20th June last year. It may be better if you take a seat,' Neville said calmly but firmly.

Jakob sat down heavily. His face gave away his guilt. He didn't possess his father's bravado.

'Will you tell us about it, or do you want me to?' Neville continued. 'You see, we have a signed confession from Danny.'

At that, there was a flicker of the infamous Lobo temper in Jakob's eyes. 'Danny? That ungrateful dog! I've given him everything. Without me, he'd be selling trinkets on a bloody beach. Son of a bitch!'

Neville waited patiently.

'And who cares what that bastard says anyway. What evidence do you have?' Jakob challenged.

'Ah yes. A police team is in your father's farmhouse now, where Eva's body was taken,' Neville said nonchalantly, as if it was a trivial detail. It wasn't lost on Bosco how subtly Neville omitted the fact that no corpse had been unearthed yet. It had the intended effect.

Jakob looked crushed. He knew the game was over.

—

SP Kerkar parked his vehicle outside the farmhouse gate. The team of Inspectors and Constables formed a ring around him as he showed the security guard the search warrant.

'Come with us,' Kerkar instructed the guard, entering the farm. 'Where is Samuel?'

'Samuel? You are looking for him?' The guard looked relieved that the police visit was about the caretaker.

'He must be in the fields or having tea in the house.'

They walked in.

The plot was at least six acres in size, from the look of it. A well-maintained farm with neat rows of cashew, banana, pineapple surrounded by a proliferation of larger trees – guava, mango, jackfruit and sapota – that Vishnu could identify readily. Whatever his character, Samuel but he was a good farmhand, he thought. In one corner, a small shed echoed with the sound of cackling. The poultry. At the centre of the plot, tucked away between the vegetation was a two-storied house. Nothing too grand, just a regular concrete construction painted in white and green. Here, too, the gardener's touch was evident: flower creepers adorned the pillars, lending an otherwise ordinary structure a more attractive quality.

'Where is Samuel's room?' Kerkar inquired, turning to the guard.

The man pointed to a garage-like structure attached to the back of the house. Kerkar signalled to one of the constables who ran across.

He returned with an emaciated man clad in a faded t-shirt with, oddly, Che Guevara's image on it. Kerkar placed him in his early sixties.

'You are Samuel?'

'Yes, sir but …'

Kerkar turned to Inspector Barwe. Pointing to the guard, he said, 'Barwe, can you take him to Samuel's room and ask him some questions while I talk to Samuel? And ensure he doesn't make any calls.'

'Of course, sir.'

'Samuel, who else is there in the house now?' Kerkar asked.

'Only madam, no one else.'

'We are here to talk to you about what happened in June last year. You sleep in that room at night?'

Samuel nodded; his expression guarded.

'Then you can tell us all about what happened on the night of 20th June after your boss returned late with two other men,' Kerkar demanded.

Samuel stared at him blankly.

'Do not pretend you know nothing. We are here with a warrant because we know what happened. If you don't cooperate, we will simply haul your ass off to the station and believe me, there you will sing like a bird.'

Samuel folded his hands. 'Sir, I am a mere gardener. I know nothing.'

'Cut out this crap!' Kerkar snapped. 'Where did you bury the body?'

Samuel's composure shattered and he was nearly in tears. The commotion had reached the interior of the house. A door opened on the veranda and a woman poked her head out.

'What is going on?' Her face changed when she saw the cops in uniform. A mischievous smile appeared on her lips.

As she walked out, Samuel wailed, 'Madam, please go back inside. Boss will be very angry if he hears …'

The woman laughed hysterically. 'Boss? Your boss is finished. I knew this day would come. It had to. Go on, show them what they have come for.'

Samuel stood frozen.

'Mrs Lobo …' Kerkar took a step towards her.

'Her ghost walks in the garden every evening. I can hear her footsteps at night. Her curse looms over this house – everything will burn down. Everything.'

'Where is her body?'

'Right over there. He knows. He dug her grave. Why, don't you remember, Samuel?'

Samuel muttered incomprehensibly, perhaps that he didn't understand what she was saying, but Mrs Lobo was not to be thwarted.

'By the second jackfruit tree. A raven perches there all day, it is her. I saw it all from my window that night. Those four wicked men laying her down. You think I don't notice things?'

With another shrill cackle, she darted back into the house, the door banging shut behind her.

Kerkar took Samuel by his arm and started walking towards the line of jackfruit trees. Standing by the second one, he asked, 'Here?'

Samuel was weeping, trembling in fear now. 'Sir, I did nothing. They woke me up in the middle of the night and asked me to dig. What could I have done?'

'We'll see about that. Show us first.'

Samuel put out a shaky finger, pointing to a spot near their feet.

Kerkar looked at the men.

One of them ran back to Samuel's room and returned with implements – spade, shovel, pick and crowbar. Kerkar pulled Samuel aside, leaving the men to begin their job.

'Yes, Samuel, you were saying that they woke you up in the middle of the night and gave you orders. Who all were there?'

The man stood silently, staring at the ground.

'Samuel, you do realize that you will go to prison as an accessory to this crime? Unless you make a clean confession and we try to get you off on the basis that your role was limited to digging a hole in the ground, under coercion from Angelo Lobo. So, speak up. We don't have time to waste.'

In halting sentences, Samuel rendered a narration of the incidents of that fateful night.

Samuel had had his usual quarter of feni and drifted off to sleep. Suddenly, water was splashed on his face and he woke with a start. The men hauled him up and dragged him to the garden. Angelo Lobo ordered him to start digging a hole in the ground between the lines of trees. How big a hole, he had asked. Angelo pointed to the body his two handymen had thrown down on the ground like a sack of potatoes. He begged to be let off but wasn't given a choice. The men joined him and they scooped out enough earth to shove the body four feet under. When Kerkar asked if the body was removed later, Samuel insisted it hadn't been.

'Was it the body of a white woman? A foreigner?'

Samuel nodded. Kerkar immediately called one of his colleagues and asked him to take Samuel to the Panjim station to record his statement. He didn't want to delay that. Samuel left, pleading and whining. Kerkar made a mental note of being lenient with him, what else could the man have done, really?

Soon, there were cries from the diggers. They had found something. Kerkar rushed over to find the skeleton of an arm, a grimy yellow band near the wrist. The body had fully decomposed, as expected. It had been in the ground, in this climate, for well over a year. Before arriving, Kerkar had left word for an ambulance backup and he called it in now. Within minutes, the entire skeleton lay exposed. Amidst the decay, a necklace of reddish beads, a metal anklet near the foot and the wristband were the only things that hadn't rotted away, or been devoured by insects. They would help with the identification. The diggers stood stupefied, staring down at the skeleton while Kerkar typed out a message for Neville, informing him of the discovery.

At that exact moment, there was a disturbance outside the gate, and they turned to see Angelo Lobo advancing, visibly agitated, with a constable struggling to restrain him.

'What the hell is going on? Who gave you permission to enter the premises?' Lobo demanded. And then he reached where they stood and saw the skeleton. He looked shocked, perhaps at what nature had done to the body of the woman he had put under the ground, virtually with his own hands.

Kerkar wasted no time. He read him his rights and arrested him on the spot. As they approached the gate, Kerkar felt a strange sensation and turned back to look at the house. There, at a top-floor window, Mrs Lobo stood with an impish smile on her face. Catching Kerkar's eye, she waved a cheerful goodbye, before disappearing into the house.

Kerkar instructed one of the constables to keep watch over her. He called the station to send across a policewoman to the house and got into his car.

—

When Neville received Kerkar's urgent message, they had been sitting quietly in Jakob Lobo's cabin. On hearing that Danny had confessed, Jakob had retreated into a state of trance. He stared blankly at the table, unresponsive to their questions, like a man in deep shock.

'Jakob!' Neville's voice rose sharply. 'We don't have so much time. They have unearthed Eva's corpse at the farmhouse. Your father has been arrested.'

Jakob looked up, finally. 'Dad? But he didn't do anything. He ... he was only protecting me. Why have you arrested him? I am the culprit.'

'Yes. We know, from Danny's statement, that Eva died at your hand. But there is still the death of Xavier Pinto to account for. He wasn't dead when his body was carried away by your father's men.'

Jakob stared vacantly at Neville. 'I need to ask you a few questions before we take you down to the station,' Neville continued. 'Now that the facts are known, I expect you will answer truthfully. On your return from Bangkok, when you heard about Xavier's death, you must have asked your father about it, right?'

Jakob shook his head. 'We didn't speak for many months after that. I lived in my room on the *Princess*. It was only in January that I returned home, after my mother's condition became much worse.'

'And after that?'

'No. It was quite clear to me what had happened. Whatever he had done, was for my sake. What was the point in creating more bitterness by bringing it up?'

'Who were the two men who came with your father to the boat that night?'

'Ronnie and Narayan.'

'Where will we find them?'

'No idea. You could try Dad's office.'

Neville glanced at Bosco, who quietly left the room.

'More importantly, Jakob, what happened to Joshua?'

Something changed in Jakob's face. He didn't reply.

'Jakob,' Neville insisted, 'you cannot remain silent. We have to find out who murdered Joshua Davies. He was supposed to join you at the boat that evening but didn't. Danny says your father messaged him from Eva's phone, probably asking him not to. That sounds believable. But later? The next morning? When he heard of Xavier's accident, he would have called Eva immediately. But Eva's phone was with your father. The next person he would have tried is you, obviously. Xavier's mother told us that Joshua stormed out of the house the moment he heard about Xavier. He may have gone to Eva's but not finding her there, he would have come here. Did he?'

'No. He called but I didn't answer. And then I left the boat.'

'Around what time?'

'I don't remember. Before noon. I had an afternoon flight – around four – to Mumbai. I went home, packed my suitcase and left for the airport.'

'But someone would have called from the boat to inform you if Joshua had turned up, right?'

'No one did. Joshua didn't come.'

'Jakob, I find it very hard to believe that Joshua wouldn't have turned up at the boat, especially after you didn't answer his calls. Where else could he have gone to look for Eva? Unless ...'

Jakob's eyes held fear now. Bosco slipped back into the cabin unnoticed.

'Even if what you are saying is true, I cannot believe that you did not accost your father about him on your return.'

'But his death was reported to be an accident ...'

'What? Eva is missing and Xavier found dead; and that evening, Joshua goes for a swim at Anjuna beach?

You want us to think that you believed that for a second? Come on, Jakob! You are wasting our time.'

Neville's voice had shed its customary civility. Jakob seemed to stir in his seat. 'Dad said he had nothing to do with it. He hadn't ever met Joshua, before or after his death.'

Neville looked exasperated. Seeing him taking deep breaths, Bosco stepped in. 'Mr Lobo, did you violate Eva Campbell sexually before strangling her?'

'No, no, I didn't … I mean, I couldn't …'

'What do you mean? Danny clearly remembered that her clothes were ripped open.'

'Yes, I did that. But …' Jakob's voice faltered.

'But what, exactly?' Neville butted in sharply.

'I tore open her blouse, touched her but there was … I mean, I didn't rape her.'

'So you molested her, but there was no penetration?'

'She resisted …'

'Despite being drugged?' Neville's tone turned aggressive. 'Danny said she could barely keep her head up at the time when he took Xavier to the toilet. What had you put in their drink?'

'Ketamine.'

'I see. Must have been a large dose, to knock Xavier out for so long.'

No answer from Jakob.

'So, Eva struggled to ward you off. And then, she spat in your face. That's when you lost your head and strangled her.'

Jakob looked aghast. 'How … how do you …?'

'You may have forgotten but you admitted this to Danny when you came out of your cabin that night.'

Jakob just sat there, with his head hung.

'Let's take him to the station, Bosco,' Neville finally said. 'Angelo should be there by now. I need to speak to him.'

Bosco conducted the formalities of arrest and advised Jakob about informing his lawyer but he didn't seem interested. All his resistance seemed to have caved in, leaving only a defeated air about him. The two officers and Bosco escorted him down to the boat parked by the yacht. On the boat, Neville sat staring at the *Mandovi Queen*. The lights were being switched on and against the dimming dusk light, it looked like a grand house where guests would begin to arrive soon, and a party would soon be under way. Neville wondered what would happen to these casinos, once their owner went to prison for a very long time.

21

IT WAS DARK BY THE TIME NEVILLE AND BOSCO ENTERED the police headquarters with Jakob in tow. Angelo Lobo had just been brought in and the entire place was in a tizzy. Kerkar was pacing around in the corridor and hurried up as soon as he saw Neville.

'We got him, Neville. You should have seen his face when he saw the skeleton,' Kerkar exclaimed, barely able to conceal his glee.

To his dismay, Neville didn't show any sign of triumph at all. Instead, he asked, 'Were there any objects on or around the body, that hadn't decomposed?'

Kerkar briefed him.

'Where is Angelo being held?'

'In a meeting room with his lawyer. I thought I would wait for you before questioning him. He is formally under arrest.'

'Thanks. Vishnu, just give me one moment, before we go in. Where is Danny?' Neville asked, turning to Bosco.

He was led to a small detention room, where Danny sat gloomily. Neville addressed him, 'Danny. Listen, I need you to tell me something. Can you remember anything that Eva wore that last evening?'

Danny looked puzzled. 'A white shirt I think. Or maybe cream. A skirt, maybe pants, I'm not sure.'

'Any ornaments that she was wearing?'

'Ornaments? No. I can't recall.'

'Watch, earrings ... anything?'

'No ... But she always had that yellow thing on her wrist.'

'What yellow thing?'

'A simple band. Looked like rubber. A friendship band, she called it. Leo had given it to her, and she never took it off.'

And then it struck him. 'Why do you ask? Have you found her?'

'Maybe. Anyway, this is useful. Thanks, Danny.'

Exiting the room, Neville sought out Kerkar. 'Vishnu, the wrist band was yellow, you are sure?'

'Yes. Muddy, but yellow,' Kerkar nodded.

'Danny remembers it. Eva wore it all the time, apparently.'

Kerkar looked relieved, though there wasn't much doubt in his mind about the identity of the corpse.

'Shall we then?'

He held the door open for Neville. Inside sat Angelo Lobo, looking uncharacteristically subdued. Not a trace of defiance in those eyes as they alighted on the policemen. They sat down across the table.

'Mr Lobo, from the physical evidence we have, it seems beyond any doubt that the decomposed body found in your farmhouse belonged to Eva Campbell. Forensic tests will only confirm that. We have signed statements from Daniel Gonsalves and your caretaker Samuel, and a confession from Jakob Lobo regarding the events of the 20th of June that preceded Eva's burial. I'm sure you will not bother denying it; the evidence is overwhelming. Ronnie and Narayan, the two men who assisted you, will also be arrested soon and brought to the station,' Neville said, in a matter-of-fact tone.

The lawyer attempted to interject, cautioning Angelo, but he waved him off bitterly. 'I have to pay for the sins of my son. That miserable idiot!'

'Not just that, Mr Lobo. There is also the murder of Xavier Pinto,' Neville continued, 'who you picked up from the boat. Your son had little to do with that. Ronnie and Narayan will tell us the details, surely, but perhaps you can save us the trouble.'

Angelo remained silent, prompting his lawyer to speak up. 'Unless you have any physical or circumstantial evidence linking my client to the death of the person mentioned, this is nothing but pure conjecture on your part. Mr Lobo has no comment to offer.'

'Really, Mr Lobo?' Neville asked, but Angelo remained quiet. 'Very well. It's only a matter of an hour or so before we will know. Meanwhile, why don't you tell us about Joshua Davies?'

At the mention of Joshua's name, the lawyer swivelled towards Angelo looking askance, as if thrown by a new angle he hadn't been made aware of. Angelo looked equally flabbergasted, throwing his arms up in the air. And it did not appear to be a pretence, either.

'Joshua? What have I got to do with him? I told you that day I've never met the man.'

'Mr Lobo, you have to do better than that. We know you messaged him that evening, from Eva Campbell's phone,' Neville countered calmly. 'We have Danny's testimony.'

Angelo's expression remained bewildered, the same baffled look in his eyes. 'Yes, I did. He was calling her incessantly. A message came saying he would be on his way to the boat shortly. On an impulse, I typed back a reply from her phone, saying she had left the boat and would call him in the morning. It seemed like the best way to stop him from landing up. What has that got to do with his death?'

'Sure, he may not have turned up at the boat but the next morning, he heard that Xavier had died in a drunken accident, and Eva was still incommunicado. Jakob claimed Joshua tried calling him but didn't arrive at the boat. And you had Eva's phone, which he must have tried constantly. Later that day, Joshua was bludgeoned to death. What should we infer?'

'You can infer what you want but I didn't see this Joshua and had nothing whatsoever to do with his death. I heard about it like anyone else in Goa did.' Angelo's tone was dismissive.

'Mr Lobo, this is the same Joshua who went to Mopa and spoke with the Aroskar family. He even had a testimony from the deceased farmer's daughter, who seems to have disappeared miraculously. You had more than one reason to silence Joshua Davies. I cannot accept your line that you had no interest in him.'

Angelo simply glared at him. The lawyer advised him to remain silent.

Neville tried doggedly to break down Angelo's defence, but the man clung steadfast to his version of events. He wouldn't deny his involvement in the burial of Eva's body, remained silent about the exact manner of Xavier's killing but stoutly denied any hand in Joshua's murder. After a while, Neville realized he was getting nowhere and signalled for Kerkar to step out. Outside the door, he said, 'Vishnu, we need to keep at it. Maybe send Bosco and Barwe in to have a go? Unless you want to continue.'

'I think I'll take over. But you look exhausted. It's been a long day. Why don't you call it a night? We will probably be here all night. Two more beauties are on their way.'

Bosco emerged, on cue, from one of the rooms. 'They have picked up Ronnie and Narayan. Should be here any minute.'

'Good. Let me know when they reach. I will do the interrogation,' Kerkar said. 'Meanwhile, why don't you and Barwe go in and talk to Angelo? He denies that he had any involvement in Joshua Davies' death. Focus on that.'

Bosco nodded and walked away. Neville sighed, 'You are right, Vishnu. I will leave you guys to it. Anyway, I think Eva and Xavier's cases will be sewn up by tonight. The two others, I'm not sure.'

'Two? You mean Leo Jarvinen as well?'

'No, Naresh Sardesai.'

'Oh.'

'But if you have a go at Jakob tonight, you could always ask about Leo. I didn't get to that.'

'I intend to. But the bureau guys in charge of that case will be here first thing in the morning. I briefed them on Jakob and Eva; they are on their way.'

'OK then. We'll reconvene tomorrow morning but please do call or message me about how it goes with Angelo's henchmen.'

'Of course, Neville. Do you want one of the cars to drop you home? You look very tired, really.'

Neville smiled wryly. 'Age, Vishnu. Been a while since I was up on my feet all day like this. Policing is not an old man's business.'

He waved at Kerkar and left the station. As he stepped out, two jeeps pulled up. Policemen dragged out two burly men in handcuffs. Neville considered going back inside for the first few minutes of the interrogation but decided against it. Kerkar was a seasoned officer, experienced in breaking down petty thugs like Ronnie and Narayan. Neville's presence wasn't necessary. He climbed into his car and drove off into the night.

Upon reaching Sossegado, Neville sat in the car outside the gate, trying to summon up the energy required to face the barrage of questions that awaited him at home. His limbs felt slack, his mind drained. He had expected to feel some relief at the Lobos being apprehended, yet all he carried was the nagging feeling of not having the answer to Mia's quest. Tomorrow, he would have to begin anew. Tonight, he needed sleep.

'Did you get them, Neville?' Mia blurted as soon as he walked into the living room.

Shehnaz took one look at Neville and her eyes softened. 'Please sit down, darling. Can I pour you a drink?'

'Yes, please. Thank you,' Neville replied wearily before turning to Mia. 'The Lobos have been arrested, Mia. We found Eva's corpse at their farmhouse. We know that Xavier Pinto was murdered. But they haven't owned up to the murder of Joshua yet. The police will be up with them all night. I will go back in the morning.'

'But how can that be? Surely …' Mia started.

'Yes. I know it looks quite obvious, but till we get them to admit, it isn't closed.'

Shehnaz handed Neville his drink. 'Dinner is ready, dear. Finish your drink and eat. You look like death yourself.'

He managed a weak smile. 'Yes. Since morning, one thing led to another and it all cascaded. I had no idea the day would unfold like this. You know how it goes – sometimes nothing happens for weeks, and then everything does in twenty-four hours.'

Neville drained his glass and they shifted to the table. The clock was already past ten. Mia looked restive, and it was extraordinary restraint that prevented Shehnaz from inundating Neville with the questions in her head. Finally, not able to contain herself any longer, it was Mia who asked, 'Neville, is it possible that Joshua's death was not related to Eva and Xavier's?'

Neville sighed deeply. 'I have thought about nothing else in the last hour or two, Mia. It would be surprising if it wasn't. The timing alone suggests a connection – everything happened within a forty-eight-hour span. And Angelo Lobo demonstrated that evening that he was willing to go to any length to protect his son. The only loose end he needed to tie up was Joshua. How could he not?'

'Then why is he not owning up? He is going in anyway, for Eva and Xavier, isn't he?'

'Ah, but in that may lie the answer. Angelo knows he cannot save Jakob anymore, but he can save himself. Jakob killed Eva and we will find that Angelo's men murdered Xavier. On his orders, yes, but not by his own hand. Knowing him, he can easily distance himself by saying that he only asked them to leave Xavier in the woods, but they were reckless. So, he is an accessory and will serve a sentence but not nearly as rigorous as that of a murder charge.'

'And that's why he isn't owning up to Joshua!'

'But surely, his political career is finished?' Shehnaz asked.

Neville smiled, not without irony. 'You know better than that, Shehnaz. Criminal records don't come in the way of political careers in our land. Sometimes, they even bolster them. We like our leaders macho, strong.'

Mia wasn't interested in this banter between her hosts. 'If not Angelo, then who, Neville?'

'It's too early to give up on them.'

'But you seem doubtful.'

'I am, to be honest with you, Mia. I keep thinking that somehow Naresh Sardesai's death is connected to all this. There is something … I just cannot figure it yet.'

Mia and Shehnaz turned towards him in bafflement, as if that was the last thing they had expected to hear, after the events of the day.

Neville's look had become distant. Shehnaz thought it was the tiredness finally overwhelming him. But it wasn't that.

The phone rang, interrupting his thoughts. Shehnaz hurried and fetched it from the sofa table. It was Kerkar.

'Yes, Vishnu ... No, that's OK ... Oh, I see ... That's good. Did you ask them about Joshua? Yes ... Oh, OK. Thanks for letting me know. Good night. And please extend my compliments to the entire team. Each one of them has been remarkable today. You must be proud of them ... Not at all. Bye then.'

Turning to their expectant faces, Neville relayed the news, 'Angelo Lobo's goons confessed. They carried Xavier to the edge of the valley, doused him in alcohol and placed him on his bike before pushing him down the slope. They went down later to check if he was dead ... But they claim to know nothing about Joshua.'

Mia's face fell. There wasn't much Neville could offer to console her.

They finished the meal and Neville excused himself. At night, in bed, Shehnaz voiced a concern. 'Neville, I was thinking, shouldn't someone inform Jennifer and Roy?'

'Yes, I was thinking of the same thing. They shouldn't come to know of it from the papers. At the station, they will all be too busy with the arrested fellows to think of this. I will go first thing tomorrow. Will you come with me?'

'Of course.'

Later, much later, Shehnaz's eyes opened. She had sensed some movement in the room. It was Neville, pacing up and down.

'What is it, Neville?' she asked.

'I think I know now. I have been such a fool, Shehnaz. That day you said it, too, but it didn't register …' Neville trailed off.

'I said something?'

'Yes, yes. It should have struck me then. Damn!'

'Neville!'

'I can't be sure, of course. And even if it was like that, how do I …?'

22

MIA HADN'T EMERGED FROM HER ROOM WHEN NEVILLE and Shehnaz drove out the next morning. It was only eight. Shehnaz left word with Agnes that they'd be back in an hour or so. Neville called Kerkar to check if he wanted to come to see the Pintos, but he was tied up with the Bureau guys and promised to send Bosco instead. It was only right for someone from the police to be present when Neville told the Pintos how their son died. Shehnaz tried to probe Neville about their late-night exchange but couldn't get a word out of him.

Bosco was waiting for them on the road outside the house when they arrived. He looked remarkably fresh for someone who had probably spent the night at the station.

'Morning, Bosco. Up all night?'

Bosco grinned.

'Must feel good to have the Lobos in the lock-up, doesn't it?' Shehnaz asked.

'Yes, ma'am.'

As they walked inside, Bosco briefed Neville about the statement obtained from Ronnie and Narayan. Xavier had been clubbed unconscious before being driven to the woods in a truck. Unconscious according to them – more likely dead. Alvares had been present at the scene.

—

The door was shut, and there was no one in sight. They knocked. A few moments passed before Roy emerged, eyes bleary with sleep.

'Sorry to wake you, Roy, but it's something important. We will wait outside. Can you please tell Jennifer as well? It's about Xavier.'

Roy looked surprised, mumbled something and retreated inside.

Neville, Shehnaz and Bosco stood outside in the bright morning sun. Shehnaz sensed a kind of nervous energy around Neville, which she couldn't comprehend. She noticed Bosco staring openly at him, as if he had picked it up as well. Jennifer came out first, a sheen of water clinging to her face. Roy followed.

'Jennifer, there is some news about Xavier's death, and I thought we should come and tell you in person. It's better if you sat down.'

'Xavier ...' Jennifer looked confused. Roy fetched one of those plastic chairs and she sat down, almost mechanically.

'Before I tell you about it, I have a few questions. That morning, when Inspector Rane came with the news, what exactly did he tell you about the accident? Did he mention that Xavier was … drunk while riding his bike?'

A look of distaste crossed Jennifer's face; Roy's jaw clenched.

'Yes,' he answered.

'That must have surprised you. It was unlike him, right? Or had he taken to drinking? Did you smell it sometimes when he came back home at night? Perhaps it was the company he had started keeping?'

Roy's eyes had narrowed. Shehnaz wasn't sure what Neville was trying to get at, nor was Bosco.

'This will come as a shock to both of you, but Xavier's death was not accidental. He was murdered.'

'What?' Roy's shout was almost a reflex.

'Murdered? How can that be? The police said he was found on his bike …' Jennifer stammered.

'Yes. But it was all staged, to look like an accident. Because he had witnessed a murder and had to be silenced.'

'Who did it?' Jennifer's eyes bore into Neville's.

'Angelo Lobo's men. The politician.'

Neville explained, very briefly, what had transpired. Roy's eyes were inflamed with anger, but Jennifer's reaction was curious.

'So, he wasn't actually drunk? They said he had taken drugs … all that was untrue?'

'Yes. He was drugged. He hadn't taken drugs wilfully,' Neville confirmed.

Jennifer turned to Roy with a venomous look in her eyes. 'I knew it. It was a lie. He was a good boy, I told you. He wasn't like that. But then you said ...'

Roy looked on in horror as Jennifer clutched her head in her hands, a strangled cry escaping her lips. 'God, what have I ...'

Shehnaz, in her confusion, turned to Neville and was struck by what she saw. He stood staring intently at Jennifer's outpouring, light in his eyes; the relief of a hunch proved right. When he spoke, finally, his voice had changed. A certainty had replaced all the tentative probing.

'In that moment, you blamed Joshua for it, didn't you, Jennifer?'

'Jenny ...' Roy pleaded, with a hand held out as if to thwart her response, but Jennifer just sat there, shaking her head silently. Her pupils dilated, she looked possessed.

'That morning, when Inspector Rane told you that Xavier had met with an accident under the influence of drink and drugs, you couldn't contain your anger, could you? Your boy – a good, God-fearing lad – had been led astray by that white vermin you had put up in your house. All those times they would ride out on a bike together, that is when it must have started, you thought. Joshua was the one responsible for tempting him down that path to ruin. You were blind with anger and hate, and he stood there in front of you. Alive, healthy, while your son was dead. Gone.'

There was no answer from Jennifer. Even Roy had become quiet.

'Joshua never left this house that morning, did he, Jennifer? You struck him down. Or was it you, Roy?'

'No, it was me,' Jennifer's hollow voice responded.

Shehnaz heard Neville exhale sharply.

'With what, Jennifer?'

Jennifer rose from her chair in the same trance-like state and walked back into the house. Roy made as if to follow, but Bosco stopped him with a gesture of his hand. She returned carrying a cylindrical stone pestle, the kind used for grinding spices on flat mortars. Bosco took it from her hand.

'How did it happen?' Neville asked, eager to get the facts out before the Pintos could change their minds. 'He stood there speaking to Roy and you walked up from behind and struck him down? But it wasn't the one blow, was it? You struck him again after he fell. Roy?'

Roy knew denial was futile. There was no mistaking the despair in his high-pitched confession. 'Jenny lost her head. I did, too. I was yelling, blaming him for everything. It was he who had taken Xavier along to those dens of vice,' he blurted, pointing a finger of accusation at a man long dead. 'They came back one evening and for the first time, I smelt alcohol on my

Xavier. And that Joshua, he kept saying Xavier only ever had an occasional beer, he could never have been too drunk. Not only did we not believe him after what the Inspector had told us, it felt like he was rubbing salt on our wounds, mocking us. I didn't even notice when Jenny went inside and got that … He fell like a log.'

'And then you carried him inside, hid him till it was dark, loaded the body into your truck, drove to the beach and flung it into the sea. It couldn't have been that difficult; even the last coastguard would have left the beach by then, right?'

Roy was silent. Jennifer stood motionless, staring at the ground. Bosco made a move, as if to take the couple away, but Neville wasn't done.

'You have a hardware store, don't you, Roy? You must keep glass cutters there.'

This, coming out of nowhere, puzzled Shehnaz and Bosco but not Roy. He looked stricken, like one whose guilt had been laid bare. Neville pressed on, with the assurance of one who knew he was on the right track. If there was a trace of sympathy in his voice when he spoke of Jenny's assault – as if he understood the depth of her anguish on that fateful day – now there was none.

'The murder of Joshua may have been a moment of madness but there was nothing impulsive about the killing of your neighbour, Jennifer. It was cold, calculated, planned in meticulous detail.'

Bosco looked like he couldn't believe his ears. Yet it had to be true, for there wasn't a murmur of protest from either Jennifer or Roy.

'Why? Had Naresh seen something that day? Or had he sensed something from your anguish, Jennifer? He must have. Yet he remained silent all this while.'

'But why, Neville?' Shehnaz cried out.

'Do you remember that first day we met Naresh? He spoke of justice. He asked Mia what she sought to gain by finding her brother's killer – closure or revenge? We will never know the truth, but perhaps he felt that what Jennifer did in the heat of the moment, upon hearing of her son's death, did not deserve to be punished by throwing her in prison for the rest of her life. But could he so easily forgive the brutal murder of a young man he was so clearly fond of?' mused Neville, shaking his head, as if lost in a vexing daydream. Then, a thought struck him, and he turned sharply towards Jennifer.

'Or was it only your suspicion that he knew? Did he ever mention it? Or was it Mia's arrival that made you fear Naresh might change his mind, out of sympathy for her and their mother? I think I know what frightened you – the last time we were here, Naresh asked me, in your presence, to come back the next day. He had something to tell me. You must have thought he would reveal everything, no?'

Roy said, in a whisper, 'He knew.'

'How can you be sure?'

'The day after Joshua's death, Jennifer got drunk and screamed about how Joshua had corrupted Xavier, that he was responsible for his death.'

'In that house?'

'Yes. I don't know why she went there in that state.'

'Did Naresh ever speak about it?'

'He didn't have to. We knew, from the way he looked at us.'

Neville shook his head, still unconvinced, but said, 'So, he had to be silenced before he said anything. And the two of you plotted it. Oh, Roy, you made one mistake but how easy it was for you to cross the line again. To save your skin, you became butchers!'

Neville had raised his voice. Even Jennifer cowered.

'It was my idea. Jennifer resisted but I told her we had no choice. Naresh didn't have much time left anyway, but we did. And I didn't want to spend the rest of my life in jail because of her stupid mistake.'

Neville continued, as if he hadn't heard this. 'You read about Naresh's speech at the felicitation and knew how easy it would be for the finger of suspicion to turn in another direction. You even went the extra yard to mislead us. The footprints … but of course, you had to. Else we would naturally suspect you as the ones who had the greatest opportunity. That was clever of you,' Neville said, with spite. 'You wore those – what were they, gumboots? – and walked on the courtyard outside, right? A few sizes bigger so that we wouldn't think of you. From your own shop?'

'They were lying here. A foreigner had left them behind some time ago,' Roy answered.

'Ah. Still here, lying in that scrapyard?'

'I burned them.'

'Of course, you did. So, you must have been in the house when Jennifer left that night.'

A faint nod from the man.

'But how …' Shehnaz asked.

'It was so easy, Shehnaz. Once you know it was them, everything falls into place. I can see it all in front of my eyes. Roy must have sneaked into the house at some point in the evening. You saw the state Naresh was in that day. He wouldn't have been walking around the house, checking corners. Roy could have hidden practically anywhere. Jennifer gave Naresh his milk and sleeping pill, maybe even an extra one, stirred into the glass …'

He looked at Jennifer for confirmation, but seeing no response, continued. 'She asked Naresh to bolt the doors from inside, as usual, and called Pramod to check. Everything was in order.'

'And later at night, when Naresh was asleep, Roy just had to step out and smother him with a pillow,' Bosco blurted, as the simplicity of the plan dawned on him.

'Yes. Then he cut the pane with a glass cutter borrowed from his own shop to make it look like the job of an intruder, stepped out and walked away in those gumboots. Roy is no stranger to household hardware, you see, Bosco,' Neville explained, in case the young Inspector wondered how someone with an average intellect like Roy could devise an ingenious plan involving tools such as glass cutters.

'Right, sir,' Bosco nodded, though he sounded a bit awestruck.

'There was only one risk – of being spotted by Pramod. But even there …' Neville was speaking to himself, as if watching the events unfold in his mind's eye and narrating them aloud for the others' benefit.

'… even there I wonder if it had been left to chance. Maybe Jennifer gave him a cup of tea, laced with one of Naresh's pills, before leaving the house. Perhaps it was a daily routine, that nightly cup to the guard. Or she may simply have lurked in the dark, waiting for Pramod to put on his headphones before giving Roy the signal to step out. It wasn't that risky, come to think of it. Not for two meticulous planners such as yourselves.'

Neville cast them another withering look. 'And for all you know, it was another big mistake, like Joshua. Maybe Naresh had never known, as you feared. Maybe all he wanted to talk to me about was what Joshua had told him about the HSS. By the way, Joshua took Xavier along with him not to bars and dives but to help him investigate the deaths of innocent people who had fallen victim to the same criminals that murdered your son.'

'No!' Jennifer cried, looking increasingly disconsolate.

'Yes. Joshua was working to expose Angelo Lobo, your son's killer. You will have a lot of time to think of that, in confinement. Bosco.'

The young man had been waiting for Neville's directive. He took Roy by the arm and instructed Jennifer to follow. Thankfully, Bosco had arrived in a police jeep with a driver. He asked Jennifer to sit in front and sat at the back with Roy.

'Tell Vishnu I will be down to the station later in the day, once I have spoken to Mia.'

The car drove off.

Neville and Shehnaz stood there on the road, staring at the two houses, their residents gone. One departed, the other two hauled off to prison. The structures looked surreal, like ghosts of the houses, which had returned to inspect the site of their ruin.

'Death haunts these houses – I remember you saying, Shehnaz, after Naresh's death. That is the moment it should have clicked for me.'

Mia was waiting for them outside when they returned. She knew, the moment she saw their faces.

'What happened?'

'We know who murdered Joshua. It wasn't the Lobos. It was Jennifer Pinto.'

'What?' Mia let out an incredulous gasp.

Neville explained. She sat bolt upright, clenching and unclenching her hands. If it was a burst of anger they had expected, that wasn't what they saw as much as a deep sense of frustration. She kept repeating, 'What a waste.'

Perhaps she would have been happier to learn that her brother had died at the hands of a villain he was trying to expose, who had now been apprehended. It wouldn't bring Joshua back but it would at least satisfy some notion of justice in her head. But then, the laws of violence rarely follow a predictable arc of reason. Sometimes, all that was required was the stirring of a baser emotion, to snuff out a precious life. A waste, as Mia put it.

Yet, it wasn't just frustration on her face but a deep sense of confusion.

'I don't understand, Neville. If it wasn't Lobo, why were the cops hell-bent on suppressing Joshua's case?' she asked.

'Yes, I thought about that too. You see, Alvares and Rane were in on the Xavier operation. The next day, they find Joshua's body and infer that the deaths are connected. It isn't hard to arrive at that conclusion, is it? And even if they had checked with Angelo, he would have definitely told them to suppress it, as any serious probe into Joshua would inevitably lead to Eva, Jakob, Xavier … dangerously close to the events of that evening. Just as all of us thought his death was linked to the other two. Of course, we will find out which of these conjectures is true, once Rane is hauled in for questioning today.'

'Neville, can I meet Jennifer once? Just for a few minutes? Please?'

Shehnaz reached out and clasped her hand. 'Mia. We feel your anguish, but don't do this. Seeing her won't help you. You came here to find who was responsible for Joshua's death. Now, you must let it go. What is done cannot be undone. Don't wallow in it. Think of your mother.'

At the mention of her mother, Mia seemed to pause. She sat sullenly, brooding.

Neville went to his room to wash up. Shehnaz followed him inside.

'Give her some time, dear. Relief will follow but it is still a shock. Closure doesn't happen in an instant,' Neville said. 'The only good thing in this case is that the actual tragedy happened a while ago, and they have had time to process that, somewhat.'

Neville himself appeared composed, but Shehnaz knew he was anything but, in the aftermath of the morning's events. She wanted to say something endearing but couldn't think of anything appropriate. She only squeezed his hand and went into the kitchen to speak to Agnes, leaving Mia alone with her thoughts.

23

AN HOUR PASSED BEFORE THEY RECONVENED ON THE veranda. Mia seemed calmer, though it could have been resignation that they mistook for acceptance. Neville pulled up a chair next to her and spoke gently, 'Mia, you are very welcome to stay on as long as you want, so please don't take this otherwise, but I think it would be better if you deliver the news to your mother in person, not over the phone.'

'I agree completely, Neville. In fact, I was just thinking the same. I should head back, if you are sure it isn't rude to leave so suddenly. After all your kindness …'

'Don't even give it a second thought. Your place is by your mum's side,' reassured Shehnaz, laying a comforting hand on Mia's.

'Absolutely, except that your mother will have a fit when she sees that cast,' Neville added with a smile.

Mia grinned. 'I intend to be economical with the truth there. An accident, maybe caused by a car, no more.'

'There are reports of a heatwave in the UK. Temperatures in the mid-thirties, apparently. Does it get as warm where your mother lives?'

'I don't think so.' Mia whipped out her phone. 'High of twenty-eight, low of nineteen tomorrow. Warm, but not hot. And I should certainly not feel the heat coming from here.'

'That's good then. You could have a short vacation at home, especially since you have leave sanctioned already,' Neville suggested.

Shehnaz could sense what Neville was trying to do. And he was doing it well. Mia already sounded better, appeared more composed. She hesitated briefly before bringing up the investigation once more.

'You had figured it out last night, right Neville? How did the penny drop?'

'Well, a niggling suspicion was always there at the back of my mind. You see, the linkages were strong – Joshua stayed there, Naresh was next door. But where was the motive? The pieces started falling into place when I heard about Xavier's accident.'

'And what happened last night to crystallize that?'

'You won't believe it, but it really was that stray remark of yours, about how death haunted those houses. I could finally look through my blind spot – the constant hunt for obvious motives such as money, land, scams, settling of scores, versus a crime of passion. Once that became clear, the second murder followed.'

'But you still have to concede it was chancy, Neville. I mean, what would you have done if Jennifer had not broken down at that moment?'

'You are right, of course. It was a gamble. But what other option did I have? In the absence of evidence, we have to hope for a confession. I was betting on the fact that Jennifer isn't a hardened criminal, like an Angelo, and the shock of such a revelation would move her. As it had, on the morning of her son's death. I concede I was lucky, but at the same time I don't think she would have withstood sustained police interrogation, if it came to that.'

There was a moment's silence, before Shehnaz spoke. 'I still cannot believe it – how that oafish Roy could pull off a calculated stunt like this.'

'You will be surprised how powerful the survival instinct can be in people. Why, look at the extreme lengths Angelo Lobo was prepared to go to.'

'What kind of sentences would you expect, Neville?' Mia asked.

'Tough to say, Mia. How old would Jennifer and Roy be now, early fifties? I doubt that they will be out to breathe fresh air again. Jakob? Hmm. I think he will get life too. Angelo will be out, but the burial of the corpse and the orchestration of Xavier's murder should result in a stiff sentence. Maybe ten, twelve years? I am guessing, really,' Neville estimated.

'They won't be up to mischief anytime soon, at least,' ventured Shehnaz, casting a cautious look at Mia.

'And it's also justice for the Aroskar family, we shouldn't forget. I do hope Swati gets to hear of this. The man responsible for their family's ruin is behind bars.'

Just then, Neville's phone rang. 'Hello Vishnu. Yes, I was about to set off for the station. What's that?' Neville laughed loudly and ended the call. Shehnaz had some idea what it may have been.

'Well, I must be off then. One last visit to the police station. I should be back for lunch, Shehnaz.'

'Please convey my thanks to SP Kerkar and Inspector Bosco, Neville. I am very grateful.'

Neville nodded and departed. Mia opened her laptop to search for flight options.

Neville arrived at the Panjim station to a hero's welcome. Vishnu received him at the gate and as he walked down the corridor, a line of officers stood murmuring congratulations or simply staring at him with starstruck eyes; a detective's post-case lap of honour. Neville couldn't help feeling a twinge of pride. They headed up to the DGP's cabin.

'Neville!' beamed DGP Chandok, as he stood up. 'I was just telling Vishnu that at this rate, we could go through all our unsolved cases in a month's time!'

Neville chuckled modestly. 'It was all the effort of your own team, Dilip. Vishnu and Bosco, particularly. They did all the heavy lifting.'

'Oh, come on, Neville! You don't have to be modest now!'

Neville decided to steer the conversation away. 'I have a couple of requests, Dilip. I made an unofficial promise to Danny, the key witness in the case, that we will be soft on him. Hope we can honour that, let him off with a reprimand. And while I doubt Angelo Lobo's men would dare to indulge in any violence now, you never know with these thugs. If some protection can be arranged for Danny's sister, I will truly appreciate it.'

'Of course, of course. Glad you mentioned it, Neville. I will personally ensure this is taken care of. But I also have a request for you. And an unfair one, unlike yours.'

Neville looked perplexed.

'Will you consider advising us on some of our difficult cases? I promise we won't trouble you unless absolutely necessary, but it would be a huge advantage even if you were to guide our investigating officers on the ones where we aren't able to make much headway.'

'But Dilip …' Neville protested, but the DGP wasn't listening.

'Of course, we will work out a remuneration structure for you. It can hardly be pro bono.'

'No, no, Dilip. It isn't about the money. Just that, this comes as a surprise. I really haven't considered such an option,' Neville demurred, aware that he wasn't being entirely honest. 'I left the force early for some peace and quiet. Now to engage again …'

'I understand, Neville. Sharmaji told me about it the other day. But you have this rare talent, it should not be wasted. If something interests you and you can find some time to look into it, we will be grateful. Think it over. Ultimately, it's your call,' DGP Chandok urged, without sounding pushy.

'That's very generous of you, Dilip. I promise to give it some thought. Right now, the head's a bit full, as you will appreciate.'

'Take your time, my friend. But remember, I will remain in hope.' The DGP laughed loudly. Vishnu cleared his throat. 'Sir, the bureau guys wanted to have a word too, on the Jarvinen case.'

Dilip flashed an apologetic grin at Neville. 'Actually, Vishnu, I think I do need that break. I'm no longer as young as you guys and this thing has drained me. I was thinking of making a short trip to Mumbai with Shehnaz.'

'Absolutely, Neville. Sorry, we are only being greedy.'

Neville felt bad turning down the request so bluntly, but he truly couldn't imagine getting sucked into another investigation right away. He shook hands with them, agreed to meet up soon for a drink with Dilip and headed down. In the corridor, he bumped into Bosco and gave him a thump on the back.

'You will make a very good officer one day, Bosco. You have what it takes. And I don't say this to everyone.'

Before getting into the car, Neville called Faye's

number. She answered in a timid voice, perhaps dreading bad news. Neville briefed her, asked her and Tony to come by to Assagaon for a cup of tea with them, later that day. She said she would.

Neville reached home to find Mia's spirits remarkably lifted. Youth, aided by his wife's miraculous powers of dispensing emotional succour, he thought to himself. Mia was chirping away merrily with Shehnaz and Agnes. In fact, they were already making plans for Mia's return to Goa, this time with her mother. Shehnaz suggested, 'Come in late January. The peak season would be behind us, the crazy crowds gone, but the weather perfect. And anyway, it would be freezing back at home for you.'

'And I will take auntie to the basilica in Old Goa, where Francis Xavier's body rests. It's quite something,' Agnes chipped in.

Neville noted, with some amusement, that Mia's mother was already 'auntie' to Agnes.

'Any luck with the tickets, Mia?' he asked, entering the veranda.

'Yes, I got one for tomorrow. Departs from Mumbai mid-afternoon. I should be in London by early evening.'

'Oh, tomorrow, is it? So, you will need to take an early morning flight out from here.'

'Yup. Booked for 8:50 a.m. Thought I would keep a slight buffer.'

Neville turned to Agnes. 'Madam is off tomorrow, Agnes. Hope you are giving her a nice farewell dinner at least?'

Agnes smiled. 'I've sent Martin out, let's see what he brings back. But Mia madam will be back soon. It's hardly the last time I am cooking for her.'

'By the way, I have asked Faye to come by for tea today. I thought it would be nice for Mia to see them before she left.'

'How nice!' Mia trilled.

Faye and Tony arrived at five. Neville and Shehnaz had only seen the two of them in faded vests and shorts and were pleasantly surprised at their appearance. Tony wore a smart printed shirt, and Faye looked fetching in a pale blue dress. Shorn of the sadness that lined her face, she was a pretty girl.

Over cups of tea the young couple shared their plans of moving to Mumbai and working with a cousin who had an East Indian eatery in Bandra, much to Shehnaz's delight. Tea spilled over into drinks, and Neville managed to persuade the young couple to join them for an aperitif before leaving.

Agnes prepared a veritable feast that night, of which the star was a stuffed squid. At some point, Rakesh Sharma called from Bangalore to compliment Neville and reiterated the same advice as Dilip – that Neville should consider maintaining a loose engagement with the world of crime detection. By the time dinner concluded, Neville could barely keep his eyes open. Suddenly, he was overwhelmed with exhaustion.

The next morning, Neville and Shehnaz drove Mia to the airport. Despite Mia's protests that Martin could drop her off, they insisted on accompanying her. The drive was subdued, filled with the quiet understanding that their farewells had already been whispered in the late hours of the night. Shehnaz and Mia had been up till late, long after Neville had gone to bed.

On reaching, Mia hugged them tightly. 'Thank you for everything. I will always be in your debt,' she said, before disappearing through the sliding glass doors.

Neville and Shehnaz drove away, past hoardings advertising Jakob Lobo's floating casinos, towards the sea which had returned Joshua's body to its shores. They discussed plans for their return to Bombay, surprised at how much they both looked forward to it.

Epilogue

ON THE DAY BEFORE THEIR DEPARTURE TO MUMBAI, Shehnaz received a letter from Cornwall.

Dear Neville and Shehnaz,

Mia has spoken so fondly of you both since her arrival that I can almost picture the two of you sitting on the veranda of your beautiful house in Goa, reading this letter. The image brings a smile to my face. Words are inadequate to express the depth of my gratitude for looking after Mia, and helping us get to the bottom of the truth about Joshua.

While my son remains lost to us, I pray that with time, Mia and I will find the strength to come to terms with his absence, enough to be able to carry on. I know that this would not have happened without your help.

I have been thinking about Jennifer's actions, and while I do feel angry, I can sense the anguish that drove her to it. We share a similar plight, after all. I'm uncertain how legally tenable this is, but I wish to write to the authorities